AF486734

What Door Will You Choose?

SMOKY MOUNTAIN MYSTERIES
BOOK FOUR

CAROLYN P. SCHRIBER

Copyright © 2023 Carolyn P. Schriber.

All rights reserved. No part of this publication may be reproduced, distributed, or transmitted in any form or by any means, including photocopying, recording, or other electronic or mechanical methods, without the prior written permission of the publisher, except in the case of brief quotations embodied in critical reviews and certain other noncommercial uses permitted by copyright law.

ISBN: 979-8-9856455-4-5 (Paperback)

ISBN: 979-8-9856455-5-2 (Digital)

Any references to historical events, real people, or real places are used fictitiously. Names, characters, and places are products of the author's imagination.

Front cover image by Avalon Graphics.

Cover design by Cathy Helms.

First printing edition 2023.

Katzenhaus Books

Cordova, Tennessee

www.katzenhausbooks.com

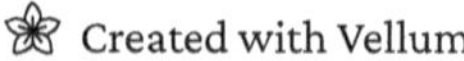 Created with Vellum

"There are two primary choices in life:

to accept conditions as they exist,

or accept the responsibility for changing them"

— Denis Waitley

Contents

CHAPTER 1

Writer-in-Residence

May 9, 2011

"You can't have it all," the retiring classics professor had said. "You young folks think new laws that recognize women's rights have changed things. You expect to be a wife, a mother, a social butterfly, and a political activist in your spare time after your job as a college professor. I'm here to tell you it can't be done. I've learned that the hard way. Being a scholar is a lifetime commitment. You take that title seriously, and you can kiss your dreams of a husband and kids goodbye."

Sarah Chomsky had been a doctoral candidate at Columbia when she heard that verdict for the first time. She believed it without question because her studies had already been consuming every waking moment of her existence. But now, her personal life was full beyond her imagination. She was newly married to the local district attorney, a handsome Harvard law graduate with academic credentials every bit as high-blown as her own. They had a delightful set of friends, a new house, and a spiritual home in the local synagogue. They even owned a famous cat, the star of a book about the meaning of the Jewish observance of Passover.

She had turned her dissertation into a seminal rebuttal of the "Cotton Is King" mantra of the southern states before the Civil War, and The University of South Carolina had picked that new book to headline their upcoming publications list. She had just passed her third-year review, and her reward had been the offer of a year's release from teaching. The proffered position of Writer-in-Residence carried with it a generous raise in salary and a once-in-a-lifetime chance to write a book based on primary documents no one else had seen in 127 years. Life was good, and if she did not "have it all," she was getting closer with every academic accolade that came her way.

Professor Julia Winthrop opened the door to the third-floor women's restroom, listened for a few moments, and then backed away. She wrinkled her nose at the history department secretary and shook her head.

"I hate that lavatory," she growled. "If no one has sprinkled itching powder on the seats, someone has scrolled hate messages on the mirrors in lipstick. There's always a lovesick student or a pregnant woman crying in one of the stalls, the hazmat crews arrive regularly to answer false alarms, and if nothing else goes wrong, the plumbing backs up."

"There's been no one in there this morning except for Professor Chomsky. Were you looking for her?"

"No, actually, I wasn't, but from the sounds of things I've probably found her." Taking a deep breath, she gave a warning shout. "Sarah, when you're finished praying to that porcelain goddess, come on out. I have some of those ginger drops in my bag. They'll settle your stomach quickly."

The toilet flushed, but the feet under the door did not move.

"I know it's you, Sarah. Who else wears high heels up here on a hot summer morning?"

"Someone who has an appointment with the dean," a voice snarled. "Besides, they're not high heels. They're just platform sandals."

The stall door banged as the occupant slammed it open. Sarah's eyes were red-rimmed from crying, and the hair around her face dripped with perspiration. "Where's the ginger? I hate the way it tastes, but I need a quick cure for this stomach virus."

"That's not a virus, Sarah. It's a baby. You can't fool another pregnant woman."

"Shut up!"

"Not until you tell me you've made an appointment with the doctor."

"I'm working on it. But first, the dean. He wants an answer on this writer-in-residence thing by this morning, and I still haven't made up my mind."

"Of course, you have. If you were going to turn it down, you would have done that last Friday. So, wash your face, comb your hair, and go say 'yes, sir' in your most grateful voice. Once you've done that, we will take a drive up the mountain to see Mama Capelli for lunch."

"Pizza? Oh, I'm going to be sick again."

"No, you're not. You don't have time. Besides, I wasn't thinking of pizza. I was thinking of that all-day soup she makes—the *ribollita*. It has white beans, bread, parmesan, beef, olive oil, carrots, celery, onion, garlic, kale—whatever remains at the end of an evening's worth of cooking. Papa

Capelli has often told me that *ribollita* can cure anything—except maybe a baby."

Sarah glared at her best friend, but she did as she was told. Worried that she was already late, she splashed cold water across her face, fluffed her curls, and headed for the administrative building.

The dean greeted Sarah with a broad smile as she entered his office. "I'm assuming your presence means you've come to accept our offer."

"Yes, sir. I'll take my year's leave from teaching, do the research, write the history of the nunnery, and serve as a good example for our writing students. But I do have one request. I'd like to be able to hire a part-time research assistant—someone who is already familiar with monastic institutions, so I don't have to waste time looking up those details. The money can come out of my stipend if necessary."

"Indeed. We did discuss adding that sort of benefit, so it should be no problem. We were talking about allowing $300 a month for an assistant, which would increase a master's stipend one entire level to that of a doctoral lecturer. And it needn't come out of your allowance. I told you the Church is throwing money at this project. You have someone in mind, I take it."

"Jean Pendergast. She spent a year in a nunnery as a postulate before entering graduate school. She has the vocabulary and the rituals at her fingertips. She'll finish her master's degree at the end of this semester, so she will have some free time. Plus, it will give her some good experience in her field of study."

"A perfect choice. That's settled then. But if you don't

mind me saying so, you look a bit pale and drawn this morning. Are you feeling well?"

"We've had a stomach virus at the house, sir. I'm over it now."

"Good. I don't want to be accused of over-working you. Oh, one more thing before you go. I've just learned that more congratulations are in order. I assume you've seen this?" He picked up a double-folded paper from the pile of correspondence on his desk.

"No. What is it?"

"It's the mock-up of the front cover of the Spring 2012 List at the University of South Carolina Press."

And there it was—a full publicity shot of Sarah holding her new book, *Cotton: Not King but Despot.* The headline read, "Young historian paints a devastating picture of South Carolina's cotton industry. Be sure to read Sarah Chomsky's interpretation of our antebellum economy."

"Oh, my! So that's why they didn't mention the book in their Winter catalog!"

"You weren't worried, were you?"

"I was afraid they had changed their minds about publishing it."

"Not a chance. It looks like they expect you to have a best-seller."

It was exciting news, but it did little to calm Sarah's jittery stomach. She took the back stairs to the third floor, hoping to avoid more questions from her colleagues. With the door to her office closed, she dialed the number of the local hospital and its information desk.

"Yes, we're new in town and looking for a family doctor. Do you do referrals?"

The receptionist was more than happy to assist. "We've just added a new doctor to our staff. Her name is Marilyn

Hammersmith. She's just finished her residency at Stanford, and we've hired her as a staff physician. She is hoping to establish an OB-GYN practice here in Birch Falls. However, until she has developed a patient base, she's taking family recommendations. I think you'd like her. She's quite charming."

"That sounds fine. Do you have a contact number for her or ..."

"Leave me your cell and I'll get a message to her. I believe she's doing rounds this morning, but I'll have her contact you as soon as she is free."

The return call came almost immediately, and before she had time to think of an excuse, Sarah had a doctor's appointment for four o'clock that afternoon.

In the meantime, the drive through the foothills of the Appalachians had the effect Julia had been hoping for. The temperature was several degrees cooler in the forest. Sunlight glittered through the leaves, and new growth gave the trees the appearance of fringe around the edges. Dogwoods still displayed their pink and white blossoms, while redbuds provided a welcome contrast.

Sarah had been staring intently out the side window, and Julia was willing to wait for her friend to break the silence. At last, the words came.

"There. Just at the edge of the road. See that dark cluster? It's a family of skunks. Do you remember, Julia? It was just about here we saw that mother raccoon teaching her kits to cross the road. Motherhood's a big responsibility, no matter who you are, isn't it?"

"Sure. But look how nature helps by providing camouflage. I would never have seen those skunks hiding amid the shadows of the trees. Only your sharp eye revealed that tell-tale white stripe."

"That white stripe is part of the trick. Most people would see it as a glimmer of sunlight."

"Hmmm. But to answer the question you had buried in your longer comment ... yes, indeed, motherhood is a huge responsibility. But it's one we accept because the rewards are so much greater than the costs. I had to learn that when Ronnie first came to live with us as a foster son. Now the need to protect him is an automatic response."

"But what if that response doesn't come? How do you learn it? How do you get good enough to do all that needs to be done? Twenty-four years in a classroom and nobody taught me how to be a mother."

"What are you imagining? Do you think that somewhere in the woods there is a great animal lecturer who teaches all the little raccoon and skunk mamas the rules of crossing the road or hiding in the weeds?"

"Of course not, and you are making fun of me."

"Not exactly. I just want to remind you that you are smarter than the average skunk. You'll get it. It'll come naturally to you, just as it does to every mother animal."

At last, Sarah laughed and relaxed in her seat. Then she pulled herself erect again and touched Julia's arm, pointing to the side of the road where a doe and her fawn picked their delicate steps through a patch of wildflowers. "They are so beautiful together."

Julia willed herself to say nothing more to break the mood of the moment until she pulled into the parking lot of their favorite restaurant.

"Mama Capelli must've been looking for us. She already has the door open."

The little Italian lady came bustling out onto the porch, her tomato-stained apron straining against her belly and her cheeks flushed from the heat of the kitchen.

"Bambinos! I thought you had left for summer vacation."

"Not this year, mama. We have too much to do." Sarah forced a smile. "I have a huge book contract that's going to keep me tied to a desk for hours every day. And as for Julia ..."

"Ach! I see it now. You have a little one coming, don't you? Congratulations. What fun lies ahead of you."

Julia's eyes widened in surprise. "How could you tell? I'm not showing at all yet."

"Ah, but your eyes. They tell the story because they look to the future, and you smile as if you knew a great secret. Your hands linger protectively at your waistline, and you are careful where you walk. All of them say, 'Hello. Here's a mama-to-be.'"

"And what about Sarah? What do you see about her, besides that crazy writing schedule, that is?"

"Sarah! Our newlywed. Still a bit shell-shocked, aren't you, my dear? Life is changing very fast for you, I sense."

"You might say so," Sarah tried to laugh it off, but instead she felt the tears begin to flow again.

"And you are pale. Are you afraid of something? Your new husband? Is he too demanding?"

"No. No. Nothing like that. We've just had a stomach virus lately. David brushed his symptoms off, but I can't seem to shake mine."

"I suggested she needs a bowl of your *ribollita*, which is why we are here."

"Well, you are in luck. I started a new batch yesterday. It should be ready to cure almost anything. Come in, come in. Have some lemonade while I turn the heat up a notch. Papa! Look who's here! Bring them some *limonata*."

CHAPTER 2

Diagnosis

May 9, 2011

Sarah hesitated outside the physician's office door. The printed legend—Dr. Marilyn Hammersmith, OB-GYN and Family Practice—appeared to be still wet. Her fingers itched to test the ink. The waiting room gave off the same sort of fresh-paint vibes. A play corner displayed new toys carefully arranged on shelves. A coffee table held copies of the latest magazines. Their lack of address labels suggested recent purchases. And the receptionist, every hair carefully in place, sat checking paperwork without seeming to move. Only one other patient occupied the room—an elderly gentleman with palsied movements.

When the phone rang, Sarah and the old man both jumped. A nurse appeared in a doorway. "I'm ready to give you your shot, Mr. Winston." As he slowly pushed himself to his feet, Sarah cringed to realize she was now going to be all alone in that room. To her relief, the receptionist spoke without looking up. "The doctor is also ready to see you, Mrs. Cohen."

In contrast to the coldness of the reception room, the doctor's smile was warm and welcoming. A quick hand-shake, the offer of water, and an efficient nurse taking a small blood sample served to ease the awkwardness of the moment. All was quiet for a few minutes, as Doctor Hammersmith glanced over Sarah's patient information sheet and waited for lab results.

"We should be addressing you as Dr. Chomsky, I believe. I am always irritated when people who have spent years of their lives studying are not given the courtesy of the title in the same way that we medical people are addressed. My mother was a case in point. She was a dentist, but her patients invariably called her Mrs. Hammersmith. She always said it didn't bother her, but it should have."

"I'll be having that conversation with my students this semester. Their bigger puzzlement will be whether they should use my new married name, Doctor Cohen, or the old Doctor Chomsky."

"I was wondering that as well. Did you keep your maiden name when you married?"

"Professionally, yes. At the university, I'm always Dr. Chomsky, but on a Saturday night at a police department party, it's Mrs. Cohen. I live two very different lives, so I might as well use different names."

"How does that work out for you—the two roles, I mean? Are you under a lot of stress as you try to balance the two?"

"Not really, no. My husband is very good at helping to keep my head on straight." Sarah was relaxing now. She smiled as she recalled some of the early conversations that she and David had about the topic.

A soft bell rang to signal a new computer entry. The

doctor scanned the list on the screen and then turned to Sarah with a comforting smile. "Your blood work is perfect—low cholesterol, good metabolic panel—sugar levels, normal sodium, potassium, oxygen. You appear to be the picture of health. So, what brought you in today?"

"Nothing special, just ..."

The doctor cocked an eyebrow. "Just ...?

"Well, I've been a little nauseated lately—unusual for me—and I thought it might be time for a checkup."

"How long since your last period?"

"Oh. Well, I'm not sure. Things have been so busy lately. I don't usually keep track of things like that."

"Uh-huh. Are you pregnant?"

"No!" Her answer came too quickly.

The doctor grinned. "Sounds like we need to do a physical exam. Why don't you slip into the room next door and change that lovely outfit for one of our fashionable hospital gowns."

"Is that necessary?"

"Yes. And we'll need one more blood sample as well."

Sarah tried to blot out the next few minutes—the needles, the hard exam table, the stirrups, the invasive exploration of her lower body. Then the nurse came back looking serious as she handed the doctor a printout.

"Are you certain? Did you double-check the results?"

"Yes, ma'am. Several times."

The doctor was still frowning as she turned away. "You may get dressed now. I'll see you back in my office."

Sarah looked around frantically. The only other available door led back to that cold medical office with all the diplomas on the wall. No escape seemed possible.

～

Dr. Hammersmith was visibly angry. "I can't help you if you are not honest with me. The biggest mistakes a patient can make are withholding evidence from her doctor, failing to mention prior treatments, and hiding symptoms. Was I supposed to guess you were pregnant? Did you think you had a big Rh-negative sign printed on your forehead?"

"What kind of sign? I don't understand what you're saying."

"Please don't play games with me. You are pregnant—probably at least seven weeks along—and your child is in imminent danger of death from a full-blown development of Rh antibodies."

"Which are ... what? I don't have a clue."

"It's part of your blood type."

"I'm an O, which makes me a universal donor, I believe. That's good, isn't it?"

"You're an O-negative, which makes your blood a threat to your unborn child. Seriously, has no one ever explained this to you?"

"I ... haven't seen a doctor since I was a teenager."

"Lord, have mercy! I can't believe it ... But I'll take you at your word. Let's start from the beginning. Most people—approximately eighty-five percent of the world's population—have a protective coating on their red blood cells that makes it possible for those cells to deliver needed oxygen and nutrients to the body's organs. That coating is called the Rhesus factor."

"Like the monkey?"

"Well, yes, the Rhesus monkey is the only other known mammal to have that Rhesus coating. The shorthand way of referring to all of this is to say that those who have the Rhesus factor are Rh-positive. Those without it are Rh-negatives."

"So, I don't have any protection for my red blood cells?"

"You do. It's just different. Your body creates antibodies against blood cells they perceive to be strangers."

"Such as …?"

"Such as the red blood cells in the developing body of an Rh-positive fetus. If an Rh-negative mother's blood mixes somehow with the blood supply of an Rh-positive baby, the results can be devastating for the child."

"And what happens to the mother?"

"Nothing, which is why you might not have known about your condition. The only danger is to the child, which only happens when the two blood systems—which are entirely separate in a normal pregnancy—come into contact with each other in the mother's body. At that point, the mother's bloodstream will begin to manufacture the antibodies to attack the baby. That process is known as sensitization, and the antibodies remain active for the life of the mother. This is all very confusing, I know."

"Three more questions: Why hasn't someone developed a cure for this?"

"They have. At least there is a partial cure. Back in the 1960s, someone developed a treatment called rhoGAM, which prevents sensitization if it is used within a day or two of the original contact. But once sensitization has occurred, rhoGAM is no longer effective. In your case, the mixing happened years ago."

"How could I have known that I had this factor?"

"Any reputable doctor who treats a woman of child-bearing years is supposed to check the blood type first. Under normal circumstances, the doctor will not only reveal an Rh-negative finding but will also recommend that the patient carry a card or wear a medical alert bracelet that identifies her condition. Either your last doctor failed to do that, or you failed to hear the warning."

"If the two blood systems are separate, how do they come in contact?"

"Several ways. A fall, an automobile accident, or another type of blow to the abdomen could cause internal bleeding. In a necessary surgical procedure, like amniocentesis, there is always the possibility of mixing. And of course, there are major events—childbirth, a miscarriage, or an abortion—although, for a first child, the danger is over once the birth occurs. If sensitization occurs during one of those events, however, subsequent pregnancies remain in danger."

"So, pregnancy and sensitization are the crucial factors. Since I have never been pregnant, the child I'm carrying now is relatively safe so long as I avoid an accident or medical intervention?"

"Theoretically, yes. But you have had at least one prior pregnancy and are already sensitized."

"No, I haven't!" Sarah was shouting without realizing it. "Your test is wrong!"

"My dear woman, you are speaking to a medical doctor. Please respect that. The evidence is quite clear. Your bloodstream is full of sensitized antibodies, visible under a microscope to anyone who looks for them. Sensitization only happens in a pregnant woman. However, a miscarriage can happen very early in pregnancy and be misunderstood as a late menstrual flow. In your case, however, your vaginal canal shows extensive scarring, which could only result from childhood sexual abuse or the blundering actions of an amateur abortionist."

"No one ever abused me. As a teenager, I may have experimented with minor petting, but I never ... I was a virgin until my marriage just months ago, and ..."

"Please stop. Your friends and neighbors might believe that story, but no doctor would."

"You're calling me a liar?"

"I'm asking that you revise a myth you've been telling yourself for years."

"And I think we're through here." Sarah stood, gathering her purse and briefcase as she moved toward the door.

"You can refuse to accept my diagnosis, and you can walk away from the help you are going to need. But you will not change the fact that you are going to miscarry this child—and sooner rather than later. Your story may well become public knowledge. All you can hope for is that the revelation happens at a time and place you choose."

Sarah froze in mid-step, her hand hovering over the doorknob. Then her shoulders drooped, and she returned to her chair.

"Can I trust you not to tell anyone without my permission?"

"In a life-threatening emergency, I may have to share certain medical information with other medical personnel. But beyond that, I am bound by my Hippocratic Oath to protect a patient's privacy, and I take that guarantee of confidentiality most seriously. I will not tell your husband or other family members if that is what you are asking."

CHAPTER 3
Emergency

May 11, 2011

Sarah moved through dinner preparations without having to think. She simply turned to her standby recipe: 'When all else fails, make hamburger gravy and mashed potatoes.' Half a pound of ground beef, some ready-chopped frozen onion, a can of sliced mushrooms, a package of beef gravy mix, and a cup of water became a savory stew. Instant mashed potatoes made with milk tasted just like homemade. And while the rest of dinner warmed, she boiled a few baby carrots until they softened and then sizzled them in butter and maple syrup until they were shiny with a candy crust. David knew something was wrong as soon as he arrived home. When hamburger gravy was cooking, one tiptoed through the usual greetings.

Sarah acknowledged his arrival with a slight lip twitch that might have passed as a smile. He rested his hands on her shoulders as an invitation for closer contact, but she did not yield.

"Bad day?"

"Um-hum."

"Want to talk?"

"Huh-uh."

"Drink?"

"No. Dinner's ready."

They ate in silence, both of them understanding that the menu spoke volumes. Sarah gathered the dishes and slid them into the dishwasher before heading for the stairs. Near the top, she turned to look down at David.

"I'm pregnant."

"What?"

"But don't start buying baby furniture. I'm probably going to miscarry soon."

"Wait! Sarah! Have you seen a doctor? Are you sure? What does this all mean?" David clutched the back of a chair, needing support as the room swayed around him.

She waited for just a touch too long, and her voice, when it came, sounded tinny and far away. "I learned today that I have some sort of genetic condition—one I knew nothing about. I brought home all sorts of pamphlets from the doctor's office, but I can't begin to explain them. They are on the kitchen counter if you want to read them. I'm going to bed."

Two nights later, Sarah awoke with stabbing abdominal pains and then a gushing flow of blood. Stumbling towards the bathroom, she screamed for David to call an ambulance.

"I can bring the car around. Hang on, love. I'll get you there."

"No," she answered. "There's not enough time. Call the ambulance. I need help now."

Sarah drifted in and out of consciousness as rough hands lifted her from the bathroom floor to a stretcher and then bounced her down the stairs and out the front door to a waiting EMT ambulance. From what felt like a very great distance, she heard David arguing with someone. He was demanding to be allowed to ride with her.

"I'm sorry, sir, but we find it easier to care for the patient if the family is not hovering. The law says ..."

"I am the district attorney, and your patient is my wife. I know what the law says. Now, move over ..."

Shadowy figures crawled through the back entrance. Someone clamped a mask over her face and told her to breathe normally. A prick in her upper arm brought on a wave of dizziness. A blur of flashing lights and wailing sirens followed as the ambulance swayed around corners and bounced over potholes.

As attendants rushed her stretcher through the emergency room door, a white-coated gentleman approached.

"What have we here?" he asked.

"I'm pregnant."

He looked at the chart lying next to her and shook his head. "You used to be pregnant. You're not anymore. The injection the EMTs gave you has slowed the bleeding, so you are no longer in danger, but you've lost the baby. I'm very sorry, Mrs. Cohen. Just lie here quietly for a few minutes. We're going to need to prepare you for an IV and a transfusion, and then we'll get you off to a private room and a more comfortable bed."

"I have to stay here?"

"Oh, I'm afraid so. You're going to need what is known as a D&C. That stands for dilation and curettage. It's a simple operation, and you'll be home by tomorrow afternoon. Oh, one more detail. Have you had your rhoGAM shot?

"It's a little late for that, isn't it?" Sarah's voice was bitter.

"A little preventive medicine never hurts."

"But it won't help, either. I'm already fully sensitized. That's what put me here."

David had been hovering near the head of her gurney, but he now put out a hand to stop the doctor. "I apologize, doctor, but I don't understand what's going on. Can you give it to me in words of one syllable?"

"I can't. It's a very complicated situation. The doctor who performs tomorrow morning's surgery will talk to you both afterward and try to explain what has happened."

A bustling nurse arrived with a small cup and a glass of water. "This is just a relaxer to help you get a little sleep tonight. Swallow it now, dear. And you, sir. Your wife is going to be fine, I assure you, but for right now, she doesn't need you here. You should head home and get as much rest as you can. You can call us in the morning to see how she's doing."

David turned to Sarah, hoping she would beg him to stay, but she was already drifting off. Her eyes closed and her mouth went slack. As for Sarah herself, she remembered little of the next few hours. Another nurse woke her at 5:30 AM to prep her for surgery, but she drifted through it barely rising out of her dream state. And the next thing she knew a doctor was shaking her shoulder and calling her name.

"Mrs. Cohen? Sarah? Come on now and wake up. Your surgery is over, and you did beautifully. You'll be back on your feet in no time. Right now, you probably need a drink of water or an ice chip to relieve the dryness in your mouth. I'll be back this afternoon to talk to you and your husband about the path you take from here on."

By noon, Sarah was sitting up, sipping a cup of chicken broth, and begging someone to help her get dressed. "I know I'll feel better once I'm home," she insisted, but the nurses ignored her pleas. "You must wait for the doctor."

He arrived, as promised, shortly after lunch and sat down next to the bed, inviting David to move in closer so that he could explain the problems Sarah was facing. "We don't see many Rh-negative patients anymore," he commented. "Now that we have rhoGAM, the number of sensitized women has dropped precipitously."

"So if this rhoGAM works so well, why is Sarah still facing the problem?"

"I don't know why she never received the shot after her first miscarriage," the doctor said, "and for whatever reason, Sarah doesn't remember either. My best guess is she was in the very early stages of pregnancy, probably as a result of some heavy petting, not even full intercourse, and ..."

"Can that happen? David asked.

"Certainly, and it's more frequent than people would have you believe. I imagine she suffered a quick miscarriage, thinking it was nothing more than a heavy monthly flow. If she didn't see a doctor, she didn't receive the rhoGAM shot, and the sensitization took place without her knowledge or awareness."

"So this could all happen again?"

"If you're referring to the sensitization, that only happens once and lasts a lifetime. But as for pregnancies and miscarriages, yes indeed, the pattern can repeat again and again. I would urge you to take every precaution to avoid another pregnancy."

Sarah's distracted mood lasted through the drive home. She stared out the windows, unwilling to meet David's eyes.

"Do you want me to carry you into the house? You were using a wheelchair at the hospital."

"Everyone gets a wheelchair. It's a liability issue. It doesn't mean anything. Thank you. But I can walk just fine."

Sarah walked past the two cats without even noticing them. Slowly she managed the seven steps to the upper level of the house but hesitated outside their bedroom door.

"Can I help?" David asked again. "Are you going back to bed?"

"No. Not here. I don't think I can bear to sleep in our big bed again for a while. I will move into my office and use the futon."

"The futon? It's hard and too narrow to share. I was looking forward to holding you all night long."

"I don't want to share it. I need to be left alone." Her voice was cold, the words sharp and clipped. She gathered a few items from a drawer and then stalked across the hall to her office, closing the door firmly behind her. David could only stare at the closed door, wondering why his warm and loving wife had disappeared.

For three days, they lived like virtual strangers in an unfamiliar rooming house. Occasionally, they passed in the hall but without comment. Mealtimes came and disappeared, marked only by someone opening the refrigerator door or gathering a finger snack. The cats began sleeping on the stairs so as not to miss the movements of their beloved owners, but neither Sarah nor David noticed them.

By Monday evening, David had had enough. He tapped

on her office door, and when there was no answer, he pushed his way in. He found Sarah huddled under a blanket as if she could hide from him forever. He pulled the blanket down roughly.

"Get up, Sarah. You've malingered long enough. It's time to face the world, unhappy though you may be."

"Leave me alone."

"I won't. I love you, and I can't bear to see you suffering in silence this way. You need to talk about what happened and how you are feeling."

She sat up abruptly, her eyes blazing with anger. "If you won't leave, I will." She padded barefoot to the closet and pulled a small suitcase from the shelf. From hangers and drawers, she gathered clothes to fill the case without even looking to see what she was packing.

"You want an explanation of how I could have let this happen? I'll be happy to tell you. Maybe it'll make life without me easier for you to face."

"I'm not going to let you go anywhere."

"You can't stop me."

"I have to stop you. None of this is your fault."

"It's all my fault." She turned to face him, and he was surprised to realize she was not shedding tears as she talked. Her voice was cold. "Do you remember the story I told you of my teenage marriage to Aaron Lehman?"

"I do, but that doesn't matter."

"It does. I didn't tell you I got pregnant almost immediately after our elopement, and I knew what that meant for the rest of my life. The Lehmans belonged to an ultra-strict Orthodox Jewish community. They didn't believe in divorce or education for women. For me, there would be no college, no career. I would be a mother dedicated to pampering my male children and brow-beating my female children into submission. So, I lied and stole my way out of a miserable existence."

"Lied and stole? You? I find that hard to believe."

"I lied about where I was going. I told both families that I had been invited by a cousin from the other family to be a part of the minyan for her wedding. One family thought I was headed for Trenton, New Jersey. The other expected me to go to Wilmington, Delaware. Instead, I headed for Atlantic City, where I knew law enforcement to be lax. To pay the extra bus fare, I stole the money by helping myself to whatever cash I could find lying around—my father's synagogue donation box, Mr. Lehman's cash drawer at the butcher shop, and even Mrs. Lehman's household cookie jar.

"The rest was easy. Homeless people tend to congregate around bus stations where they won't be so obvious. Once I penetrated Atlantic City's cardboard box community, several folks were willing to point me toward a cheap abortionist. His clinic was a shack down a narrow alleyway. The abortionist himself was a middle-aged guy with greasy hair and a beer belly that sagged over his pants. He gave me a shot of whiskey to calm my nerves and then told me to get on the table, put my feet in the straps, and spread my knees.

"I don't remember much after that, but I know I bled for three days before I could go home. I tried to keep a smile on my face, but I knew I had killed my child. I had also destroyed my parents' and my in-laws' desires for a grandchild. The only thing I didn't know was that I had also killed my future babies."

Sarah's voice was beginning to rise and crack with hysteria. Her words came in phrases rather than sentences. "Leaving you ... For your own good ... Divorce ... Grounds of desertion ... Nice Jewish girl ... Remarry ... Lots of babies ...

Never see you again." By this time, she was screaming, her mouth twisted into an unrecognizable sneer.

David slapped her. Her eyes widened in shock, and then the dam broke. Her words faltered, the tears flowed, and her breath came in wracking sobs. David gathered her into his arms and held her tightly until he felt her muscles relax. When he realized she had cried herself to sleep, he tucked her carefully into the futon and then lay beside her, his arms protecting her from whatever phantoms might haunt her during the night.

CHAPTER 4

Back To Work

May 14-15, 2011

Sunshine poured through the windows as Sarah and David woke the next morning. After several days of clouds—gloomy weather that had reflected their sadness—the bright sun and deep blue sky were particularly welcome. David propped himself on one elbow and stared down at Sarah's still tear-streaked face.

"Good morning, beautiful. Did you sleep well?"

"I must have. My limbs still feel too heavy to move. Can I stay here all morning long?"

"You may do anything you wish today, my love, but I thought you might be interested in some breakfast first."

"Oh! Breakfast? You know, I think I might be hungry. I think I'm starving."

"You haven't eaten much of anything for days. You'll need to begin slowly. How about some poached eggs on toast to start your recovery?"

"Heavenly. You're so good to me, even when I'm not at all

sure I deserve you. I seem to remember throwing a terrible tantrum at you not long ago."

"Must have been some other bloke. I don't remember anything of the sort." David was laughing at her description of hysteria as a tantrum. "Whatever you may call that little storm we had last night, it's over now, and we don't need to talk of it ever again. Understood?"

"Yes, sir, but ..."

"Hush! Go wash your face while I hunt for the eggs."

They spent the weekend together, often hand-in-hand—walking, watching pictures in the clouds, window shopping, and nibbling at whatever caught their fancy. On Saturday afternoon, a new office supply warehouse attracted Sarah, who had realized that the room she called her home office was nothing but a catch-all junk collection spot.

"During those days when I shut myself away in there, I couldn't imagine using the space to write a serious book. I couldn't even see the surface of the desk."

"Well, let's fix that! Look, here's a desk pad with an insert for a half-sized write-on calendar. And it has matching accessories—cups for little things like paper clips, a letter holder, a pen and pencil tray, a tape dispenser, and a mini-hot plate to keep your coffee warm. What color combo do you like best? There's the cold steel version, the great outdoors in blues and greens, or the sunset symphony of reds and oranges. Choose carefully because they have the same shades of thumbtacks, book markers, and erasers."

"Not to mention the paperclips, post-it notes, and index cards. I love the nature themes—with maybe the addition of a couple of house plants that don't mind being neglected."

"You've got it! You'll also need a comfortable desk chair and a moveable desk extension to hold your laptop. Now, then. Will it feel more like a spot you can settle into for the long haul?"

"Yes, but you're running up a huge bill."

"So what? The writer-in-residence has an expense account, doesn't she?"

"I'm not sure it covers pastel paper clips."

"Anything to make you smile, my love."

The shopping trip was therapeutic, and Sarah returned home Saturday night tired but happy with her identity as a writer. On Sunday, she and David tackled the office itself, moving furniture, cleaning out piles of old magazines and expired mail, and gathering up forgotten cat toys. Sarah did not want to remember the nights she had spent sleeping on that old futon, so they moved the futon downstairs to the lower office to be used as an emergency bed for unexpected guests. Then in its place, they brought in a rocking chair that had belonged to Sarah's grandmother. Once they added a cushion, a throw rug, and a flexible floor lamp, it provided a perfect reading nook. The final adjustment involved moving the desk to the window to provide a view over the trees at the edge of the porch. The natural setting provided a perfect counterpoint to the blues and greens of her new office decor. When they were finished, Sarah stood in the doorway, breathing deeply. "That was a lot of work, but I'm ready to start writing," she said. "This is the perfect setting."

"I think you would be wise to work here for a while before returning to campus," David said. "Put some time between last week's events and your research efforts so that you don't have to answer too many personal questions."

"I agree. And because there is almost no evidence for the

first few weeks of the nuns' arrival in Birch Falls, I can let my imagination run free."

"Have you decided on an overall design for the book yet?"

"Not really. I'm hoping it will develop as I go along. I haven't given up on Jean's suggestion of using the liturgical hours as an organizational pattern for the chapters, but I don't want to overdo that aspect. I do know I want my readers to feel an identification with the women who came here to establish the nunnery. To do that, I have to turn them into real people, even if I exaggerate their feelings. This office is going to help. Once I sit in my desk chair and look out the window, I see nothing but trees, just as they must have done. So, give me a few days to let the creative juices start flowing.

The phone rang, interrupting Sarah's concentration as she paged through the first volume of the mother superior's journals. She ignored it, but after several insistent buzzes, she reached for the receiver.

"Yes? What is it?"

"My dear sister-in-law, must you always snarl when you answer the phone?"

"Hannah? Sorry. Thought you were the little guy who is so worried about my expiring car warranty."

"Well, I'm not calling with good news, I admit, but first, how are you? Are you up and about? And emotionally? How is it going?"

"I'm fine, Hannah. It was an easy miscarriage, so early that I didn't have time to realize I was pregnant before I wasn't. So, I'm back at work, at least in front of the keyboard, if not yet on campus. Now, what's your bad news?"

"It's Elijah! We've been can... Oh, that's not the right

word. We're not canceled. We're still under contract but indefinitely postponed, which is why I'm calling. If you haven't started writing the Yom Kippur book, don't bother. We won't need it for a year or more, if then."

"OK. But I don't understand. What happened?"

"Some overly-clever woman in Montana is what happened. She saw our *Elijah, The Passover Cat* book, thought she could do as well as we did, and borrowed our idea. She just published a little book explaining Passover for Jewish children. It's called *Elijah Gets a Seat at the Seder*. She even won a prize for it."

"How did you ...?"

I didn't. But The Questioning Mind Company has people who do nothing but watch publication lists to make sure no one tromps on their ideas."

"Is it a copyright case?"

"I thought it might be, but I called Dad, and he says it's not. She was clever enough to change most of the details. It takes place in Montana, not New York City. It's snowing, not raining. The cat is white, not black. It's the mother who wants to keep the cat, not the father. He is all for kicking the kitten back to the curb."

"But she calls the cat Elijah?"

"Yes, but that's a biblical detail she can't change. The story doesn't work if they call the cat John."

"I suppose not, but it's so obvious a copycat."

"Obvious, maybe, but not illegal. Anyhow, our publishers will not move ahead until they have a chance to analyze this year's sales during Passover and see whether this woman follows up with other books. They are worried that our intended audience is just not big enough to support two separate series."

"I don't know whether to feel angry or relieved. It does

give me the time I need to work on the nunnery book, so I should be grateful, but it is insulting when someone just walks off with our idea."

"I know but I do have an idea about how to get even."

"What are you thinking about doing, Hannah?"

"I'm not telling you because I don't want you to get in trouble but keep your eye on the internet for the next few days, particularly the Friends and Family section of Faces."

A few days later, Sarah opened her Faces page to discover the following exchange:

WEBMASTER: We usually hold a space open on Mondays to allow our friend, the Brooklyn Zoo Python, a chance to speak his mind. But this month, he has asked that his space be turned over to his buddy, Elijah the Passover Cat, who has a warning he needs to pass along to his readers.

ELIJAH: Thanks, Python. I need to warn my fans that we have an interloper in our midst. Some woman I've never heard of has discovered the story of how I came to be adopted at a Passover Seder a couple of years ago. She has taken that story—which is true, by the way—and written her book using the same general theme. She changed a few details, but the hero is still a cat, the setting is a family Seder, the weather is terrible, and the bedraggled cat is so hungry that he makes a mad dash for the empty chair at the table, helping himself to the scraps that family members offer him. The new title is Elijah Gets a Seat at the Seder. *Yep, you read that right; she even named her cat Elijah. The nerve! Hiss!*

PYTHON: Hey! I thought only snakes could hiss.

ELIJAH: Not so. Cats have a great hiss. When a mama cat

hisses, her kittens take cover. But be that as it may, I want my readers to be careful to buy the real book, not the fake one. My picture on the cover comes from a real photo, showing my silky black fur and my manly physique. Don't fall for the Elijah book with the wimpy white kitten on the cover.

WEBMASTER: Thanks for the warning, Elijah. You readers, be careful out there.

Sarah laughed, but she suspected Hannah was not through. Two days later, Elijah was back, this time at the invitation of the Webmaster, who had been overwhelmed with messages protesting the fake book.

WEBMASTER: Elijah, our readers want to know what you intend to do about the interloper. Are you going to charge her with a copyright violation and take her to court?

ELIJAH: No, we can't do that. Copyright law applies only to a body of tangible written work. You can't copyright an idea, a character, or even a storyline. She didn't copy our book. She only told a similar story.

WEBMASTER: What about the name Elijah?

ELIJAH: It goes back to the Bible. Anyone can use it. All we can do is tell readers that her book is a copycat. Grrr.

WEBMASTER: Well, here's one message to make you feel better. It says:

'Remember that imitation is the sincerest form of flattery.'

ELIJAH: Oh, I like that! Purr. Purr.

Sarah began work on her nunnery book in a way that only another writer would have understood. After breakfast the following Monday, she bustled through the house—straightening, dusting, sweeping, tidying. And while she worked, she was talking to herself. The dean had once commented that writers often found their best ideas while scrubbing a sink, and so it was with Sarah. Suddenly she had a mental image of a group of intrepid ladies arriving in a frontier town in the middle of the night and immediately sitting down to talk about what they needed to do first.

Sarah could hear their voices. One sounded mature and authoritative, while others were younger and more hesitant. One of the younger ones sounded positively giggly, while another was afraid of her shadow. There was a whiner who was already positive that nothing was going to work out the way they hoped. And there was the lazy one, who didn't want to hear about anything that involved hard physical labor. The characters had no names as yet. Their facial features were still fuzzy. Their backstories were private, and their futures as cloistered monastics remained very much in doubt.

Still, these characters had arrived, and Sarah knew without being able to explain it that these women would guide the development of her new book. Eager now to get started, Sarah headed for her new office, powered up her laptop, and opened the file that would become *The History of Saint Walburga's Nunnery.*

CHAPTER 5

Matins—The First Hour

From the journal of Mary Frances McMurtry, later known as Sister Francesca, and now, by the grace of God, as Mother Francesca, Mother Superior of this Convent of Our Lady St. Walburga:

August 1843

It was midnight when we arrived in Birch Falls. The coach driver apologized for keeping us out so late. I just smiled, realizing that he had no understanding of the liturgical schedule that religious orders followed. For us, being awake at midnight is part of the natural custom of two periods of sleep. Our predecessors went to bed when it got dark, slept for about four hours, and woke up to a world that had stopped bustling about. It was quiet, dark, and peaceful —a perfect time to think, to meditate, to have a heart-to-heart talk with a friend, with one's conscience, or perhaps with God.

On this day, my sisters and I had slept through the early

hours of darkness as the stagecoach covered the last few miles of our journey. Now we had arrived, and we were awake and alert, ready to talk about what lay ahead of us. The innkeeper wanted to show us to our beds. We asked for tea and one more log on the fire.

"What will happen on the morrow, Mother Francesca?" one of the sisters asked.

"We'll start slowly. No rush. We want to approach the building of our new home in the right frame of mind. My only real goal for tomorrow is to visit the site of our new nunnery. Father William tells me the church is already finished and waiting for services to begin. I'm hoping we'll be able to walk through the rest of the site, mapping out where we want to build our chapter house, the refectory, and the cloister gardens. We will be leading double lives for a while—both nuns and architects. We'll begin to observe our seven liturgical hours almost immediately, wherever we happen to be. At the same time, we will do what we can to help design and plan the layout of the nunnery as a whole."

"How do you envision our liturgical schedule, Mother Francesca? You referred to seven hours instead of the usual eight."

"Here's how I hope we will develop our daily routine, based upon the most recent papal directive."

"MATINS: We start as we have done this night, observing Matins for an hour or two around midnight. After sleeping for several hours, we awaken to a quiet world. This break between two periods of sleep gives us time to ask what God expects of us as a new convent. The liturgy itself is built on the biblical text of Christ's midnight prayer at Gethsemane:

'Not my will, but thine, be done.' It is a reminder to be ready to do whatever God will ask of us.

"LAUDS or PRIME: We return to sleep between 1:00 and 2:00 AM, feeling surer of our plans, and we rest until the ringing of Lauds at sunrise. Depending on where you began your spiritual journey, you may know this particular service as Prime. Also, it is a reminder that it is the beginning of our physical workday as well as our spiritual schedule. The biblical text is based on Christ being brought before Pontius Pilate. It asks us to rejoice in the day we have received and to praise God for his generous gifts, whatever his plans for us may be.

"We will adjust our times, depending on the season of the year. Here at the beginning of summer, the sun creeps over the horizon around five o'clock. But during the winter, we may offer a pick-up breakfast—tea and toast—in the kitchen, while we wait for daylight to make our work possible.

"TERCE: Actual work begins at six and continues till the ringing of Terce at nine. At this third hour of our working day, we take an abbreviated break for breakfast and remind ourselves of Saint Benedict's injunction: '*Laborare est orare*— to work is to pray.' Depending upon the developments of any particular day, we may offer a quick invitation to private prayer as a substitute for the readings of the day.

"SEXT: Three more hours of work brings us to noon and the main meal of the day. If our physical workload is heavy, the same provisions for an abbreviated service may apply to the hour of Sext. The assigned biblical passages and liturgy may be read during the meal. Except during the period of Lent, the Cantor may substitute an inspirational story of a saint's life.

"NONE: Our final physical work period ends with the

ringing of None, the hour that marks the death of Jesus on the cross. This is also the last of the abbreviated liturgies. From three o'clock on, we return to the full liturgy.

"VESPERS: This service comes at sunset, or around five o'clock in winter. A light dinner—perhaps bread and soup or a cold salad—follows. The emphasis is now not on work as a form of prayer, but on prayer for its own sake. The themes include thanksgiving, praise of God, self-evaluation, and confession of failures. We stress the glorification of God.

"COMPLINE: The last service of the day is Compline, bringing with it the closure of nightfall and sleep as an image of death. The childhood prayer, 'Now I lay me down to sleep' captures the meaning of Compline. And thus, we make our way through the days, following the path our Savior laid out for us."

I had several other announcements to make as well. I chose the five ladies who accompanied me on this first trip to Birch Falls for the roles I intended them to fulfill.

Sister Agatha had already been assigned the position of Prioress. The title is rather misleading because it will be many years before we have grown large enough to need a separate priory. But in the meantime, Sister Agatha will serve as my second-in-command. She will enforce any needed discipline within the convent and will handle much of the routine business of the nunnery.

Sister Scholastica is properly named, for she is the scholar among us. Her official title is Cantor, and as such, she will lead the choir in the singing of the hours every day. In addition, she will be responsible for the library and any work being done in the scriptorium. Right now, she will focus all of her efforts on the liturgical hours. Later, when we are fully functioning, she may need an assistant to help in the library and scriptorium.

Sister Martha will be our Cellarer. She will be responsible for all of our food and drink. She will supervise a staff of cooks and kitchen workers. Within the rest of the convent, she will oversee the employment of guards, porters, and other workmen. She will supervise all activities involving the buying and selling of goods.

Sister Juliana will be our Almoner. The title puts her in charge of charitable activities within and outside of the convent. That includes distributing food to the poor and helping those who come to us with simple medical needs. In addition, because we will be shorthanded for a while, Sister Juliana will take charge of training any novices and offering hospitality to our visitors.

Sister Elizabeth will serve as our Chamberlain. She will supervise the distribution of clothing and bedding, take care of the laundry, and, for the time being, set up an infirmary should any of our nuns become ill.

These are all more or less permanent positions to be held so long as the sisters can do the work involved. For the younger women coming into the convent in the following months, we will make assignments on a rotating basis so that each woman may find a position that particularly suits her abilities and interests. If one of our newcomers has a particular interest she wishes to develop, someone will let me know so that we can find a suitable job for her.

~

"Have you seen the site of our convent, Mother Francesca?"

"No, I haven't. I'll be seeing it for the first time with all of you tomorrow. I have, however, received a complete description from the architect who is managing the construction. The church, as I have mentioned, is already finished. It is built of a locally quarried stone to last for centuries. The building follows the standard description of a Christian church layout. Two great doors open at the west end to allow parishioners to enter the nave and participate in the worship services. It has a traditional transept, representing the cross, with north and south entrances and chapels for private prayer. The choir, with its holy altar, is at the eastern end of the building, where the first sunlight will illuminate the stained-glass windows. The choir is slightly off-center, with a slant to the right, recalling Christ's bowed head.

"I've been told that the grounds were once farmland. The original owner spent most of his life clearing the plot we purchased, but he did not live long enough to enjoy the fruits of his labor. We will benefit from his efforts. He has left us a barn with an adjoining pasture, a hillside with several straggly fruit trees in need of some loving attention, and a central well that gives promise of a refreshing water supply for all of our needs."

"A barn? What will we do with a barn? So far, we don't even have a place to stay for ourselves." Speaking as the prioress, Sister Agatha gave voice to what her younger colleagues were thinking.

"Wrong on two counts, my dear sister. First, we do have a place to stay. The innkeeper recently bought a house directly behind the inn. The original owner decided to keep moving west, and he offered the innkeeper a chance to purchase the building at a reduced price. The owner of the inn plans to turn that house into an extension of the inn, but for the next several years he will not need the additional space. He is renting the building to the church for a minimal sum, and it will be our home away from home while the convent is being built.

"Moreover, we do need a barn. Right now, I suspect it will be little more than a ramshackle structure, but it will remind us that we can have a cow who will provide us with fresh milk. We will have room for a mule to help us transport our goods, a chicken coop for fresh eggs, and shelter for other beasts who come our way."

"A cat and her kittens?" A soft voice came from the back of the room.

"Oh, most definitely. Cats will be a part of our family. We need them for rodent control as well as companionship. As for the layout, you must envision a square plot of land. The church already defines and fills the southern edge of the property. The western edge of the plot borders a road that runs back into town. We will have a stone wall along the western edge of the property to provide some privacy for our nuns as they go about their business. But there will also be a welcoming set of doors giving access to our central cloister gardens, and those doors will open every Sunday to allow entrance to the church.

"On one side of the doorway will be a small office for our porter, who will act as a go-between to connect our sisters and the outside world. On the other side of the doorway will be a small room from which I can conduct any daily business with the townspeople. When we finish all other construction, I will consider building an abbess's house, with a formal reception area for visiting family or prospective members, along with my private office and sleeping quarters.

"Paralleling the church, our refectory and kitchen will lie along the northern edge of the grounds. The refectory offers a central gathering spot, where we come together at least twice a day to share our bounty, refresh our bodies, and hear some edifying lessons. Separating the kitchen from our living quarters is, of course, a safety precaution against fire. It also makes it possible for our cooks to grow summer vegetables and flavorful herbs right outside the kitchen door.

"The last side of our quadrangle—along the eastern edge of the original plot—will be our chapter house. On the first floor, the chapter room will contain an Arthurian roundtable, which will allow us to talk to one another as equals. Two smaller rooms, along with a small kitchen, will serve as our infirmary and guest quarters. Our dormitory and lavatory facilities will occupy the second floor. The third floor with its banks of unshaded windows will contain our library and our scriptorium, although their completion will be somewhat delayed until our daily accommodations are in place.

"All of our buildings will open onto a covered but open-air walkway to allow us to pass from one building to another in times of bad weather. On pleasant days, this cloistered walkway will invite our nuns to stroll outside for a view of our gardens or to find a quiet place to read and write. The central area, of course, will contain our cloister garden, an ongoing project full of beautiful flowers, relaxing aromas, and small vistas that surprise and delight the eye.

"That takes care of the edges of the central plot. The barn, the orchard, the pasture, and an interesting hillside all lay behind the original quadrangle, suggesting opportunities to expand our grounds. As one example, I am considering turning those old fruit trees into an area that also serves as a cemetery for nuns who do not wish to be buried in the crypt. If we decorate each new grave with a young fruit tree, we will eventually leave an amazing orchard for the following generations.

"What I have just described is, of course, pure speculation at this stage. As we explore the grounds, I hope you will bring to us any ideas you may have. This is a unique opportunity to create a convent from the ground up. Let's make it something extraordinary. But for now, it's time for a second sleep. Scurry off to bed and rest before tomorrow's grand adventures."

CHAPTER 6
The Accident

August 1843

The grizzly old bartender shook out a wet towel and took a final swipe at the plank he used as a counter. Then he leaned on both elbows to survey his customers.

"Hey, fellas, heard some news today you'll be interested in. The Padre came in for lunch. He tells me he's discovered that a whole bunch of unmarried women arrived in the neighborhood recently. Seems they are looking for a place to settle."

"Wooh, wooh, wooh. 'Bout time we had some female companionship around here."

"There's just one catch. These women? They're . . . nuns."

"Aw, crap!"

"You mean those tight-jawed old biddies with the funny hats and long black robes? Like the teachers with sharp-edged rules to rap our knuckles the way they did in grade school?"

"Them's the ones. Like I said, "Crap!""

May 15, 2011

David looked up after reading Sarah's opening page. "Wow. Makes me want to learn more, but what will your strait-laced Catholic bishop think of the language?"

"I'm hoping he'll recognize that it suits the time and characters."

"You continue to amaze me, my love. How do you do it? How do you create a story—a scene or a character—out of your imagination? I mean, where do you start? When I begin to work on a criminal case, I have a clear starting point. Bang. Someone pulls a trigger, and I have a murder to deal with.

"But look what you've done. You've been given an assignment: Write the history of a nunnery. So how do you know where to start—to use a bunch of frustrated long-shoremen in a makeshift bar?"

"It's the historical mindset, I suppose. While I was cleaning house the other day, I wondered what Birch Falls was like before it was a town—when it was nothing but a raging waterfall that stopped all boat traffic on the river. Then I began thinking about why the town developed and what kind of people were the first settlers. I kept going back until I reached the 'nothing but trees' stage. That was my starting point—my gunshot if you will."

"But how do you get from trees to longshoremen in a bar?"

"Having a couple of good courses in economic history helped. And I have to admit I went back further than the trees. I started with the river system. If you look at a map of the United States, you'll see that the waterways form a giant tree-like shape in the center of the country with all rivers headed eventually to the great Mississippi and then out to the Gulf of Mexico. Our Birch River flows north and west, which sounds contradictory, but the water is headed for the Tennessee River, then to the Ohio River, and then to the Mississippi.

"If you were a farmer in Northern Mississippi or Alabama or southern Tennessee, you would be looking for a way to ship your cotton crop to market. The Birch River seems promising until you load your boat, start down the river and suddenly realize you're headed for a waterfall with a 20-foot drop.

"At the foot of the falls, you can see that another boat has a similar but opposite problem. It's facing a 20-foot wall. Is there a solution? Of course. Trade boats. All you need is a good, solid road working its way down the side of the mountain and a crew of longshoremen to unload your boat, transfer the goods around the waterfall, and reload them onto the other boat for their continuing journey. But how do you find dockworkers in the middle of a mountain range?

"You advertise for them. That's what newspapers are for. Workers will come because it's good money, and once the longshoremen come to build the road, a dozen other needs will pop up. Where will they sleep? Where will they eat? What if they need new boots? What if one of them tears his pants? What if there's a fight? What if one gets sick? Anywhere that people come together, others will join them to serve their needs. *Voila*! A town! Someone with an empty building to fill with beds. Cooks. Merchants. Craftsmen. A sheriff. A lawyer. A schoolmarm. A doctor. A minister."

"A nun?"

"Why not?"

"Is the history all a part of your plan for the book?"

"No, not at all. You know, as a historian, I hate writing

history because it is so dull. I want to tell a rousing good story, and in this case, the story belongs to Sister Francesca, mother superior of the nunnery. My evidence comes from her own words and I must use that evidence to the best of my ability. I'm planning to tell her story from her point of view, including only what she might have known at the time she lived. If some detail of historical evidence needs to appear within the story, I'll slip it in, rather like feeding a cat a pill by concealing it in a bit of raw calves' liver. That introduction I gave you to read is a good example. I'll probably use the longshoremen and the news of the nuns' arrival as a kind of preface before the story begins. It's vitally important, but the reader may take a while to recognize that fact."

Sarah was not eager to talk further about the book, so she was grateful when the sound of a trucker's air horn interrupted this conversation. "Listen to that racket, will you? The fellow who developed the trucker's horn ought to be hung up by his ears."

"It does get your attention, doesn't it?"

"Are you aware that we come in for special treatment from local truckers? Mrs. Blackburn next door has a brother who drives an eighteen-wheeler, and he tells her that they are encouraged to pull on their air horns for all they are worth when they drive by our neighborhood. They're hoping to get your attention, I gather, so that you will do something about the lack of signage on that blind curve out there."

"Me? Why would I ...?"

"I told her the road signs were not a part of your job description, but I don't think she was listening. She's concerned that there will be a serious accident there, and it could be one of us involved in it."

"Do you remember my telling you that if I was elected as the new DA, I would come to regret it? This is one of those times. She's right, but there's nothing I can do except mention it once more to the road department."

Their discussion was interrupted again, but this time the air horn sounded more frantic than usual as the driver pulled its handle repeatedly. Then came the sound everyone dreaded—squealing brakes followed by the crumpling of metal and the shattering of glass. David and Sarah were on their feet before the sounds subsided. Then, out of the unnatural silence that followed, came the low moaning of a car horn sounding a single extended note.

"That's a bad sign, Sarah. It usually means someone or something is leaning on the horn button. You had better stay here while I investigate."

"No way. You may need help."

They ran around the side of the house side-by-side until their feet faltered when they saw the devastation. On the far side of the road was an eighteen-wheeler jackknifed across the highway, the cab tilted precariously with two wheels in the far culvert and the trailer still shaking back and forth as if it could not decide whether to stop or go on. As they stared, the cab door opened, and a white-faced driver lowered himself gingerly to the ground, tears running down his face. "I couldn't help it. I tried. He was on the wrong side of the road, and ..."

On the nearer side of the road almost in the Cohens' front yard, a late model SUV had wrapped itself around the trunk of an ancient oak tree. It had hit with such force that the engine block had been pushed completely into the passenger compartment. David held out his arm once again. "Stay here, Sarah. It is going to be an ugly sight. I don't think anyone could have survived that crash, but I need to check."

He approached the wreck from behind and peered in the side window before he realized that the windshield was gone and he could look directly into the passenger compartment. A young couple had occupied the front seats. Now their eyes stared past each other without seeing. Their jaws hung slack as if they had been trying to scream, and their heads were twisted at impossible angles. David forced himself to reach under the dashboard and pull the wire that controlled the horn. Then he backed away, his vision blurred.

"Dead. Both of them. It looks like their necks snapped with the impact. At least they died together and instantly."

"David! Listen! There's a whining sound coming from the back. Could you see into the back seat?"

"No. Everything is compressed—like an accordion. I hear it now, too. Maybe there's a dog back there. It could have survived."

"Can you open the sliding side door?"

"No. It's jammed."

"Try the back lift gate. There is probably a button to lower the seat back."

"It doesn't work."

"Here. Maybe I can crawl over the seat. I'm hearing a funny hiccupy sound now. There's something else trapped in here."

"Be careful, Sarah. If it's an injured animal, it may attack out of fear. Stay back. I'm calling dispatch now to get crews out here to clear the wreck." He turned his attention to his cell phone.

"Denice? DA Cohen here. Listen carefully. I have a horrible wreck to report, and it's practically in my front yard. Highway 126 at that blind curve. There's an eighteen-wheeler jackknifed across the road, blocking traffic in both directions, and it may take a crane to lift the tractor out of the culvert. We'll need to set up temporary detours around the mess. The truck driver is out and moving, but injuries are unknown. The truck appears to belong to something called 'Allied Home Goods, Inc.'

"The second vehicle is an SUV, now wedged headfirst into a tree trunk. Luckily, I can see the license plate. It's a Tennessee registered plate, number Q31 95L. Two victims, male and female, both dead with broken necks, so we'll need the coroner. There could be a gasoline leak, so send the fire department, too. And we're hearing unidentifiable sounds suggesting one or more additional victims, human or animal. We need ambulances, human services personnel, animal control—pretty much everybody you've got."

For the moment, he had forgotten Sarah. Now he turned back to the wreck to hear her shout, "Oh, my living soul! It's a baby—no, two babies, still carefully strapped in their car beds."

"How old?"

"They're tiny—infants. One in pink; one in blue."

"Don't move them, Sarah. Those infant carriers provide good protection, but you can't be sure the children have no injuries. For now, you might try singing to them, or just talking, so they hear human voices."

"I'm coming out. It's scrunched back here. And I'm smelling something odd."

"They're babies, Sarah. With dirty diapers, no doubt."

"No, it's not that." She finished wiggling over the seat back and jumped to the ground.

"David, look. See that drip? That's gas. It's already spreading. One stray spark and the car goes up in flames. We have to get them out."

"It's a risk either way, but give me a shot at reaching them." He stretched himself along the top of the back seat and felt blindly for a way to grip one of the carriers.

"There should be a carrying handle. But be careful of your shoulder repair; don't re-injure yourself."

"The shoulder is strong, Sarah. And I just found the handle. One carrier coming up." He handed the first baby to her and went back for the second. She carried them to the house, setting the carriers on the porch furniture, where they would be out of the way and protected from any further disturbance. David joined her there, the sweat on his brow demonstrating the amount of stress he was feeling.

"Now we wait."

CHAPTER 7

It's Only Temporary

May 15, 2011

The Cohens heard the sirens and emergency horns long before the vehicles appeared on the scene. Route 126 was blocked by the accident, and several of the bigger vehicles were having trouble finding their way through the narrow neighborhood streets. It felt as if they had been waiting for hours, but it was probably only a few minutes before the first help arrived.

Emergency medical technicians stopped their trucks next to the crumpled SUV, and two uniformed techs jumped out and peered into the car windows. Then they returned, shaking their heads, and drove on to the location of the jack-knifed semi where the truck driver was sitting on his running board, leaning his head on his hands.

"Headache, sir?"

"Just feels a little funny—floaty or shimmery."

"Not surprising after an accident like this. Do you mind if we take a look at your eyes? Oh, yes, a bit of disorganized vision, I'm guessing. Hit your head, didn't you? We will be transporting you to the hospital in a few minutes where they can get a better look at what's happening."

"Do I have to go to the hospital? I need to get my rig straightened out. I'm on a deadline."

"I'm afraid you're not going anywhere tonight. You may have a serious concussion, and your truck will not be ready for a release, anyway. We will call your company and deal with your boss's expectations. You just relax here while we check for other victims, and we'll be back to get you in a bit."

The EMTs then moved to the front porch of the house where their chief took over.

"DA Cohen, I'm Jake Tappitt, head EMT on this shift. We are sorry for disrupting your peaceful Sunday evening."

"How long is it going to take to clean up this mess?" Sarah asked.

"Well into the night, I'm afraid. There's a lot to be done. We can't move the SUV, for example, until the coroner arrives and gives us his verdict on the two bodies in the front seat. At best, we hope to have the road cleared and open again by the time rush-hour starts in the morning. Now, where are these babies people have been telling me about— the ones who survived the crash?"

"They're right here, sound asleep despite all of the racket going on around them."

"Thank goodness they were in these safety-approved car beds. We're going to have to wake them to check their vital signs, but young as they are, they should go right back to sleep. Has anyone told you what's being done to take care of them?"

"Not yet. The police have the license number of the SUV, however, so they should be able to trace the owner of the car and find out where the family belongs."

"Ah, here comes a staff member from family services now. She should be able to help. I wouldn't worry about the children. They seem perfectly fine to me. Lucky little guys."

Bea Randolph was an experienced social worker. She had seen almost every terrifying situation one could imagine, so she was well prepared to take charge of the two little orphans who now awaited her on the Cohens' front porch. She introduced herself and pulled up a chair. "I'm going to give you the whole story," she said. "Please understand that I'm using people's real names only because you are the district attorney. The possibility that you may have to deal with these matters in court means you will need to know their real identities.

"The young people who died in the crash were Joseph and Miriam Schantz. They run—ran—a small delicatessen in downtown Muddy Bottom. They've been married for seven years but have no children. For the last several months, they have been working with the Jewish Children's Home in Nashville to settle the details of open adoption. An expectant mother of twins knew she would be unable to care for them and wanted only to know they would be raised together in a loving Jewish home. The twins were born five months ago, and today was the first day of their adoptive parents' six-month trial. They were returning home after picking up their new babies.

"Both Joseph and Miriam have living parents, but when we contacted them to let them know about the accident, neither family showed any interest in following up with their potential grandchildren. I gathered from our conversations that the parents were not entirely on board with the idea of adoption. Or perhaps they're just overcome with grief. In an instant, after all, they went from being new grandparents to being childless themselves. Their minds may change as they adjust to their new realities. However, in the meantime, the babies will return to the Jewish Children's Home until someone adopts them.

"The only problem right now is that it's much too late tonight to find anyone willing to drive them back to Nashville. We will probably have to admit them to the hospital overnight, although I hate to expose them to that long admission process, especially since they are technically nameless and indigent." It was a blatant play for sympathy, but it worked.

"They can stay with us tonight," Sarah offered.

"I can't ask you to do that. You're not equipped to ..."

"They have everything they need with them—bottles of formula, diapers, blankets, clothing. I saw it all when I was helping to get them out of the car. And it is safe to go back into the car now that the firemen have finished washing away the leaked gasoline."

"Sarah, are you sure ...?"

"Don't even think it, David. We have empty dresser drawers that make perfect cribs. My mother used to do this for family visits all the time. It's settled."

"Well, then, we shall pick them up at 9:00 in the morning. And thank you for your help." David had already moved off the porch in response to a shout from the police chief. Sarah picked up a carrier in each hand and then stood helpless in front of the closed front door. Bea Randolph had turned to leave before she realized the problem.

"Here. Let me help you. This is not a job for a single person." Together the two women moved the babies from the porch to the guest room, where they pulled out dresser drawers to serve as makeshift cribs.

"Are you sure about this? Will your husband be able to help, or will he be tied up with the accident?"

"I'm sure he'll be back soon."

"In the meantime, you had better let me stay to help. These little guys are about to quit making polite whimpering sounds. They will soon use their full-blown lung power to demand diaper changes and bottle refills."

"I can manage."

"What makes you so stubborn? You can't do it all."

The phrase offered uncomfortable similarities to Sarah's greatest fear—her inability to do everything that needed to be done. Her jaw tightened, and she grabbed the nearest diaper, determined to handle the tasks. Chaos reigned for a few more minutes, but eventually, the children were dry and fed and headed back to sleep. Sarah and Bea relaxed in the matching armchairs near the window.

Bea looked around the neat house and smiled at what that neatness suggested.

"You and your husband have no children," she commented.

"It's that obvious, is it? No, we've only been married for three months. But your observation is correct. There won't be children. I have a ... a blood disorder ... Rh-negative with full sensitization." This was the first time Sarah had given someone the medical explanation, and she felt rather proud of how calmly she had been able to admit her problem.

"There are alternative methods of creating a family, you know—fostering, adoption, hiring a surrogate."

"Yes, we've heard all the lectures, but so far nothing feels quite right for us. We have close friends who are applying to become foster parents, but I'm not sure they will go through with it. The wife is worried about what a child of any age will do to their marriage."

"That sounds like a self-created problem. Most prospective fosterers are more concerned that they won't have enough time with a child to make a difference in the child's life. In many cases, fostering is just a temporary bandage on a festering wound."

"You've had lots of experience with this sort of thing, haven't you?"

"Well, I've seen lots of families struggling to form permanent bonds with children who are afraid to trust them. Children who need parental love the most are also the ones most likely to test those bonds by acting out. They're rather like a cat who pushes a vase of flowers onto the floor in front of you and then rubs against your ankle as if to say, 'Do you still love me?'"

"How do you feel about adoption? Is it more likely to be a permanent solution?"

"No guarantees. Even raising a child from infancy to age eighteen is only temporary. Think about your own life—and I'm assuming here that you had a fairly standard upbringing."

"I did, and I still do. My parents remain a part of my life."

"Really? When did you see them last?"

"Uh ...This is June, right? About three months ago, at Passover."

"And when will you see them again? Yom Kippur? Hanukkah? Several more months? I'm not criticizing. Yours is a normal pattern. Eighteen years of daily interactions, and then the time you spend together is short—temporary. Even with a child of your own, you would spend only a fraction of your life in active parenting."

"So, you still think adoption is a good thing?"

"Do you mean, why do I think it's the most important development since sliced bread?"

"I'm sorry to sound so naïve, but when I was growing up, adoption was something people didn't talk about. We had a girl in my third-grade class who was adopted, and I remember the talk that went through the classroom as one kid whispered to the next, 'Have you heard, she's—ppssstt—adopted?' They made it sound as if she had done something terrible."

"Luckily, the term has lost its stigma. But most people don't realize how many parentless children we have in our society. We still hide them away in orphanages, children's homes, private schools, or disciplinary workshops. I also have to admit that our adoption system leaves much to be desired. When a young couple comes into one of our institutions to consider adopting a child, they have a preconceived notion of their future child. They want a bright, energetic, athletic, talented, three-year-old, blue-eyed blonde. Introduce them to a dark-haired eight-year-old with several missing teeth and watch their eyes glaze over."

"The blue-eyed blonde is still the ideal? I understand some of that description, but why the emphasis on the three-year-old?"

"You'd be surprised to see how many people will turn down a child who is not potty trained, simply because they don't want to have to bother going through the drill. It breaks my heart to see how many children are passed over as not quite the perfect child."

"I can understand why a parent might not be willing to take on a child with major problems. But what happens to the children who don't make the grade—the ones who don't get adopted?"

"'They compensate for the missing parental love after a

while. They develop other interests and make friends. And then when they turn eighteen, we release them into society to survive as best they can. A few will enroll in, say, a junior college, or a trade school. Others, I'm sorry to admit, simply go downhill and come back to other safe and protective institutions, like the local jail."

"That's awful!"

"Of course, it is. If I had my way, every orphaned child would be adopted. We all deserve to have at least one person who loves us unconditionally and creates a supportive home —one that values character as well as reading and writing. But what are you really asking? Should you adopt? I can't answer that, but I would hope you might see an adopted child as one way you can make our world a better place."

"Even if it's only temporary?"

"Even then."

Sarah allowed herself a period of contemplation, and Bea respected her silence. A short time later, David returned to find both women with their eyes closed.

"Sleeping on the job?"

Sarah opened one eye and glared at him. "All is quiet. Don't break the spell."

One of the babies whimpered, and Bea stretched out her experienced hand to jiggle the right cradle.

As the whimper turned into a sleepy sigh, the social worker stood to excuse herself. "Now that you have an extra pair of hands, I must get back to my office. We still have a transfer to arrange for the children in the morning."

Sarah mouthed a silent thank you and waved her on her way.

David smiled. "All is well, I take it. The situation isn't bothering you?"

"Not at all. I'm just happy to have been able to help. It

has made a nice break from the work I've been doing all week. And after all, it's only temporary. They'll be gone in the morning."

"You've been working hard on the book, I know. Is it going well?"

"I won't go that far, but I'm feeling better about it. I have started to take Jean's advice about using the seven liturgical hours of the convent as an organizational feature. The nuns handled the monotony of their lives by turning the day into manageable chunks separated by the singing of the hours. The patterns of daily life in the convent also make more sense when I can think of them in terms of their inspiration, development, and measurable conclusion.

"This week I've been working on the original plan—the meditative period in which the mother superior lays out her organizational plans. She must decide which liturgical hours God will find most pleasing, which of her sister nuns will best serve as members of her staff, and the best way to organize the buildings of the new convent.

"I've been interested to notice that in everything that happens, she sees a message from God. And for her, the liturgical hours provide a reminder to be ready to do whatever God asks of her. For example, she would have believed this accident was meant to spur her to some course of action. I'm not sure what message she would read into it, but it does help me understand her better."

CHAPTER 8

Solving Problems

June 27, 2011

Sarah spent the next few weeks at home working on her book plans. She had been pleasantly surprised to discover several books on monastic practices in the college library, and she hauled them home to have their details at her fingertips as she worked. She did a lot of reading about monastic institutions in general and how they function. She mastered the layout of the liturgical hours and began to understand the rules and regulations of monastic life. But no matter how neatly she organized her home office, something was missing in this atmosphere. It was all too easy to walk down the hall and pick up the latest magazine, snap on the TV, or end up in the kitchen making a snack. Home, no matter how comfortable, did not provide the scholarly atmosphere she needed.

And so it was that by the last week in June, Sarah found herself packing her briefcase and moving to the archival collections section of the college library. The patrons' room offered all the amenities she had missed—the individual desk lamps, the bookstand with its braces and elastic bands to hold the pages of a reference work open, and bookshelves from floor to ceiling.

One of the privileges her contract offered was the use of a library carrel so she could leave her work out from day to day, but she did not take advantage of it. She preferred to join the other scholars at the long worktables. As she felt herself becoming a part of that working group, she also began to identify herself with the mother superior whose words she was reading. Her status as a member of the faculty gave her a similar air of authority. She was someone who would be consulted for advice on many levels.

It was now fully summer, and the only people on campus were a few younger faculty still working on that first book and a cluster of work-study students who were earning their tuition by working all summer. Sarah had failed to hire a research assistant during the chaos of her health crisis. So, on the third day of her full-time return to campus, Sarah summoned Jean Pendergast to her desk.

"How is your workload, Jean?"

"My workload? Everything's done. I finished my master's thesis and passed the oral exam. Now that summer is here, the library science students have pretty much taken over the indexing projects, so I'm just reading for pleasure."

"There's much to be said for that, you know. What about the coming fall semester? Are you still planning to teach at your husband's school for boys?"

Jean grimaced. "Probably not. The teacher they thought they were losing may change her mind, so there is no definite opening. I may do some substituting, but it's not a regular job." She made a small sound—half snort, half chuckle.

"Truth be told, I don't know what I'll be doing next fall, and that scares me."

"What do you want to do?"

"I want to be back in a classroom, but not as a teacher. I still have much to learn, and I don't know how to do anything except be a student."

"Still no chance of going to grad school to earn your doctorate?"

"Not unless you know something I don't. Smoky Mountain isn't going to offer doctoral-level courses yet. And the schools that do are all too far away to allow me to commute."

"I may have some suggestions, but I also have an offer for you. Let's talk about that first. One of the provisions of my contract as a writer-in-residence is that I may hire a research assistant at a very attractive salary. It would be about $300 a month more than you are currently earning as a work-study student."

"To do what?"

"Explain Catholic doctrine to me. Look up details I'm missing. Handle correspondence. Pursue lines of research I don't have time for. Keep track of the sisters within the nunnery. I suspect you'll find lots of details I would completely overlook. You would be my right hand, and I'll make sure you get a by-line for your resume."

"Full-time?"

"Yes and no. Your working hours will be as flexible as mine, although you will get a regular monthly paycheck. There will probably be big gaps during which you'll have nothing to do, and other times when you'll be swamped. But I promise to be reasonable about what I ask of you."

"You know I'll love helping with the book. Thanks for trusting me."

"You're perfect for the job. Everyone agreed, even the

chair and the dean! But now let's talk about your doctoral possibilities."

"I just don't see any way to make that work. The boys are eight and ten now, but it will be years before they are mature enough that I can leave them for days at a time."

"No one's going to ask you to do that. You need to understand how the doctoral degree differs from your current studies. Up to this point, your goal has been to gain broad general knowledge about various historical periods. You've also been learning methodology. Now it's time to put that knowledge to work.

"To become Dr. Jean Pendergast, you will leave the classroom behind and become an independent researcher. Your goal must be to become the country's leading expert on a specific and limited topic."

"That's impossible. I'll never ..."

"No, it's not, and we're all here to help you do it. Moreover, no one expects you to accomplish that in less than ten years—five years of coursework (mostly reading) to prepare for your comprehensive written exams and five more years to write your dissertation and pass your orals. And if it takes longer than that, so be it."

"But what do you mean by 'leading expert' on something?"

"It's not hard to do if you narrow your topic enough. Let me give you an example—one my advisor suggested to me. I wasn't interested in the topic, but it was a viable option. Start narrowing the time frame—not American history as a whole but the era of the nineteen-sixties—narrowed to the presidency of John Kennedy—narrowed to the Bay of Pigs Crisis—and then to the question of who originated the plan that put an end to the crisis. Was it Kennedy, his advisors, a think-tank, or a long-range plan?

"Kennedy gets the credit, but so far as I know, no one has asked where the ideas originated. The evidence is probably in the Kennedy papers somewhere, but no one has looked for it. You could do that and write a book about it. Voila! You're the new expert on the Bay of Pigs."

"Why weren't you interested?"

"Two reasons. The Kennedy Library is in Boston, which was just a little too far from New York City to be accessible. And anyone working on the Bay of Pigs has to be fluent in Russian, which I am not."

"Whoa! So that's why everyone kept insisting that we start learning foreign languages."

"Exactly. If you want to be an expert on a topic, you need to know what the rest of the world has said about the topic. And the rest of the world does not always speak English. I spent two years between my master's degree and the beginning of my doctoral studies looking for obscure characters who might make good dissertation subjects. Two years was not an unusual break. Some folks take much longer. You need to have a clear idea of your topic and all the tools you will need to do the research, including the pertinent languages. When I don't need your research skills, you can fill your time mastering languages and exploring the dark alleys of history."

"I'm stunned. I never realized ... I thought I'd just be back in a classroom for years."

"Depending on the school you choose, you may do most of your coursework as independent studies. They may only require you to be on campus for one session a year. So, you can schedule a course to take during the summer when your husband is freer to take on child-care responsibilities. Or the boys might go with you for a month-long session. Lots of possibilities exist.

"Most of your study time will be spent reading all the scholarly work done up to that point. At the same time, you'll discover what other languages you may need, and you will be able to fill those gap years by auditing language classes. That's how I learned German, by the way. I sat in on German 101 classes right on my campus. Remember all those discussions we had about where language training could be found?"

"So, even if I were free to start my doctorate, I'd need a couple of years to prepare?"

"Maybe longer. You're still young, so there's no hurry."

"OK. So, when do we start?"

"Right now. You need to head to the HR office to fill out the employment paperwork. They are expecting you.

The next morning, Julia Winthrop tapped on Sarah's office door but did not wait to hear a response before poking her head around the door frame. "Gwen told me were here, and I wanted to catch you before you went charging off to your Special Collections hideaway. God, I've missed you!"

"Good morning to you, too. Why don't you come in instead of keeping one foot in the hallway? I'm not going to run you off."

"I'm ashamed to be pestering you on your first week back during your writing hours. I have some idea of what you've been through, and I'm awestruck that you're here at all. I don't have any business adding to your concerns. But if I don't talk to someone soon, I'm going to implode."

"Julia! Sit! Calm down! I'm here because I'm feeling good again. And yes, I will be headed off to the library soon. But you're my best friend, and I always have time for you. Now, what's going on?"

"Well, the good news is that family court has granted our petition to serve as foster parents for Ronnie Baxter while we wait for our formal certification to untangle all the red tape involved. But the bad news is that Ronnie reacted strangely when he got the news. As soon as it appeared that we had full parental rights over him, he rebelled. He's reverted to the typical, smart-mouthed teenager I feared he would be."

"They all do that now and then, don't they? I certainly did."

"Ah, but not to this extent. He's accusing Will of being just like his father—trying to ruin his running career before he can get started."

"How so?"

"You're probably not aware of it—I wasn't—but the next Summer Olympics take place in June 2012 in London. Ronnie wants to move to a training facility in Colorado Springs now and apply for a place on the 2012 Track Team. Will has tried to explain that the training facility will not take potential runners unless they have a proven track record in competition. Ronnie does not have any sort of record because he hasn't been allowed to compete this year. And the wind sprints he does with Will don't count because there's no official record of them."

"That's not Will's fault. He's been training the boy during his off hours, hasn't he?"

"Yes, and that's part of the problem. Ronnie accused him of deliberately holding him back to keep him out of contention."

"How old is Ronnie?"

"Barely fourteen."

"Much too young to be going off on his own."

"That's what we've tried to tell him, but he won't listen. Will has even made what I consider to be an incredibly generous counteroffer. He's willing to take the whole family to London next summer to see the Olympics in person. He says he can get tickets so Ronnie can see all the various running events. He may even be able to get him in to talk to some of the runners."

"What a wonderful idea!"

"Not according to the foster-child-from-hell. He says he won't sit in the stands with his parents and their squalling baby because he would look like a 'dorky wannabe.'"

"I think I know what Bea would say about this."

"Who's Bea?"

"She's the social worker we met the night we took in those two babies from the wreck in our front yard. During a few breaks when the twins were both asleep, we talked a lot about adoption and the difficulties families face. She would say that Ronnie is testing you. He is being mean and making impossible demands, while at the same time he wants you to prove you love him. He's offering you an excuse to get rid of him if you want to change your mind. If this one doesn't work, he'll try something else, which could be worse."

"So, what do we do?"

"Keep telling him you love him. Praise his good qualities if you can find some. And about the Olympics—You might try switching his focus to the 2016 Games in Rio de Janeiro. He'll be eighteen, with at least three years of competitive running behind him. Encourage him to tell his coaches next year that he wants to participate in the 2016 Olympics. Give him an attainable goal and help him reach it. Prove your love."

"Thanks, Sarah. I'm not sure my husband will buy into this, but it's worth a try. I wonder if you can buy Olympic tickets four years in advance?"

CHAPTER 9

Building Relationships

July 1, 2011

It was Friday morning, and Sarah was well aware that she was looking at a long four-day Fourth of July weekend. She had come into the office early hoping to get her research materials sorted so that she could spend most of the weekend writing in her home office. The building was empty, and she had left her door latched rather than wedged open. She had also considered leaving the lights off, but she needed to see what she was doing. Still, all was peaceful for a while until a rustling and whispering commotion began in the hall outside. Sarah could hear the conversation but did not recognize the voices.

"What's going on?"

"We were checking on Professor Chomsky. We heard she won't be teaching in the fall."

"Why not? She's not leaving, is she?"

"I hope not."

"Is she in there? Did you knock?"

"When she closes the door like that, it usually means she doesn't want to be disturbed."

"The lights are on. She must be inside."

"Try knocking, Chad. Maybe ..."

Still irritated but also amused to recognize one of her favorite students, Sarah pulled the door open. "Can I help you?"

"You're still here! I'm so relieved." Olivia Cartwright had been Sarah's first advisee, and the two had a long history of friendship. "Are you working?"

"Not anymore. Come on in, you two. She gave a quick, dismissive nod to the student she did not recognize, and then re-closed the door against further interruptions. "And before you ask, I'm not going anywhere. I've been given a release from teaching so I can write a new book for the college. It's a long story. You'll hear about it later."

"If you're busy, we can come back another time, but we're so eager to share our good news ..."

"What's going on? The last time we talked, you mentioned you were working on some big plans, but you weren't ready to talk about them."

"We wanted you to be the first to hear about The Cartwright Foundation."

"The Cartwright Foundation? That sounds a bit over-whelming."

"It's a big idea. But let me start from the beginning. You may remember that after my father died, one of the suspects in his murder was Jack Dunlap. He was able to clear himself almost immediately because he had spent that entire day in Knoxville negotiating with the athletics department at UT. They were discussing a new product line aimed at the college crowd."

"I remember Jack Dunlap, but I thought ... Is he still around?"

"I know you disliked him because of the way he treated me, but he's an absolute genius at marketing. Since I became a business major, I've learned a lot about selling a product, and I've gained a great deal of respect for Jack and his talents. So, yes, he still works for the company, and he's a part of this story."

"OK. Go on."

"His idea is that our Pencil Pets line is getting a bit old. The little kittens and puppies still appeal to grade schoolers, but they soon outgrow them. And we've about exhausted the other characters, like farm animals and the zoo. Jack is proposing a whole new line—called 'Helmet Heads'—to appeal to high school and college students. These new pencil toppers would be modeled on the design of a school's football helmets. They would be sold in campus bookstores or used as fundraisers, or promotional giveaways. But they would also have a certain nostalgic quality. A college guy isn't going to put a poodle puppy on his pencil, but he might like a UT helmet to show his school spirit."

"Would they be collectible or limited to individual schools?"

"Either. Or both. We can put together all the colleges from a single state or a conference like the Big Ten. Jack's working on that now. Anyhow, that's what we were doing last winter. We ran test markets in several parts of the country, and the results were phenomenal. People grabbed them up. So, we'll be going into full production soon."

"I'm still not hearing anything about a foundation."

"That's the other half of the story. I'm not my father's daughter when it comes to money. I am not interested in how much cash we might bring in. I want to know what we are going to do with the income. There's a clear and natural solution. You know Chad's story—how his football career was wiped out by a traumatic brain injury after a bad tackle on the football field. Student-athletes need better equipment and better ways of treating their injuries when they occur. The profits from our Helmet Heads will go directly to the Cartwright Foundation to make that happen."

"Forgive me if I sound a little skeptical, but how exactly do you plan to do all this?"

"Chad, tell her about our think tank. I'm not explaining things as clearly as you do."

"Sure. We've been playing 'Secret Squirrel' with this idea for over a year now, and we've put together a group of talented specialists to help us along the way. We meet in the evenings at the plant, and we don't discuss the foundation in public—yet. But I know Liv's been dying to tell you about it. Here's the group we've called the Helmet Heads Think Tank.

"Olivia, of course, is the *de facto* owner of the Cartwright Company, so any final decisions must get past her, and she then runs them past her board of directors. She's careful to outline what changes will occur so that no one can later claim surprise. We've been able to demonstrate that our current equipment is capable of handling the new designs and that expenses will drop because the helmet designs are simpler than, say, the difference between a bloodhound and a Pekingese.

"My role will be as the spokesperson for the foundation. My major is in radio and TV journalism, and I've done several courses in public speaking, debate, and motivational pep talks. I'll be recording spots of different lengths for public service announcements and filming longer segments for news broadcasts. I see my role in two ways. I'll be passing information to a broad public audience, but

I'll also be announcing by my presence that TBIs can be overcome."

Olivia was smiling at Chad's attempt to downplay his role. "What he's not mentioning is that he's drop-dead handsome and has a dreamy voice to go with it. His sex appeal is one of our biggest assets."

"Come on, Liv! Let's not overdo this. I'm just a part of the group. Jack Dunlap is still head of marketing for the company as a whole, but he'll be doing double duty by helping us market the helmet heads themselves. Within our group, the other person employed by the company is Rick McBride. You probably remember him from one of your classes last year."

"Sure. He's the junior high football coach who wanted out of coaching before one of his students got injured. I introduced you to him, didn't I, Chad?"

"Yes, but then he changed departments. You haven't seen him lately because he's doing catch-up work in chemistry and physics. He quit his teaching job and came to work for the Cartwright organization. He's being paid by the company as Head of Research and Development. He oversees a whole staff of scientists looking for ways to immobilize the human head within a helmet.

"Olivia has added two other women to our private group. Beverly Jacobs is the former assistant district attorney who made such a good impression on the judge during the whistle-blower trial. She's still a lawyer but is looking for a cause. We're offering her one, and we can use her legal expertise. The other is a new doctor in town. Marilyn Hammersmith recently moved here from California where she did an internship and a residency in TBI. I've been told her first love is OB-GYN, but she's seen the latest developments in trauma care. We hope to keep both women in advisory roles."

"I've met the doctor. She seems quite talented."

"She's already been helpful. Last, a local star will be handling our corporate outreach. We're hoping to get other like-minded companies to join our effort, and Bert Wheeler, the former Harlem Globetrotter, is just famous enough to fill our needs. Those seven people form our Think Tank."

"Good plans! But I think you're missing coverage of one other area. What about the ordinary folks—the father whose son suffered a concussion in a high school basketball game or the grandmother who worries about her cheerleading granddaughter when she's part of one of those human pyramids? They're going to care about your efforts, even if they can only afford to send you a few dollars."

"I think you're asking two different questions. First, we're not limiting ourselves to football. We want to see all athletes protected. And second, we will, of course, be open to individual donations, no matter how small."

"That's great. But do you have someone to handle those small amounts—someone to send a thank you note or an annual reminder to send another $5.00?"

"You're right. It's called customer appreciation. But there's a lot of detailed accounting paperwork involved, and right now we don't have anyone with enough free time to handle it."

"Don't you know someone like that? Someone with time on his hands? Somebody who likes working with figures and keeping records?"

"Not right off hand ... oh, wait! Mr. Gillespie!"

"That's the one I was thinking of."

"But he's retired ..."

"And probably bored, as well as being interested in the company he worked for all those years. You made his retirement years financially stable, Olivia. Now how about making him feel important again?"

"I'll visit him this afternoon."

Sarah stood in her doorway and watched as Chad and Olivia headed toward the stairs, shoulder to shoulder and fingers interlaced. She was still smiling at their devotion to one another when a man's voice startled her.

"They're something, aren't they? I see lots of couples on this campus, but those two stand out from the crowd. You couldn't pry them apart with a stick."

"Not that I'd be likely to try it," Sarah replied. "What are you doing back here, Gabe? I thought you'd be well on your way to Havana."

"Well, today, I was looking for you. I need a favor."

"Name it."

"Maria Hernandez has decided to apply for a White House Fellowship, and I offered to help her solicit the three required letters of recommendation. You are our first choice."

"Hold on. You're losing me. I have no idea what a White House Fellowship is."

"It's the most prestigious award a political science major can receive. Less than twenty people qualify each year, and most of them are in their thirties before they do so. The winners spend a year working in the White House in positions tailored to their talents and interests. They are paid a respectable salary equivalent to that of a regular governmental employee in the same position. They travel, meet heads of state, sit in on conferences, write policy papers, chair committees, and learn what responsibilities a governing official must fulfill. The qualifications are pretty generalized, but the applicants must demonstrate a high potential for future government service. Beyond that, the crucial requirement is that the candidate must have completed an undergraduate degree before starting the application process.

"And that's the issue for Maria. She will graduate with her political science degree at the end of the fall semester. Graduation is set for December 17, and the deadline for submitting all fellowship application materials is January 7, exactly three weeks later. That schedule is too tight, especially over the holidays, unless she has all the paperwork ready to go ahead of time."

"Then why doesn't she wait a year or two, get some graduate courses out of the way, and seek practical experiences ...?"

"I've suggested that, but she is determined, not just to win one of the fellowships but to use it to work on the 2012 election campaign. She idolizes the Obamas, as you probably know."

"Can Maria do it? Can she win? Or is she setting herself up for a huge disappointment?"

"I think she can win. She's exactly what they look for—a brilliant student coming out of an impoverished minority background, a self-starter with a successful election campaign under her belt, and the support of important people like the head of COGIC. If I didn't think she could do it, I wouldn't let her try."

Sarah could not control her reaction. "You wouldn't LET her try? What gives you that right? You sound like my grandfather—right out of the fifties."

"I don't mean to control her, but I care what happens to her."

"Maybe that's what is bothering me, Professor Ramirez.

You seem to care too much."

"Are you asking …?"

"Let's not do this in the hall." Sarah pushed the door open and held it to usher the younger man into her office. She closed the door firmly and then faced him. "Now, then. let's try this again, remembering that you are the authority figure in this little scenario and Maria is the impressionable underage child. What am I getting into here? What is the relationship between the two of you?"

"You mean, besides the obvious fact that I'm head-over-heels in love with her?"

Sarah's eyes widened with surprise that he was so open and honest about his feelings.

Gabe shrugged and continued. "Sure. I can't deny it. But I can also assure you that there is nothing inappropriate about our relationship. I have never had Maria as a student, nor will I allow her to take a class from me. We don't date. We have no physical contact. I've never so much as held her hand if you can believe that. I simply adore her. She knows it, and I think she feels the same as I do. But we wait. And if she wants this year in the White House, I'm willing to support her effort."

"And when she goes off to work with all these high-powered people and you're still here in Birch Falls—what happens then?"

"You want an honest answer, I assume. I will probably quit my job and follow her to Washington. There's always a job there for a historian."

Sarah shook her head. "I'll be honest with you as well. I'm uncomfortable with this situation, and I don't think I'm the right person to write the letter you're asking for—as least not at the moment. Give me some time to think about it, OK?"

CHAPTER 10
A New Course

July 2-5, 2011

Sarah's copy of the University of South Carolina Press brochure arrived in the next day's mail, and she displayed it above the kitchen sink to remind herself that there was more to her life than washing dishes and reading other people's journals. But when David wanted to tell their friends about her featured appearance, she pulled away.

"This is nothing new," she explained. "I finished that book over a year ago, and the sad truth is that I've done nothing since. I keep expecting someone to say, 'That's nice, Sarah, but what have you done lately?'"

"I think you're being too hard on yourself. You're working on a great topic right now."

"Yes, but only because someone offered me a bunch of money to do so. What I miss is the feeling of excitement I used to get at the beginning of a new project. I've given up on fascinating ideas in exchange for financial gain, and I'm ashamed of that."

"I don't understand. What have you given up?"

"You want a list? Start with the idea of having a baby. I may not have said it out loud, but I was excited to think I might be pregnant. Then that possibility crashed around my heels, and I had to accept the idea that motherhood was not in my future. I just gave up the whole idea."

"But you don't have to give it up. We haven't talked about adoption, but it's a real pathway if that's what you want."

"You're not hearing me. I've already rejected the possibility. I quit, and I gave up on my other projects, too. Hannah called to tell me about the Elijah publishers putting our contract on hold, and I simply shrugged and said, 'Fine. I won't start writing.' I had promised myself I'd find an interesting woman and build a historical novel around her. I quit looking for her. The dean offered me a year away from teaching, and I mentally locked my classroom door. I'm boring. I even bore myself."

"Why are you browbeating yourself? What's happened to make you so discontented with your life?"

"I'm not sure. I've been reading about the first nuns, the ones who founded the convent. They are all so dedicated to a cause. Each one of them has a role to play, and they do so with a willingness I find both puzzling and amazing. I envy their belief that they are doing the will of God. It gives them a purpose and makes their smallest tasks worthwhile. They have this mantra: 'To work is to pray.' For me, work is just working."

Sarah had started to pace around the room. Now she paused at the front door and looked out across the lawn at the tree that still bore the scars of the recent crash.

"Sometimes life seems meaningless. We go along day after day without thinking about much of anything. And then someone plants a tree in our path and we crash blindly into it. Our lives end in an instant, and we've left nothing behind to show we existed. So why do we bother?"

"Whoa! Whoa! This isn't like you, Sarah. Surely, you don't believe that image."

"It's how I see myself at the moment. In the past few days, I've talked to a bunch of folks who have great plans for their futures. I envy them, but I can't figure out how they find the courage to risk everything for the possibilities of the future. All I can do is duck and cover, hoping it's not my turn to hit the tree."

"Who have you been talking to?"

"Start with Julia. She's been telling me about Ronnie and his goals. He's determined to become an Olympic athlete, and he's ready to start training right now for next summer in London. He's only fourteen, but he knows what he wants and is willing to challenge everyone who gets in his way.

"Then there are my graduate students. Both Matt and Jean are planning to get their doctorates, and they don't even blink when I tell them what is involved. Ten years of work? OK. Learn two more languages? Can do. They know what they want, and they're ready to do whatever it takes.

"Chad and Olivia came in yesterday to tell me about their newest project. They are starting a national foundation to support the development of safer equipment for student-athletes. They are planning to raise millions of dollars and save thousands of lives. I can't even comprehend the boundaries of their vision for the future.

"And before the end of the day, I also talked to Professor Ramirez. He is so in love with one of our students that he is willing to sacrifice his professional career to help her compete for a valuable fellowship that would take her away from him.

"They all have wonderful dreams. Maybe they'll never accomplish what they have set out to do, but their dreams inspire them to be better at what they do every day. That's the feeling I miss, but I don't know how to find it again."

David's face reflected his concern. "You know, my love, we've had this conversation before. You've talked about your goals and problems and how they conflict with one another. You've admitted you're not sure what you want to do with the rest of your life. Will you be a career professor, leaving your mark on the future by the way you inspire your students? Will you become a great American novelist or write beloved books for children? Will you give up the other goals to be a stay-at-home mother? Or is there some other role out there—a dream you haven't discovered yet? Maybe the problem is not that you don't have a dream but that you have too many smaller goals."

Sarah chuckled. "You may be onto something there, but I don't see it that way."

"Doesn't the discovery of the nunnery records still excite you?"

"Not any longer. It was just a fluke. I have wondered about something, however. I'm still looking at the seven canonical hours the nuns follow as a sort of road map for the well-spent life. They begin their day by contemplating what God wants of them. Then they give thanks for the day to do what is required of them. Then they go and do it—in neat little chunks of the day, broken up only by meals and prayers. They come to the end of the day with gratitude for the opportunity to do the work. And then they go to bed feeling satisfied with a day well spent. Maybe there's an answer in there somewhere.

"You know, just from reading the mother superior's journals, I've been getting a pretty clear notion of their take on life. In one sense, all their days are alike, but they are also clearly separated. They start with a plan; they carry it out; they finish at the appointed time. They don't carry problems over from one day to the next. Each morning is a fresh start; each evening has a satisfactory conclusion. It's a good formula for sleeping well."

"It is, indeed."

"Do you think that's even possible in today's world?"

"I don't know. Maybe. You have a free day or two coming up. Why not try it?"

"I can do that. I'll designate tomorrow as 'Elijah Day.' He needs a good comb out and claw clipping. More important, he deserves some play time, a few treats, and some serious cuddling. Maybe he and I can also discuss how we should handle the contract problems with our publisher. That's another one of my dreams postponed. I'm sure Elijah has an opinion, if only I could read his mind."

As if Elijah could read her mind, her little black cat awakened Sarah early on Sunday morning by pressing his cold wet nose on her cheek. Her first reaction was to swat him away, but she pulled him toward her once she was fully awake and gave him a long cuddle.

"Good morning, my beautiful pussycat. Did you hear me talking yesterday about spending my day with you? Are you ready? Or are you just hungry? if I have to guess, breakfast wins out."

For the first time in a long time, Sarah faced the early morning sunlight with a smile on her face. Instead of impatiently pushing the hungry cat out of the way, Sarah slowed her steps to enjoy the brush of soft fur against her ankles.

"Since this is going to be our special day, I have a new treat for your breakfast. The packet is labeled 'chopped chicken livers in a special savory broth.' It doesn't come with a bagel, or I might be tempted to join you. But what do you think? Does it sound good?"

"Meow!"

"That's a yes, I take it. Well, here you go. Enjoy it while I have some coffee and a bear claw. And no, it's not a real bear."

As was his habit, Elijah finished his breakfast and headed off to find a sun puddle to take a short warming nap. That gave Sarah some time to get dressed in a comfortable lounging suit and collect her cat-grooming tools. She sat cross-legged on the floor next to him, sharing the warmth of the early morning light. She stroked him gently, her fingers testing to spot any mats or scabs that might interfere with a comb. Then she began the long brush strokes that turned his shaggy fur into a silky and shiny coat. She used a damp cloth to wipe the corners of his eyes and a q-tip to remove a little waxy build-up in his ears.

"What a handsome boy you are," she told him. "But what do you say we trim those lethal claws before you snag them on something—like the back of my hand?" This was not Elijah's favorite grooming step, but on this peaceful morning, he tolerated it well. Then he and Sarah both stretched, relaxed, and closed their eyes in contentment.

Coming down the stairs from the bedroom, David spotted this little tableau and tiptoed past to reach the kitchen without disturbing them. David had always adored Elijah, but he did not doubt that the cat preferred Sarah's attention. Seeing the two of them together gave him hope the animal's affection could lift Sarah's mood.

Sarah had been a cat owner long enough to understand that one never awakened a sleeping cat. So, when she discovered Elijah had fallen deeply asleep in the sun, she continued her reverie on the downstairs patio. How long has it been, she wondered to herself, since she had put her feet up and done nothing but relax?

It was still Elijah's day, and her thoughts immediately returned to memories of his kittenhood, starting from the moment she opened the door on the first night of Passover and discovered a wet and bedraggled kitten who dashed to the empty seat at the table and helped himself to scraps of meat. Sarah's rabbi father, however, was the one to declare this little creature just might be Elijah, the wandering prophet. The name stuck. Other memories crowded in—the drive across the Appalachians to Birch Falls and Elijah's first taste of a hamburger and fries; the night the cat decorated her hotel room with toilet paper; his first exploration of their new apartment; and the catnip-laced courtship that soon made David his second-best friend.

Then came the often-repeated story of the origins of his name, several invitations to Passover dinners, and eventually, the suggestion: "You really ought to write a book." David's artistic sister pitched in to do the illustrations and almost without effort they had a children's book. It received much acclaim at the local level and made Elijah the most famous cat in town.

Sarah's jaw tightened as she remembered how the dream of publishing a whole series of Elijah books crashed down around them. At the time, the news that another author had stolen their book idea and published a very similar children's volume came as a shock. When the publisher said, "We're sorry but under the circumstances, we can't take a chance on publishing more volumes," Sarah and Hannah had both simply accepted the ultimatum. And as she remembered that day, Sarah realized it might have been the origin of her loss of confidence. She had turned away from friends, colleagues, and even Elijah. Her energy and enthusiasm faded. She had been going through the motions of her life but without purpose or enjoyment.

Now, just at the right moment, Elijah emerged from his nap and jumped into her lap. Sarah hugged the cat and then put him firmly on the floor. "You're right. It's unfair, and I'm going to do something about it." She reached for her cell phone and clicked the speed dial for her sister-in-law and collaborator on the first Elijah book. When Hannah did not answer her phone, Sarah left a cryptic message: "Meet me for lunch at the Filling Station tomorrow at noon. Bring Elijah sketches."

CHAPTER 11

Dream Deferred, Not Denied

July 6, 2011

When Hannah arrived at The Filling Station, she found Sarah already seated at their favorite table behind the hollyhocks. "Good morning," she quipped, "and what brings us out on this fine Wednesday morning?"

"Didn't you once say you never needed an excuse to eat lunch here? After a four-day weekend during which I cooked all the time, I am eager to be pampered through one delicious meal."

"That's not a good enough excuse. I know you better than that."

"Maybe so, but we had better get our order in before we get down to business. Our server already brought us their favorite fruit-infused tea and informed me that today's specials are a quiche Lorraine and a French onion soup. It all sounds wonderful, and watching the other customers eat their salads has been making my mouth water."

As Hannah reached for her napkin, she noticed a handle sticking up from beside Sarah's chair. "What is that?" she asked. "A suitcase? Are you running away from home?"

"No. Not this time. I just brought a little helper to make my argument."

"Which is? I'm still trying to find out what's going on."

"Sorry. Look. I've changed my mind about publication. I want to move ahead with writing the other Elijah books. I'm ready to do them, and I'm not willing to let some stranger in Montana drive me out of the bookstores."

"And the suitcase …?"

"It's Elijah's carrier."

"Do you have a cat under there?"

"Say 'Hello,' Elijah."

"Meow-w-w."

"What's he doing here?"

"He's here to remind you of how cute he is. If you turn us down, I want you to have to do it straight into his furry little face."

"Sarah, I've already explained. We can't do it. Our publisher has the right of first refusal. We can't go to another publisher unless Questioning Mind releases us."

"Which they've already done. We had a signed contract with a date. They broke it."

"I don't think that was their intention when they asked for a postponement."

"Yes, I know. I checked with David. He said it might not have been their intention, but it was nevertheless a refusal to honor the terms of our contract. Still, I'm willing to give them a second chance before we jump to another publisher or even self-publishing."

"What makes you think they'll change their minds?"

"A better proposal from us, and the realization that we can take the books elsewhere."

"Let's hear your new proposal."

"OK. We're going to use the full power of the internet—a 'Faces' account, like the one we borrowed from the Brooklyn Zoo Python, along with a web page belonging to Elijah Cohen, the Passover Cat. We'll use social media to answer questions, post pictures of the real Elijah, announce publication dates, and sell books and a stuffed Elijah. That will give us national publicity, not just the local coverage we had with the first book. We're not going to mention that other woman's book; she will get no more publicity from us."

"You do realize, don't you, that we have less than three months before the High Holy Days? That's not enough time to get a new book printed and into bookstores."

"I know we don't have time to create a Rosh Hashana or Yom Kippur book this year. We can have Elijah explain that he isn't old enough yet, even in cat years, to participate in the High Holy Days. And then we'll jump straight into bringing out a Hanukkah book, which will have a big holiday appeal to children. It's also the day for which we have lots of pictures and a ready-made storyline."

By the time Sarah stopped to catch her breath, Hannah's eyes were shining with excitement. "I love it! We have several lessons to teach the 'Questioning Mind' people. And if they don't go along, we could self-publish on Amazon, couldn't we?"

"Indeed, we could, and it's easy enough to do, but I'm hoping we don't have to."

Sarah smiled as the waitress arrived. "I'll have the chicken and brie sandwich on French bread."

"And I am having today's quiche." Hannah looked at

Sarah curiously. "I'm surprised you're having the sandwich instead of one of the daily specials."

"A favor for Elijah. I can slip him a few bites of chicken and no one will notice. He would make a mess with quiche."

"That's what you get when you raise a cat to think he's people."

"Make fun if you like, but he's going to earn you lots of money this year."

"I hope you're right. I'm willing to give the new book a shot. When we finish lunch, why don't the two of you come back to my house? I'll put the phone on speaker, and we can call The Questioning Mind as a team. It's known as ganging up on them."

"I have one more request. Do you think Benny would be willing to answer some questions about his impressions of Hanukkah for us? I would like to be sure we are seeing it through a child's eyes and not some jaded adult view."

"I think he'll be flattered to be asked. Why don't we plan to get together on Saturday? We can talk with him and maybe map out the entire book."

By the time David arrived home that evening, Sarah was dancing around the kitchen with a smile on her face and the makings of a fancy dinner waiting on the counter.

"There's a pitcher of sangria in the fridge," she told him. "Why don't you take it out to the patio with you while you heat the grill? I'll be down in just a few minutes with a couple of rib-eye steaks and some vegetable skewers."

"Are we celebrating something? This is quite a change from hamburger gravy."

"You might say that. Go on outside and pour a glass of sangria for me. I'll propose a toast when I bring out the rest of dinner."

Never willing to argue with a happy wife, David headed for the patio. Sarah followed with a food-laden tray.

"Those steaks look wonderful. Where'd you get them?"

"Wegman's. They get credit for the veggie skewers, too. They contain zucchini, summer squash, huge mushrooms, cherry tomatoes, Vidalia onions, and multi-colored pepper strips. Everything's been marinated. All you have to do is turn them over once in a while."

"And what's in that foil-wrapped packet?"

"This? Only a couple of pre-fried spring onion latkes. They just need to be heated until their edges get crisp again."

"Latkes? We only have those on Hanukkah."

"Hey. Haven't you heard all the TV commercials about Christmas in July? I figure, if the Christians can celebrate a second Christmas when it's ninety degrees outside, we Jews can fry up a summer latke for a special celebration."

"OK. Spill it! What are we celebrating?"

"The upcoming publication of *The Hanukkah Gift*—book two in the Elijah Series for Jewish Children."

"Really? Your publishers changed their decision?"

"Well, let's say your sister and I sort of changed it for them. I wouldn't say we threatened them. We just gave them a 'put up or shut up' choice. When they heard what we had planned, they decided they could manage to handle a couple more books after all."

"That's wonderful. What's the schedule?"

"We plan to start using the selling power of the internet by the end of this month. Elijah will have a website and a 'Faces' account so he can keep his fans apprised of what's going on. The publishers had already commissioned a stuffed Elijah, so they're putting production back on the fast track, and his little doppelgänger should start appearing in bookstores around September first. We have guaranteed a completed manuscript and page proofs for the Hanukkah book by the end of October. Publication will follow in November in time to hit the stores on Black Friday, the day after Thanksgiving. We'll begin work on the High Holy Days volume in 2012 with publication sometime in August. So, here's to a successful publishing campaign. And to Elijah!"

David clicked her glass and then threw his arms around her. "Congratulations, darling! I'm so proud of you."

"Careful. Don't spill my sangria. I've earned every drop of it today."

"You have been doing what we talked about?"

"I spent Monday with Elijah and let him remind me of how much fun we had with his first book. On Tuesday, I called Hannah and made a lunch date to discuss our choices. And today, we met, talked, and agreed to move ahead. We called the publisher this afternoon, gave him our proposal, and let him know we would go elsewhere if he did not agree. He never even protested. I'm guessing he was waiting to see if we were serious about the Elijah series. Once he knew that, everything fell into place—and what a wonderful feeling it is."

"You're going to be busy, but that's part of the fun, isn't it?"

"Absolutely. We're holding a planning session on Saturday, by the way, and Benny is going to join us. I want to hear him explain his understanding of Hanukkah—not that he thinks like a cat, but because he's still at that childlike stage where he notices the details we forget to pay attention to."

"I'll try to stay out of your way. Maybe I can schedule a golf round with Dad."

"Really? Are the two of you finally making some progress on becoming friends as well as family?"

"I hope so. I haven't had a chance to tell you, but the

courts have made some scheduling changes—ones that give us both some free time on Monday afternoons. Dad offered to use that time to show me what the law firm is working on, and I'm enjoying seeing some familiar cases from a different point of view."

"Such as ...?"

"Remember Dotty and Smitty?"

"Who? Oh, you mean the tire salesman and the hot dog lady? I thought they ended up in jail somewhere in Georgia."

"So they did. But one of the local cops started to notice some oddities about the case. He did some investigating and discovered that Smitty is not who he says he is. He's a highly dangerous fugitive. In his twenties, our Smitty robbed several national banks. He got caught and was sentenced to thirty years in federal prison. Then he staged a jailbreak and disappeared, killing a prison guard during the breakout."

"Wow! And you were dealing with this guy? That scares me."

"Me, too, if the truth be known. He has gone to great lengths to disguise himself. He had all his teeth pulled and got dentures that changed the lines of his face. He went from glasses to contacts and had several tattoos removed. I hope that hurt—a lot! I understand he dyes his hair and uses lifts in his shoes to make himself taller. He filed his fingerprints, too, but that didn't work as well. Once the police realized how much of his appearance was faked, they started looking for criminals who had disappeared, and some of Smitty's prints still matched. His name isn't John Smith, either, as it turns out. He was born Clyde Brogdovich."

"So, where is he now?"

"Locked up in a maximum-security prison and under 24-hour guard until he undergoes a new trial for murder and jailbreak. Even Dad is fascinated by the story."

"But he won't be tried here?"

"No, he's being held somewhere in upstate New York. On the other end of the ridiculous scale, do you remember the divorce case we couldn't settle because the couple could not agree on custody of the dog?"

"Oh, who could forget that one? Someone kidnapped the dog, didn't they?"

"Yes, and Dad and I ended up on opposite sides. The wife charged her husband with the kidnapping and demanded that we prosecute him. And the husband hired the Cohen Law Firm to defend his good name. We never went to trial because no one could find the dog, who was the only witness, after all."

"So, what happened to them?"

"Well, the husband and wife were so distraught that their friends thought they were both nuts. So, the couple turned to each other for comfort because they were the only ones who understood how terrible the loss was. Eventually, they got back together in their grief and dropped the divorce proceedings. Once that was settled, a distant relative returned the dog."

"And they all lived happily ..."

"Nope. The dog settled things by running away. He's never been found. I visualize him living in the middle of a homeless community, where he can maintain his anonymity by rolling in mud puddles and garbage piles. Dad and I agree —we hope he's happy as a little clam because everyone loves him, no matter what he looks or smells like."

"And with that bit of good news, I suggest we finish this sangria and enjoy our celebratory dinner. We have much to be thankful for tonight."

CHAPTER 12

Lauds—The Second Hour

From the journal of Mary Frances McMurtry, later known as Sister Francesca, and now, by the grace of God, as Mother Francesca, Mother Superior of this Convent of Our Lady St. Walburga:

June 1847

I always open the shutters on my eastern window before I go to sleep. I do not wish to miss that wonderful moment when the first rays of light break through the darkness of the night. Some call that moment the false dawn. I prefer to think of it as God's promise of another day. Sometimes that first display manages to streak the sky with bands of color that light up my heart. I see it as a demonstration of the power of God's control of the universe. Some say those colors foretell the coming of bad weather. I'm not sure that's true, either, mainly because I suspect God's perception of bad weather is quite different from our own. He knows when we need rain, even if we object to getting wet.

This morning, however, there will be no rain, for it is a special day in the life of our nunnery. We will gather for the last time on the eastern porch of our borrowed house to greet the rising of the sun and the gift of a new day. That has been our practice since arriving in Birch Falls. But today, after four years of construction, the chapter house is ready for occupancy. It will be my pleasure to declare that the middle hours of our liturgical day need not be observed in full while we make the move from borrowed house to Saint Walburga's Convent. Private prayers of gratitude, of course, will fill our hearts.

What delights await us? From this day forward, we will have access to our beautiful church, not just on Sundays but seven times a day. We will come down from the chapter house and along the cloister walk to the southern portico. From there, we will enter the choir where we will raise our voices in everlasting praise to God the Father Almighty. And at this hour every day—call it Prime or Six AM if you will— we will watch the stained-glass windows of our apse. We will wait for the first rays of the sun to rise above the horizon and cast beams of vibrant color across the sanctuary. No matter how beautiful it may seem, the light from our windows is but a poor imitation of the handiwork of God across the sky. May it serve as a reminder of His majesty and power.

The nunnery of Saint Walburga is now fully functional. As of this summer, there are eighteen of us, with others waiting for the chance to join us. The original group of six women with whom I traveled made up the administrative staff. Each of those women bore heavy responsibilities in the beginning, but each of them gained a helper from the second group.

Sister Benedicta arrived from a teaching order in Pittsburgh. She fell naturally into a position with Sister Scholastica. Both are now skilled in literary matters. Benedicta has already memorized much of our Book of Hours, knowing almost instinctively what readings, scriptures, and responsive prayers are most appropriate for each of the liturgical hours. If and when Sister Scholastica decides to take over the library and scriptorium, Sister Benedicta will be ready to step into the role of Cantor.

Sister Hildegard also comes to us from a teaching order in Knoxville. She was happy to be offered the job of novice mistress, thus relieving Sister Juliana from that portion of her duties. Did Hildegard realize that the next group of six newcomers would all be novices? Perhaps not, but she has accepted the young women with a healthy mix of open-armed comfort and insistence on strict adherence to the rules. A true teacher, indeed.

Sister Magdalen is a transfer from the Sisters of Mercy. Her experience in caring for the sick and infirm will benefit all of us. Her special interest lies in the use of herbal remedies, and when she has no patients in the infirmary, she can be found in the apothecary's shop. Within days of her arrival, she began to prepare a plot of ground at the back of the cloister garden where she now grows her medicinal plants.

Sister Teresa comes to us from an urban setting. Her original order found its calling in reaching out to travelers, the homeless, and the struggling poor. Although she may be best qualified to deal with our charitable efforts, I have asked her to take responsibility for visitors to our house. Many of those unexpected arrivals will be travelers looking for assistance and encouragement as they make their way toward the frontier. Her training should serve her well.

Sister Ursula grew up as the daughter of a local merchant. Although a lifetime as a shopkeeper did not appeal to her, she has had much experience in buying and selling. We have asked her to become the assistant to Sister Martha, our cellarer. Martha's real talent is managing people, not food supplies, so she willingly turned over the tasks of providing our food and drink to Ursula, while she manages the workers who help keep the convent running.

Sister Helena is the oldest of fourteen children, so she grew up helping to raise her brothers and sisters. She is an organizer, a disciplinarian, and a manager—the ideal helper to step in when the details of everyday life grow too complicated for our novice mistress, Sister Hildegard, to handle on her own.

Do things ever get that complicated? Oh, to be sure they do, particularly with a new class of novices. Is it possible to make nuns out of all six of them? I doubt it, but all of them have some redeeming qualities that might serve them well in the community.

Sister Agnes is the quiet one, and in a community consisting entirely of women, finding silence is often a blessing. I worry about Agnes, however, because all too often she appears to be not just quiet but frightened into speechlessness. I once sat down beside her and felt her shrink into herself, pulling her arms closer to her body, hunching her shoulders, and hiding her face from view. What might she be afraid of? Has she been threatened? Abused? Forced to come here under duress? Before we accept her, we must break down the walls she has built around herself.

In contrast, Sister Catherine is a strong, outspoken, and mature young woman, wise in the way of the world and sophisticated in her tastes. She hates the plain habits we wear day after day. I have already had to reprimand her for shortening her skirt and pushing her sleeves above the elbow. She finds our early bedtime inconvenient and our meals unappealing. No matter how sincere her love of God may be, a nun must conform to the rules of the order. If Sister Catherine cannot do so, we shall have to dismiss her.

Sister Priscilla also gives me cause for concern. She is lazy and wrinkles her nose as a very thought of work. Ask her to sweep the floor and she pushes the dust under the rug. She shakes her head every time she hears one of us repeating the Rule of Saint Benedict that work is prayer. She has argued with me, holding that work interferes with prayer, although I've heard her use that same argument to avoid something as common as doing the dishes.

That leaves us with three viable candidates. Sister Bridget is young and silly, but she's fun to have around. Sister Veronica needs to alter her eating habits and lose some excess weight. I've caught her hoarding food in her bed and accepting gifts of candy from her family when they visit. She is, however, working on her self-discipline. And finally, Sister Joan is our best candidate. She is a peacekeeper and a diplomat, guiding her sisters to be better at this novice business.

These seventeen women have become my family, and, as we watch the sun come over the mountains on this day, we share the excitement of having a real home at last. We must never forget, however, that when the sun rises on a new day, it brings with it a call to our duties. Every day has its schedule. We will follow the Hours, recite the prayers, heed the Scriptures, and then go to work. Only if each of us contributes our share of labor will the nunnery flourish.

Five years of effort have brought us to this point but the end is not in sight. We have only a vision of what we may become. We are called to become an example to our community. We must use our gifts to help those around us. Some of us will work within the nunnery to keep it functioning, while others will reach beyond its walls to those in need. As the

Gospels tell us, we must offer education to the young, care to those who are ill, food to those who hunger, guidance to the confused, help to those who labor, and comfort to those who mourn.

And now it is the first hour of our working day, and we are loading the wagons to carry our nuns and their belongings to their new home. Each woman has an assignment today, each one designated to add the final touches that will turn these empty buildings into our permanent convent. Sister Elizabeth, our chamberlain, directs the first wagon out. She is responsible for all clothing and bedding; but for this day, she will share those duties with Sister Hildegard, the novice mistress, and two novices, Sister Agnes and Sister Veronica. The dormitory floor has four rooms, each with six cubicles. The nuns will randomly assign the cubicles and provide each one with sheets, a blanket, a pillow, a towel, and a candlestick. The cubicles cannot be closed, but they provide some feeling of privacy. Each nun may keep at her bedside her prayer book, a rosary, an extra candle, and one personal item, such as a family portrait.

The next group of wagons is headed to the refectory. Sister Martha, our cellarer, and her assistant, Sister Ursula, are in charge of the kitchen, supplying foodstuffs, cooking utensils, silverware, and dishes. Sister Martha will be training our hired cooks, while Sister Ursula takes charge of inventory. Two novices, Sister Bridget and Sister Priscilla, are setting the tables with plates, spoons, and salt cellars. The first meal they will serve will be tonight's supper.

A third group is at the church, making sure the candelabra are full, the altarpieces are polished, hymnals and prayer books fill the racks in the choir, and kneeling cushions are in place. As mother superior, I am responsible for this work crew. Sister Benedicta will be observing my every move in case she may one day need to step into an official position. My two novices, Sister Catherine and Sister Joan are the oldest and most trustworthy. We will assemble there for the first time this evening for our Vespers service, and I want everything to be perfect.

The rest of our experienced nuns are busy setting up their assigned stations. Sister Magdalen is stocking her infirmary, and Sister Teresa has prepared the visitor's quarters in case a church official should decide to stay over for the second day of observation. At the chapter house, Sister Agatha and Sister Scholastica are comparing notes to be sure all is going according to schedule.

At Lauds, God offers us a beautiful new day, full of dreams and opportunities to achieve our goals. And at the end of the day, we shall be required to assess our efforts. May He be well satisfied.

CHAPTER 13

Hanukkah Memories

July 9, 2011

The doorbell rang early on Saturday morning. Sarah grabbed a housecoat and trundled downstairs, expecting to see the paper boy or a set of missionaries bringing their good word from door to door. Instead, the caller was Benny, Hannah's 11-year-old son. "Good morning, Aunt Sarah," he said. "Mom says to tell you she'll be here by ten, but it's OK for us to start without her. Have you had breakfast? All I had was some cold cereal." He looked at her, wide-eyed, trusting Aunt Sarah to be able to fix the immediate problem.

Sarah grinned at his seemingly innocent question. "I was just planning to stir up some blueberry pancakes. Would you be interested in sharing some?"

It was a small lie, but then what harm is there in indulging one's favorite nephew?

"Oh, boy, I love blueberry pancakes. Do you have some maple syrup?"

"Sure. You can help by getting it out of the fridge for me. And find the butter, too."

The clattering in the kitchen brought David to join them, and soon all three were happily mopping up blueberry juice and crunching bacon strips. After finishing five pancakes, Benny leaned back in his chair.

"Yum. That was good. Thanks, Aunt Sarah. Mom said you had some questions for me—something to do with Elijah's new book. How can I help?"

"That's my cue to go mow the yard," David laughed. "If the women finish their interrogation, Benny, you can always join me with a rake."

"I have a better idea," Sarah said. "Why don't you two clean up the dishes in the sink while I get dressed and find my note-taking stuff? The grass can wait for a little while, and so can our neighbors who are still trying to sleep."

Hannah's arrival in mid-morning required another kitchen trip to brew a new pot of coffee, but eventually, the two authors and their informant sat down to talk about Hanukkah.

"I still don't understand what you want from me," Benny said. "I'm just a kid."

"Exactly. And I need to know what kids think Hanukkah is all about. You're older than our readers but still young enough to remember what puzzled you about the candles and spinning tops and special meals when you were five or six years old."

Benny giggled. "Remember the year I thought it was my birthday, Mom? I kept blowing out the candles, and Dad got really mad."

"I think that has happened in a lot of families, but what do you know about those candles now?"

"Not much more. I don't try to blow them out anymore,

but I sometimes worry that Elijah will catch his tail on fire as he walks by. I've never understood why we use candles. All the psalms and readings talk about oil lamps. And I have no idea why someone wanted to light them in the first place."

"OK. Let's start with the Hebrews living in Israel in the second century before the Roman Empire. Their land formed a bridge—and sometimes a barrier—between eastern Europe and Africa. Do we need a simple map, Hannah?"

"I can arrange that."

"A nasty Syrian king named Antiochus wanted the Hebrew people out of the way so he could make Israel a part of his Syrian-Greek kingdom. He had a huge army at his disposal, but the Jews of Israel preferred a kind of guerrilla warfare, attacking at night, sabotaging Greek traditions, and refusing to fight on the Sabbath. The Syrians responded by harassing Jews because of their religion. They made it illegal to pray or go to Temple. When the fighting came to Jerusalem, the soldiers released a bunch of pigs in the temple and destroyed the holy books kept there. They even sacrificed a pig on the altar."

"Mom ought to draw a picture of a dead pig. Kids love gory stuff."

"Maybe." Hannah wrinkled her nose at the thought.

"The Jewish leader was Judas Maccabeus. He and his followers took back what the Syrians had tried to destroy and slowly restored the Temple. But as part of the re-dedication, they needed to burn an oil lamp in the window every night from sunset until the last straggler had left the streets."

"OK. How about a picture of a street with nobody around but a little cat?"

"That's better."

"To their dismay, when they locked themselves into the Temple, they could find only enough pure olive oil to burn the lamp for a single day. They knew it would take eight days to create more pure olive oil for the lamp. Some wanted to give up, but Judas urged them to have faith in God. Miraculously, at the end of the first day, the oil lamp was still full, and so it remained for all eight days. When the dedication was complete, the Jews came out and discovered that the Syrians had left. It was a great miracle."

"So that's what the candle flames stand for—one for each day the oil lasted."

"Today we don't use oil lamps, and electric light bulbs are not a good substitute for a flame. So, we light candles instead. When we light each one, we remember the re-dedication of the Temple and the great miracle of the oil. That's the meaning of Hanukkah."

"But what of all the other customs, Aunt Sarah—the foods cooked in oil, like latkes and those jelly doughnut things—*sufganiyot*?"

"Fried foods are traditional, so you'll find fried fish and fried chicken, too. They serve as a reminder to rejoice in always having enough oil for cooking as well as lighting."

"Whatever. It all smells wonderful. Elijah thinks so, too. You can see his nose twitch as soon as he comes inside. What about the dreidels? He likes those, too. But that's such a silly game."

"It wasn't silly at the time. Jews who gathered to pray could be killed for doing so. The Jews invented dreidels to use when the Syrians tried to punish them for praying. They would say, 'We're only playing a little game of tops.'"

"And the giving of gifts?"

"That's mostly for children. We do it because it makes both the giver and the child happy. Hanukkah is always a happy time. That's why we have parties and visit our friends and family."

"Cats, too. Remember last year when Elijah got a Hanukkah gift?"

"Ah, that's a story to remember."

As if he had heard someone call his name, Elijah entered the living room and curled up in Sarah's lap. She stroked his silky fur as she told the story.

"Since both David and I went to work every day, Elijah was left by himself for long hours. We knew he was lonely and bored because he often got into trouble while we were gone. We would come home to find small objects knocked to the floor, the newspaper torn apart, or food spilled in the kitchen. We kept buying toys that were supposed to keep a cat from getting bored, but they didn't work for Elijah. He has always preferred the company of a crowd.

"The first time I suggested that we get Elijah a kitten, David was dead set against the idea. 'That's just asking for more trouble,' he said. 'Two of them would come up with twice that many ideas about what to destroy next.' I suspected he was correct because I remembered my mother's two kittens. During a friendly game, they chased each other up to the top of her giant rubber tree plant, stripping every leaf along the way.

"One day, our department secretary announced that her cat had produced a litter of five kittens. They were almost six weeks old by that time, and she was looking for gullible folks to adopt them. I couldn't help myself. I went to see them, and I fell in love. The liveliest kitten of the litter was completely white except for a little black circle on the top of her head. It made her look like she was wearing a yarmulke. 'She's a flirt, too,' Gwen had said. 'She teases every man who visits us. We've started calling her Delilah.' When I took David to meet her, she immediately crawled up his pant leg. He couldn't resist.

"Elijah met Delilah on the third day of Hanukkah last year. The whole family came to our house for dinner that evening, and we began the festivities in the usual way. David lit the candles on our menorah, placing three candles in the menorah from right to left. He used the ninth candle, (the *shamash* or the one who serves), to light the three candles, moving from left to right. David's father read the Hallel, Psalms 113-118, and Rabbi Leibowicz read the description of the re-dedication of the Temple, found in Numbers 7:1-8:4. To complete the ceremony, the assembled guests joined in singing 'Mighty Rock of my Salvation,' a medieval German hymn. Then it was time for fun, celebration, the giving of gifts, and a festive dinner. The highlight, however, was a Hanukkah gift for Elijah."

"I remember, Aunt Sarah. You sent me out to the porch to find the cat, and when I brought him in, there was a basket sitting on the floor in one corner of the room. Elijah was still half asleep and not paying much attention until a little white creature crawled out of the basket. Then I felt him push against my arm, and he kicked off, jumping to the floor in full alert mode."

"It was quite a scene, wasn't it? The black cat and the white kitten stared at each other, while every person in the room waited for a cat fight to break out. Instead, we saw a demonstration of cat poses. Elijah turned sideways and arched his back until a ridge of fur stood up along his spine. His tail crooked into a question mark. He looked quite formidable, but Delilah showed no fear. She did, however, try to copy his threatening pose until she over-arched and fell over. Embarrassed, she gave a quick lick to her hindquarters and then turned and crouched into a stalking posture. Elijah yawned again before giving her a warning hiss. Delilah attempted a hiss of her own, but it came out like a sneeze and sent her tumbling backward again. I was certain I heard Elijah laughing."

Benny was thoroughly caught up in the narrative, unaware that he was mimicking the cat's postures. He turned to his mother, his boyish fingers still curved into imaginary claws. "You were scared, weren't you, mom? I heard you whisper to Aunt Sarah, begging her not to let Elijah hurt the kitten."

"You are right. I was scared until I saw Elijah flop over on his side and stretch out. What an insult to that baby cat!"

"I didn't have to worry," Sarah said. "I knew Elijah didn't have a mean hair on his body. But that Delilah! She just wouldn't give up. Elijah's tail was wagging slowly in what I think was a peaceful message, but to Delilah, it was a giant snake and she pounced. Elijah's front paw caught her in mid-air and sent her flying tail over teacups toward her basket. There are limits to a grown-up cat's patience, after all."

"Even I was a little nervous when I saw Elijah get up and follow her to her basket," Benny admitted. "but all he did was sniff at her, the way mom does with me after I've been playing outside on a hot day."

"My favorite photo is the one that shows him giving her one giant lick from head to tail. Then she relaxed, and he gave her a thorough bath. When he finished, they curled up together with one of his paws stretched protectively across her tummy. They have been joined at the hip ever since. And there you have the stories of Hanukkah—little guy versus big guy, utter bravery, faith, dedication, the bonding with family, and a great miracle.

The conversation about Hanukkah continued for most of the morning. Benny particularly enjoyed the family stories about funny things that had happened during the holidays, and Sarah took notes each time a memory struck her as something that might go into the book. The conversation continued through lunch, but when David announced that he was off to spend the afternoon on the golf course with his father, Hannah and Benny also got ready to move on to a local softball game.

CHAPTER 14

The New Normal

Evening, July 9, 2011

"That does it, I think. I have our whole conversation recorded on tape. I'll sit down next week and divide it into thirty-two pages, some of which will be two-page spreads. I'll get those to you as soon as possible, Hannah, so you can start matching drawings to the narrative."

With the house empty except for two sleeping cats, Sarah went upstairs to type her notes. If this was an example of her new schedule, she approved it. Family time, no clock-watching, permission to do as she pleased, and a book project that made her laugh—all combined to help her enjoy her new normal.

She smiled to herself when she imagined a new Elijah book. In the quiet of the afternoon, she allowed herself to remember last year, when *The Passover Guest* had come out, and Elijah had become the best-known cat in all of Tennessee. She had to admit she had enjoyed his popularity.

The need to have him travel with them had simply been an excuse to buy a cute little stroller with his name on it. As a bonus, it would pass the airline's rules and regulations about animals traveling in the passenger compartment. Book signings had been great fun, too. Elijah usually slept through the boring business of selling copies of his book, but Sarah never tired of watching children press their noses against the screen of Elijah's carrier to get a look at their feline hero. She giggled as she remembered the day David had presented her and his sister with rubber stamps containing the imprint of Elijah's paw so they could sign his books for him.

As if he could read her mind, Elijah wandered into her office, still yawning as he awakened from his nap. He rubbed up against her ankles and when she didn't pay enough attention, he gently tapped her knee.

"I see you, my furry friend, but I'm supposed to be working. If you want to have another Elijah book, you'll have to learn not to interrupt the creative juices." She leaned over and scratched him briefly behind his ears, which he took as an invitation to leap into her lap.

"Oh, no, you don't. I can't type with you between me and the keyboard. This may be a book about you, but I'm the one who has to write it. So, you can get down and go on about your kitty business." She watched him fondly as he paused to lick his shoulder and then nonchalantly tromped off to check out his food dish.

"I probably ought to be working on the nunnery book," she reminded herself," but that's just something I do to earn enough money to pay the bills for all of that expensive cat food. My job may keep us warm and fed, but Elijah and his books are the ones that fuel the fire in my heart."

~

Sarah worked happily through the afternoon and was surprised to see how late it was when David finally arrived home. She called to him from upstairs. "That must've been quite a golf game, but don't look in the kitchen expecting dinner to be ready. I'm planning to order Chinese. When I get conned into cooking pancakes at seven o'clock in the morning, I go off kitchen duty before suppertime." She was laughing as she spoke, but her smile faded as she got her first look at David's face.

"What's wrong?"

"Nothing, actually, but ..."

"Something, I suspect. You don't usually take a golf game that seriously."

"We never made it to the golf course. Dad begged off, first complaining it was too hot and then admitting he was tired. I don't think I've ever heard him use that word. But he was tired today. He flopped into his recliner and hardly moved. He talked about several cases his firm handles but without much enthusiasm for them. Then he turned on the TV and dialed up a PGA tournament, saying maybe it was time he visited golf courses from a distance.

"At one point, he dozed off, and I cornered Mom in the kitchen, asking her if she thought he was coming down with something. She admitted she thought he looked a little pale. I would have said he looked gray—not his hair but his face."

"Maybe it's just a little bug going around with the change in the weather."

"Come on, Sarah. Don't try to minimize this. The man has never been ill a day in his life that I can remember. Nor has he seen a doctor for anything like a regular checkup. Plus, he's sixty-six years old, over-weight, and overworked—a perfect candidate for a heart attack or something else equally lethal."

"Did you ask him how he was feeling?"

"Of course, I did, and he did nothing but snarl at me. He accused me of wanting him out of the way."

"That sounds like his own fear, not your reaction to his appearance."

"That's right, it was. But what's making him feel that way? That's what is worrying me."

Sarah had no ready answer to his question. "Maybe you'll see it differently once you've had something to eat. How do fresh spring rolls sound, along with a shared dish of 'Happy Family' over fried noodles?"

"'Happy Family?' What is in that, anyhow?"

"It's nothing more than a traditional Chinese stir-fry, except it has a little bit of everything in it—steak, pork loin, chicken, shrimp, maybe even some tofu—to keep everyone happy."

"Does wishing make it so? And, yes, I get the message. Mom was cooking something complicated, Dad wanted to watch TV, I was looking forward to the golf course, you were book-planning, Hannah was sketching cats in her imagination, and Benny had a softball game. Saturdays have something for everyone, and I should mind my own business."

Sarah smiled at his understanding and reached for the phone to call in their dinner order. but before she could lift the receiver, the phone rang. A glance at the small screen told her the call was coming from David's parents. She backed away and nodded to David to answer it.

David listened briefly, his eyes widening in alarm. "Mom, please. Slow down and tell me what happened ... Did he black out or was he awake ...? Where is he now ...? No, don't try to help him get up ... You need to call 911 ... No, you can't drive him to the hospital. You're too upset. Besides, the EMTs are equipped to start treatment immediately rather than waiting to get to an emergency room. I'm on my way. You call 911 and then try to keep him calm until we all get there."

David ended the call and turned to Sarah, letting his panic show for the first time. "It's Dad. He fell getting out of his recliner and may have hit his head on the table. Mom says his face looks funny and his speech is mumbled. It sounds like he might have had a stroke. I've got to go."

"I'm coming with you. I may be able to help your mother."

The ambulance was already there when they reached the family home. A crowd of neighbors and gawkers had gathered to stare at the emergency vehicles, and the police seemed to be losing the battle to control the scene.

David elbowed his way through the onlookers to reach the open ambulance doors. Inside, one of the EMTs looked up and sighed. "It's the district attorney again," he grumbled. "Better let him on board. Otherwise, he'll delay us with arguments." Forcing his smile, he raised an eyebrow. "Who is it this time, sir?"

"My father, and yes, I'm riding along."

"Can you do anything about that woman out there who is crying and demanding that we do something?"

"That's my mother, and my wife will handle her. Just a minute." Summoning his best crowd control voice, he shouted, "Step back, folks, and let the ambulance get on its way. Sarah, take our car and bring Mom to the emergency room. We'll meet you there."

As he re-boarded the ambulance and the door slammed behind him, his father spoke from the stretcher. "I must be dying. That's the quickest you've ever come when I called you."

David laughed in relief. "You sound good, Dad. What's going on?"

The EMT attending pushed David away and replaced the oxygen mask on his father's face. "We don't want to make him talk, but the speech thing coming back so quickly suggests nothing more than a small TIA, not a major stroke. The doctor will explain once we get to the ER."

The news was good. By the time the ambulance reached the hospital, Mr. Cohen's vital signs had already returned to normal. The attending physician gave him a quick check-up and then sent him off to an examination cubicle. "I think your father is going to be fine," he told David. "But something happened. One doesn't just fall over without cause. It's good you came in. This will give us a chance to catch a small problem before it becomes a serious one."

Now time seemed to drag as the family was shuffled off to a waiting room while a series of technicians, nurses, and other doctors did mysterious things with odd-looking instruments and took unreadable notes. Almost an hour passed before a doctor entered the waiting room asking for the Cohen family. David was the first one on his feet, but the doctor turned to Mrs. Cohen as the spokesperson.

"You are the wife, no? Your husband is doing just fine. As far as we can tell right now, he seems to have had what is called a TIA—a transient ischemic attack."

"I have no idea what that is," she admitted.

"Ah! It is sometimes called a mini-stroke. It happens when something—a bit of plaque or a tiny blood clot—temporarily blocks a small artery in the brain. It may produce stroke-like symptoms, but they disappear quickly as the clot breaks up and moves on. You described a drooping eye and garbled speech—both common stroke symptoms. But by the time Mr. Cohen reached the emergency room, we saw no sign that anything had occurred."

"So, we don't have to worry about anything?"

"Well, things aren't quite that clear. Brief periods of neurological dysfunction can often be a warning signal of further trouble to come. They tend to occur when the patient has other coronary problems, such as high cholesterol, lack of exercise, or excess weight. The good news is that if we catch the small problems, the bigger ones may never develop.

"I'm going to keep Mr. Cohen here overnight, and I'll ask the nursing staff to keep a close eye on him to ensure there is not another attack. On Monday we will schedule an MRI, which will allow us to see into his brain and identify any trouble spots, past or future. Then we will have a better idea of what he needs to do to avoid further difficulty."

The doctor seemed to be getting ready to discuss the matter further, but a sudden outbreak of shouting voices from down the hall brought the family to their feet again.

"That's enough, I said. Where are my clothes? What have you done with my clothes? I'm going home."

"If you do, it will be with your bare backside hanging out of that hospital gown. Now lay down, Mr. Cohen. You're not going anywhere."

"You can't keep me here."

"Oh, yes, I can. We need an MRI, and that can't be done until Monday."

"Now see here. I'm a lawyer, and ..."

"And right now, you are just a patient—a disagreeable one, at that, and we can use restraints if necessary."

"Oh, my stars, he's on a rant. Excuse me while I see if I can help."

She pushed past the doctor, her heels clicking on the tile floor as she headed for the examining room. Her voice carried for all to hear.

"Shut up, Leonard. You're being insufferable. These

people are just trying to help you. Now quit being a pain in the behind and get your behind back in the bed. In a few minutes, they are going to find you a nice private room where you can be as obnoxious as you like without disturbing the whole floor. You're staying here for a few nights, and I intend to spend the night on the couch in your room making sure you stay put. I'm sure these nice ladies can find me a blanket and a pillow. Now I'm going to go back out there and send David and Sarah home so they can get some dinner and rest."

"Humph, I have not heard anyone offer me dinner," he grumbled. "Normally I'd be eating by now."

"Shut up, Leonard. This is your new normal."

CHAPTER 15

The Girl on the Porch

July 11, 2011

Mr. Cohen's tests lasted until late on Monday afternoon, by which time his wife and two children had nearly exhausted themselves with worrying about the outcome of his MRI. His mood as the attendants shifted him from the gurney to bed did little to encourage their hopes for a happy outcome. "Ouch! How many patients have you guys dumped on the floor?"

"Not a single one, Mr. Cohen. You're in safe hands."

"Humph. After that experience in the MRI, I don't trust any of you. I thought sure they were going to cook me alive."

A gentle nurse intervened. "You can relax now, Mr. Cohen. It's all over. Let me see if I can find you something refreshing to drink. The doctors will be in soon to explain your results."

"Why can't somebody just say 'yay' or 'nay?'"

"It's not quite that simple, sir." The warning came from a middle-aged doctor standing in the doorway. "I'm Dr.

Fenwick. I will explain what's going on as soon as my interns arrive. Ah, here they are now. Your admittance record shows that this was your first fall. Is that correct?"

"Yeah, I guess, except that time I tripped over the hose somebody left in the yard." He glared at David, who cringed at the memory.

"But no blackouts? No short periods of failed memory? Sharp headaches? Dizziness?"

"No. I told you. I've never had a problem like this."

"Well, sir, your MRI tells a slightly different story. It shows several small lesions in your brain–spots where a blood vessel has leaked and left scar tissue. That suggests you have been having a series of TIAs or what we call 'silent strokes.' They may have occurred without your being aware of it—while you're asleep or, for example, when you're watching a dull TV show and drift off for a few minutes."

"Nothing to worry about, right?"

"On the contrary, sir, I find it deeply worrying. It suggests you are headed for a much more serious event—a full-blown stroke that could leave you paralyzed, unable to speak, or even dead."

"No," Mrs. Cohen wailed. "He's always been healthy."

"I'm sorry to put it so bluntly, but Mr. Cohen is not healthy and hasn't been for some time. I want you all to understand how serious a matter this is because it's going to take all of you to keep him on the straight and narrow path back to good health."

"Meaning what?' Mr. Cohen growled. "I won't have a bunch of nursemaids dogging my footsteps and telling me how to live my life—even if they are members of my family."

The doctor was fast losing his patience. "It means you're overweight and lazy and more than a little ignorant if you'll excuse my bluntness. You need to be exercising, like walking a mile or more every day."

"I do that. I play golf."

"Once or twice a month? And riding in a golf cart between holes? That's not exercising. That's a lazy man's excuse. I mean taking 10,000 steps a day and proving it by keeping a counter on your shoe. You can do it playing golf but only if you play every day and walk between holes."

"I don't have time to do that. I'm a working man. I have a law firm to run. I can't be out on the golf course when someone's life is in the balance. And I'm not overweight, either. That's good solid bone and muscle you're seeing. I've been big-boned ever since I was a kid."

"Nonsense! It's flab. It's not only unattractive. It's like carrying around a forty-pound bag of rocks every place you go. We are going to put you on cholesterol-lowering medication and a cardiac diet, one heavy on fish and vegetables instead of your usual meat and potatoes. And once you're retired, we will put you on a regular exercise schedule."

"I'm not about to retire, and I don't plan to follow this nonsense you're suggesting."

"Then, the next time we meet, you will be in the morgue, and I'll be telling your family to plan your funeral and get on with their lives."

"Out! Get out!"

"Oh, we had better add some anger management classes to the prescription."

"Get out, all of you. I want to see a new doctor."

"Good. I don't like treating patients who are killing themselves."

Mrs. Cohen was crying softly as her daughter and son helped her out of their father's room. "He's just upset, mom. The protocol of an MRI is impossibly hard to deal with. I am sure once he is settled, he'll see the wisdom of what the doctor is demanding."

A young nurse interrupted Hannah's efforts to console her mother. "Look what I found for our patient. A glass of cold lemonade should make him feel much more comfortable." She pulled a straw from her pocket and set the glass on the bedside table. Mr. Cohen took one look at it and hurled it across the room.

"When I asked for a cold one, I meant a cold beer, not some five-year-old's street corner concoction." The sound of breaking glass followed the Cohens as they left for the night.

Sarah took David's arm as they headed to the hospital's parking lot. "We have had a long and stressful day. I think we deserve something scrumptious for dinner. How about checking out that new Chinese restaurant in town? It's owned by the former chef at Isolde's, so it should be a special experience. Besides, we never did get the Chinese dinner we were going to order on Saturday."

"Good idea. But don't try to convince me to try any dish called 'Happy Family.' I would have trouble believing in it tonight. In fact, after that lecture we heard about a healthy lifestyle, I am thinking of ordering steamed fish with broccoli."

"Sounds good to me. I just hope they are still open this late."

As it happened, the restaurant owner met them at the door, his hand still reaching to turn the 'open' sign to 'closed.'

"Ah, the esteemed district attorney, Mr. Cohen, and his lovely wife, the professor. You are our last customers of the evening but do come in. How is your father? We have heard he was ill."

"He is doing better, thank you, but how does news like that travel so fast?"

"It's a small town. Small events make a big noise. Now, what can I bring you to start your meal?"

"How about a couple of Tsingtao beers?"

"And could I interest you in an appetizer of fresh spring rolls—on the house? I have several made up in the kitchen and they are going to go to waste since you are our last customers of the evening. What you don't eat I will just have to put out for the girl on the porch."

"What? I didn't notice a girl out there."

"No, no. It's just an expression—bad translation from Chinese."

"I don't get it."

"I will try to explain. You see, in my part of China. we cannot afford to waste food as you do here in America. We also believe that no one should go without enough to eat. So, when someone has leftover food, they do not just throw it away. They look for someone hungry. And those who need food wait outside for someone to offer a meal. We call those waiting for food 'the person who sits on my porch.'

"Here in America, I see many who are hungry, and I try to help as I learned in my childhood hometown."

"Is that what's in that pile of boxes on your side porch? I couldn't help but notice it as we came in. Most of our businesses leave their trash in the back alley, Mr. Chen."

"It is unsightly, I know. I must find a trellis or something to block the view. I apologize, but you see, we are remodeling this old house to make a cozy restaurant. When this was a family home, the only door in the kitchen led out to a side vegetable garden, so for now that is what I must use for daily grocery delivery and garbage pickup. We keep it as neat as possible during the day, but by this time of night ..."

"I understand, but the city does not want you attracting vagrants and vermin to a residential neighborhood. And if I'm not mistaken, this is also where you leave your leftovers."

Mr. Chen nodded. "But where you see vagrants and vermin, I see the poor, the hungry, the suffering. I package my leftovers carefully and put them out in a cooler, separately from the garbage. Someone hungry—the girl on the porch—finds them and eats well. But you frown. You still do not approve?"

"I think there are food safety laws against that sort of thing. Don't worry. I know you mean well, and I won't turn you in. But be careful how long you allow the extra food to sit out if there does not happen to be a girl on your porch."

"Do you realize how much you sounded like your father just now?" Sarah watched David closely, worrying about the way he was handling the news of his father's health problems.

"That was my official DA's voice you were hearing, not Dad's. I can't ignore a city code violation, even if most of my thoughts are elsewhere."

"But what's so terrible about Mr. Chen feeding someone who is hungry?"

"Nothing, so long as there's only one girl on the porch. But if others start joining her, we could soon have a crisis. Mr. Chen can't afford to feed every hungry passer-by. And then there's the issue of food safety. He could lose his restaurant if those vagrants we discussed start coming down with food poisoning."

"I think you're creating problems that don't exist to avoid thinking about the family crisis that is your real concern."

"Maybe so. But you saw for yourself how quickly Dad's anger erupted. That in itself is a matter of concern. I don't want to be the one who asks the wrong question and triggers a full-blown stroke."

"What would you have him do? Do you want to see him retire and take up mall walking as his new preoccupation?"

"Why not? He'd be fairly safe there, with people around to call 911 if necessary. More important, an orderly retirement would give all of us time to think through the implications of his absence. My biggest worry at the moment is that he will drop dead suddenly, leaving all the hard decisions up in the air with no one to take charge. I know for certain he doesn't have a will."

"This discussion is getting us nowhere. It's too soon for any of us to be thinking clearly. Moreover, we're sitting here picking at the food we don't want and taking up the restaurant's time and space. Let's ask the waiter to wrap up the fish to take home. If we don't eat it, Elijah and Delilah will."

As Mr. Chen locked the door and turned on the closed sign behind them, David hesitated at the edge of the porch. "Wait here. I can't just turn my back on this mess." He moved quietly to the side porch and a pile of boxes awaiting removal. Then he kicked the pile and shouted, "Police! Come out of there now!"

After an initial silence, a tousled head emerged from the pile, and a girl's soft voice asked, "What do you want? I'm not hurting anything."

"There's a law in this town about sleeping on public property."

"It's not public property, and Mr. Chen doesn't mind if I sleep out here."

"Well, he's about to care. What's your name?"

"Janice."

"Do you have a last name, or are you some kind of royalty who only needs one label?"

"Janice Highsmith. And before you ask, I'm nineteen and I'm from Huntsville, Alabama That's the place with all the rockets and German restaurants. Anything else you need to know?"

"Anybody in there with you?"

"What? Do you think I'm some kind of tramp or lowlife streetwalker? No, there's nobody here—except Baskerville. He's my dog, but he won't bite. He's more likely to lick you to death."

"All right, Janice. You look chilly. Do you have a sweater or something? I'll give you a couple of minutes to gather your belongings, and then we're going to find you a nice warm cell to sleep in tonight."

"What about Baskerville?"

"We'll drop him off at the Humane Society with a 'Hold As Evidence' tag. That'll keep him safe for a while."

Sarah had been listening from a distance, but she could not control herself any longer. "David! You're not taking that poor girl to jail! How can you?"

"Back off, Sarah. Remember Mr. Gillespie and what he once told me about the threat of jail? He said it was better than the place he was living at the moment. The same is true here. Would you rather a young woman have a shower, some clean clothes, a cot, and a blanket—or should I leave 'The Girl on the Porch' sleeping in a cardboard box?"

His question made Sarah's breath catch in her throat. While she had been worrying about Mr. Cohen's health and trying to finish the next Elijah book, she had let the details of the nunnery book slide by unnoticed. She had read whole years of memoirs without registering the details. She remembered now, and now she knew why the incident at the Chinese restaurant had made her uncomfortable.

The mother superior had a version of the girl on the

porch. Hers involved a girl in the sanctuary. On Monday morning, Sarah returned to her notes and re-read Mother Francesca's struggle over how to help the female vagrants in their little town. The nun's answer vindicated David's decision and made Sarah feel ashamed of her intolerance.

CHAPTER 16

Terce—The Third Hour

From the journal of Mary Frances McMurtry, later known as Sister Francesca, and now, by the grace of God, as Mother Francesca, Mother Superior of this Convent of Our Lady St. Walburga:

Autumn 1848

The morning I learned I had been named mother superior of the new Saint Walburga nunnery in Tennessee, I sat in the archbishop's office and dreamed big dreams. I imagined an enclosed quad of buildings, all of them facing the central garden area. I didn't think about the surrounding landscape or the community in which our little cloistered group would dwell. I assumed we would spend our days celebrating the liturgical hours and filling the time in between services with the work of God; that is, in silent prayer and private contemplation. My sisters would be strong, healthy, and devoted to their calling. The local church would provide for our physical needs while we sang hymns of gratitude.

That was the first day and my first impression. How wrong it was! I soon learned my days as mother superior would be filled with personal crises, logistical nightmares, and cantankerous old ladies struggling to subdue the joyful spirits of our novices. We had a cloistered garden and a protective wall, but the world outside had little interest in our activities. There was no provision for meeting our physical needs. The local priest viewed our church as competition rather than a co-worker. I had expected the town to help us. As things turned out, the town turned to us for help with their problems.

Here is an early example. It was the first break in our working day—the hour known as Terce. It corresponded to nine AM and the third liturgical service. After the reading of Scripture, the singing of a hymn, and the appropriate prayers, our nuns would have a quick cup of tea and a piece of toast to fuel their next three-hour work assignment.

I entered our church to make sure the prayer books had been set up. To my surprise, I discovered a young girl curled up asleep on a bench in the nave. Her clothes were well-worn and much too thin for the coolness of this September morning. Her hair had not seen a comb for days, and tears had left muddy streaks down her cheeks. She was not one of ours, and my first thought was that she had no business in our sanctuary. I shook her shoulder to awaken her, and she jumped in terror.

"Who are you," I asked, "and what are you doing here?"

"I am Gretchen Butcher, and I was looking for a place to sleep last night. A woman on the street told me I would be safe if I came in here. It is a church, isn't it?"

"This is a nunnery. We are not open to the public. You must leave before our next procession."

"I have nowhere to go."

"Where is your home, child?"

"I have no home anymore. My father kicked me out because I am evil, or so he says. I've been living on the street and begging for food from passers-by. I can manage during the day, but nights frighten me." Her tears begin to flow again, and I had no idea how to help her.

I am ashamed to admit I didn't even offer her a piece of toast. I simply handed her the burlap sack into which she had stuffed a few belongings. "The sun is up now," I told her. "You must leave before the sisters arrive for prayers."

"Will you ask them to pray for me?"

"Go along."

In my dreams every night now, I see her—that bedraggled child—as she clutched her burlap sack and shuffled her way to the door. I thought I would never see her again, but I was wrong.

As I had promised my ladies from the beginning, we open our church doors to the public every Sunday morning. That is, of course, one of the things Father Jason Miles complains about. He says we are stealing his parishioners. In truth, I suspect those who come to us on Sundays have never visited St. Mark's, his small Catholic church. They prefer us because we ask no questions. We don't demand they submit to baptism or come to confession. And we don't pry into their family affairs.

Several weeks after my initial encounter with Gretchen, I looked up one Sunday morning to see her sitting in the back row of the nave. There was no doubt now as to the reason for her homelessness. Her round belly showed clearly through the thin rags she wore. I tried to catch her attention, but she kept her eyes lowered throughout the mass.

Shortly after the service concluded and the congregation departed, I received a disturbing visit from Ron Morrison, our local sheriff. Now, don't get me wrong. I like Sheriff Morrison. He's a good man, and he performs his duties well. The crime rate in Birch Falls is quite low. Our streets are safe for women and children even at night. We've never had a murder. And if our jail occasionally overflows with overnight guests, the charges seldom go beyond drunk and disorderly. Still, having him turn up in my office on a Sunday afternoon was a bad sign.

"What can I do for you, Mr. Morrison?" I asked. "Surely you're not selling tickets for a policemen's ball."

"Nothing quite so innocent, I'm afraid," he responded. "I have a serious problem with my jail capacity. Until now, one large holding cell has been sufficient to corral all the drunks on a Saturday night. But the assumption behind that statement is that all of the prisoners will be men. Lately, I have had a problem with a female vagrant. She keeps turning up on our streets; she's hungry, cold, homeless, and needing protection. I can arrest her, but then where do I take her? I can hardly throw her into the same large holding cell with a bunch of drunks. One night I locked her in my office, but that's where I keep my accounts and ready cash."

"I can understand your problem," I answered, "but I'm not sure what you think I can do about it."

"Wait. I'm not finished. Lately, the cause of her problem has become obvious. The lady is quite pregnant."

"You're referring to Gretchen Butcher, aren't you? So, why aren't you talking to her doctor or her family?"

"She can't afford a doctor, and her family won't even speak to her."

"That's a pretty strong reaction to a fairly common problem, isn't it? Why won't the family help?"

"I have been trying to work with Mr. Butcher but without success. He is as strict and strait-laced as they come. He is demanding to know the name of the father of the child. She insists that the man responsible is a middle-aged man, one of Mr. Butcher's friends who boards his horse in the Butcher's stable. According to Gretchen, this fellow has been forcing himself on her for years, but she has not told anyone because she knew no one would believe her. The present situation proves her right, of course."

"I still don't see how I can help. The young woman may not want to be pregnant, but I am pretty sure she doesn't want to be a nun, either."

"I need a safe and secure place to hold her long enough to let her get her life straightened out. Your nunnery is ideal. Safe and secure, it certainly is, but more than that, you and your nuns would set a great moral example for her to follow. No one will ask her to join the order, but she will be able to see what a good life is all about."

"What would we do with her? We do our work as part of our prayer mission, and for those things we cannot handle, we have already hired local people to fill the positions. We have a call to charity, but that does not mean we must make permanent room for a stranger in our midst. We are an enclosed order, intentionally shut off from the outside world."

"Since you have done this for one of the least ..."

"Yes, yes, I got the message, but I worry about setting a precedent. I feel sorry for Gretchen and I would like to help, but I can't let you turn my nunnery into jail cells for all the wayward women of this town. We can't afford to ..."

"First, there aren't all that many. Gretchen is the first female prisoner that I have not been able to handle. Second, I've already hired a contractor to build us a separate holding facility for women. And third, the state pays me a set amount for each incarcerated individual. The payments for any woman you take in will come directly to you to offset your expenses."

"I don't like the term payment. We do not sell our services. Each of us—individually and collectively as members of the convent—has taken a vow of poverty."

"Then look at the state's money as a gift for the upkeep of the nunnery."

"And what is to be done about the baby? We have a nurse among us who can probably handle the birth, but what if Gretchen doesn't want a child? What if you release her, and she leaves the baby behind? What do we do then?"

"Don't worry about problems before they occur."

"But we must be prepared for any eventuality. Will the nunnery end up with a baby to care for?"

"Since you have done this ..."

"You've already used that line. Look, sheriff, Gretchen came to me for help several weeks ago, and I turned her away. I have felt guilty ever since, and I've prayed for an answer to her problems. God always promises to answer our prayers, but he doesn't promise we will like the answer. In this case, I don't like the answer one bit, but I will do what I can on a day-to-day basis. Bring her to us, and I will find room for her in our infirmary. She will have small chores to do each day, and we will expect her to observe our daily routines. You will need to make it clear to her that she is here as punishment and that she must obey the rules. If she does not, I reserve the right to send her packing."

And just that quickly I broke my own rule by breaching our enclosure. Gretchen was a model prisoner. Once she was sure no one would force her to become a nun, she settled into our routines. She worked in the laundry, where Sister Elizabeth gave her sewing lessons. She quickly learned how to darn stockings, sew on buttons, and mend small tears in a habit. One of the novices was also teaching her how to knit little booties and bibs. All were skills she could later use to earn a living in the outside world.

During the working day, she went quietly about her duties. I only asked that she walk to the refectory for meals. She needed the exercise and the socialization as well. She did not disturb us during our liturgical services. For weeks she simply stayed out of sight, but then I noticed that she had started attending Vespers each evening. That service offered respite from the day's responsibilities and thankfulness for the blessings bestowed. The rituals seemed to offer her comfort as her pregnancy progressed.

I had never discussed her baby's future with her. That's another of my failings. I tend to avoid conversations that make me uncomfortable. Had I probed a bit deeper, I might have learned that she was determined to keep her child. Instead, I stewed over the sheriff's latest request that we take in two more young women whose lifestyles had brought them into conflict with the rules of matrimony before pregnancy. I realized that I had been standing on a slippery slope from the moment I accepted Gretchen. And now I was sliding deeper and deeper into a situation I had vowed to avoid.

St. Walburga's was no longer a cloistered house, devoted solely to prayer and contemplation. We were now a part of the Birch Falls community—a place of refuge for unwed mothers and a nursery for their babies. Most of my sister nuns were delighted with the development. The town was grateful. The babies and their mothers were safe. But I wondered what God thought about it. Would He commend me for my mercy or condemn me for my failure to keep my vows?

CHAPTER 17

Time Rushes On

July 13, 2011

Mr. Cohen came home from the hospital on Wednesday afternoon. He was reluctant to admit how shaky his legs felt after spending several days in bed, but his discomfort revealed itself in another spurt of bad temper. Each time Miriam asked him how he felt, if he wanted to stretch out on his recliner, or if he would be more comfortable going back to bed, he snarled at her. "Quit treating me like a hot house plant. If I want something, I'll ask for it."

By the time David stopped by to see how things were going, his mother had retreated to the kitchen.

"What's cooking?" David asked innocently enough.

"It's a recipe for snacking suggested by Doctor Fenwick —roasted chickpeas seasoned with salt substitute and garlic flakes."

Mr. Cohen was passing through the kitchen. He peeked into the oven and shuddered. "They smell revolting and look worse, rather like rabbit droppings. I'm not sure why you're bothering for me. I have no intention of eating them."

"Well, you need not hold out for chocolate-covered peanuts or cheddar-flavored potato chips, because such indulgences have all disappeared from our shelves. So long as I'm cooking, you're going to follow the diet prescribed by medical experts, not by your taste buds."

"Did you ever find out what that Mediterranean diet is all about, mom?"

"Whatever it is, it's a lie," Mr. Cohen shouted from the living room. "Italians live on pasta, bread, olive oil, and wine."

"That's what they serve in America's Italian restaurants. In Italy, you would be eating vegetables, beans, nuts, and seafood. The olive oil and wine are all right, but you would also be getting eggplant, kale, Brussels sprouts, octopus, and mussels."

"Humph. I'd rather starve."

"That can be arranged," Miriam snarled back at him.

"And I'll tell you what else I am not going to do. I am not walking 10,000 steps a day. I'm not giving up my golf cart. And I'm not about to retire."

David shook his head, admitting to himself that this was not the time for an argument. He headed for home in hope of finding a friendly voice.

Sarah shouted a greeting from her upstairs office, followed by a warning. "Don't open the door. I'm on a ladder, and you'll tip me over." After a short pause, she opened the door from inside. "Come on in, but don't move anything."

"What in the world is all of this?" he asked, staring at walls now covered with little sticky notes.

"It's Elijah's schedule for the next few months. He starts his Faces page on August 1. The green notes are his topics. The stuffed Elijah makes its appearance on September 1, and the pink notes are personal appearances at local bookstores. The white notes are my deadlines, including page layouts in mid-October and page proofs by Halloween. Then it's production time when all we can do is wait. But the gold notes indicate Thanksgiving and our trip to New York City with the Birch Falls band. The gold note with a black stripe around it is Black Friday, the release date for *The Hanukkah Gift*.

"We will start doing bookstore appearances on Saturday, November 26. Those dates will get blue notes. The eight days of Hanukkah, December 20-28, are our prime selling dates, and I expect Hannah and I will both be on call. Our appearances—and Elijah's—will appear on purple notes. Clear?"

"As long as you understand it. It's quite a commitment, isn't it?"

"Yes, but worth it."

"Are you sure about that? It seems like a lot of work for someone who also has a scholarly book to write."

"It's not a problem, David. I spend the mornings working in the archives and trying to see things through the eyes of a middle-aged nun. Then by mid-afternoon, I'm ready to take a break and play around with silly ideas for Elijah's talk shows. The two balance each other quite nicely."

"Starting to get a handle on the mother superior, are you?"

"I hope I'm interpreting her correctly. She's a good person, well-educated, and sincere in her beliefs, but she's finding her position of authority more of a challenge than she expected. Of course, that's true of most of us, isn't it? We all think we know how something ought to be done, right up to the time when we're the ones who have to do it. I have to admit, though, that I was surprised when I started realizing the depths of her anxiety. What's more important was my realization that I faced the same issues. I didn't see that coming."

"Authority sucks sometimes. I could have warned you of that."

"' Well, thinking about people who throw their authority around—how is the young woman you tossed in jail the other night because she turned out to be the girl on the porch?"

"You still think I made the wrong decision, don't you?"

"Not any longer. I understand that she needed a bath—probably a flea treatment as well. But I'm concerned that clean clothes, several good nights' sleep, and some nourishing meals don't go far enough. They don't change the fact that she comes from a dysfunctional family with a drug addict for a father and an alcoholic mother. She is well out of that environment, but you've offered her nothing but jail as a substitute."

"I have good news on that score. With the help of my mother, Sheila Leibowicz, and the combined services of the local YWCA and the Jewish Women's Federation, our Miss Janice Highsmith will be released from jail first thing tomorrow morning, and all charges dropped. She will move into a room and board accommodation at the YWCA, and next week she starts a three-month training class to become a licensed home care provider."

"That's a really weird coincidence!"

"What is?"

"I spent the morning reading the mother superior's

memoirs, in which she discusses the first steps she took toward altering the nature of the nunnery. It had been intended as a cloistered community, shut off from the rest of the world. Then she discovered that in Birch Falls, that kind of seclusion was almost impossible.

"There was a girl in her story, too. She was a teenager, unmarried but pregnant, and her father had kicked her out of the family home. She lived on the street until the sheriff arrested her as a vagrant and then realized he had no room in his jail to house her. He asked the nunnery to help, and the mother superior eventually agreed to take the girl in and give her some training so that she could support herself and her child. Doesn't that sound somewhat familiar?"

"It does, particularly as in both cases it is church women who provide solutions to the young girls' problems."

"The difference, of course, is that now there are established programs just waiting for someone to need them. In the case of the nunnery, it was up to the mother superior to invent a plan. Her one saving grace was that the state paid a set amount for the girl's room and board, just as if it were a jail cell. But who pays for Janice's support? Surely, she has no money."

"That's why the church women are involved. They guarantee her room and board for three months, after which she will repay their investment by working for an additional three months as an assistant instructor. The clients she will work with pay for the service, but their fees go back to the church ladies to support the next batch of trainees. By next spring Janice should have certification as a caregiver and be on her way to becoming self-supporting."

"What do they train her to do? Three months is not long enough to earn any sort of nursing credentials."

"No. It's not intended for that. These women simply offer

an additional hand to people who are struggling to hold their families together. The first month of training is pure housekeeping—how to do laundry, load the dishwasher, cook simple meals, mop floors, or run errands. The second month covers basic childcare—how to change a diaper, burp a baby, bandage a cut, or deal with emergencies like choking. And the third month expands into helping care for injured or ill adults. For example, they make it possible for elderly people to live their last days at home or for a parent to go back to work after the birth of a child. The work sounds simple, but it is vitally important."

"I'm a little surprised that Janice is going along with training as a caregiver. I didn't get much of a sense that she was looking for employment. She seemed happy enough living in her box and eating the handouts Mr. Chen provided."

"She was less enamored of living in a jail cell than Mr. Gillespie suggested. She brightened considerably when I suggested that success as a caregiver might help her become a licensed practical nurse, something she could do as an independent contractor. At any rate, she will be under supervision for the next six months. Then we will see if the experience has changed her attitude."

"It's too bad there isn't a program like that for people like your father who need to change their basic lifestyle."

"You're right about that. I worry about placing all the pressure on mom to force him into diet and exercise changes."

"As Dr. Fenwick said, it is going to be up to all of us to help."

CHAPTER 18

Facing the Future

August 2011

For the next couple of weeks, Sarah and David were little more than ships passing in the night. David, of course, had a full-time job as a district attorney, but he was also trying to keep a foot in the door of his father's law office. He checked every day to make sure the junior partners and law clerks were functioning normally. When they faced a problem, he tried to do a quick fix. If a complicated issue arose, he took the time after work to stop by the family home and discuss the problem with his dad. As far as he knew, no clients had complained about delays in their cases, but he worried about potential slip-ups.

Meanwhile, Sarah continued her practice of working on the nunnery book in the mornings and switching to Elijah's story in the afternoons. She had finished the textual page layouts for *The Hanukkah Gift* and passed the drafts on to Hannah, who was ready to insert the illustrations. They had agreed to reserve the last week of September for final revisions.

Sarah's other project involved establishing Elijah's presence on the internet. She had opened the homepage for him on *Faces*, and his first August posting had been his photograph with a caption: *Who Is This Handsome Fellow?* In the next few days, she followed that with postings giving the usual *Faces* information:

- *Elijah F. Cohen*
- *Born in New York City*
- *Resides in Tennessee*
- *Dropped out of Feline Obedience Academy after one semester*
- *Employed as a poster boy by The Questioning Mind Publishing Company*
- *Single but in a relationship*
- *Enjoys kitty bags from fancy restaurants, bouncy toys, and catnip mice*

A second picture followed, with a clickable bar inviting readers to join the Elijah Fan Club. An asterisk opened a warning: *Must be over three years old. Members under the age of twelve must have parental permission.*

Despite his busy schedule, David found time each morning to check *Faces* for Elijah's thoughts of the day. When the fan club announcement appeared, David came home laughing. "I like it," he announced. "How many cat lovers have signed up?"

"Would you believe it? Elijah's page has 417 followers, and 348 people have registered for the fan club. I've been planning to send out special little messages to fan club members, but I'm going to have to get an e-mail service like Mailchimp to handle these numbers."

"That's a good idea, but a couple of cautions—check costs and volume cut-offs. You may end up with a great many more customers than you bargained for. And don't volunteer to send people things other than messages. You don't want to be mailing 348 packages containing stuffed Elijahs, for example."

"Gotcha! But you have to forgive me for being excited by my early numbers."

"I'm thrilled for you. That plagiarizing lady in Montana doesn't seem to have hurt your business a bit. She may have helped publicize your books. Anything else going on in your world?"

"Well, I have been doing some thinking about the best way to help your mother cope with a crotchety old man. I don't have time to go over and relieve her during the middle of the day, but I can give her a break on weekends. I asked Dr. Fenwick for suggestions to help your father alter his diet, and he had one of the nurses give me some recipes—things that are flavorful and filling without being fattening. I'm going to invite your parents to dinner in a few days after your dad has settled into some acceptance of his new circumstances. I'm thinking of next Friday evening after prayers at synagogue when the menu can be light and informal. I want to try a bean and tomato stew with lots of fresh herbs and seasonings. With a French baguette and some extra virgin olive oil for dipping, it should make a filling late-night supper."

"You are great, Sarah. Thank you. Now if you could just come up with a way to force Dad to talk about retirement ..."

"Hmmm. That's your problem, my love. You handle the office; I'll stick to the kitchen."

~

Leonard Cohen was in a great mood when he and his wife Miriam set out for the synagogue that Friday night. It was his first outing since his mini-stroke, and he had taken all afternoon to prepare—a leisurely shower, a close shave, a stylish sport coat with contrasting trousers, and a pair of freshly polished loafers. He had even taken a pair of scissors and trimmed his sideburns and the hair on the back of his neck. "Do I look healthy enough to be out and about?" he asked Miriam.

"You look quite handsome, my dear. No one would ever know you just got out of the hospital."

Unfortunately, the whole town knew of his recent attack, and friends and rivals alike wanted to get a word or two with him.

"Hope you're feeling better. Are you sure you should be out so soon?"

"My husband had the same thing. That's what killed him."

"They didn't put you on one of those namby-pamby diets, did they? That bland stuff will kill you faster than the healthy food people admit. It's all made of wood pulp, you know—fit for nobody but beavers."

"What about your golf game? Want to make up our regular foursome next Saturday, or is that off-limits to you?"

"I called your office last week and they said you weren't coming in. Are you planning to retire now?"

"Did somebody say retire? Are you planning to close the office?"

"If you die soon, can I have your Tennessee Titans season tickets?"

Leonard's cheerful mood faded quickly, trampled by thoughtless people and their rude remarks. "Get me out of here," he whispered to Miriam, "I'm about to kill someone."

He was still fuming by the time they reached David's and Sarah's house. Sarah headed for the kitchen, whispering to David to open a bottle of wine. "There's a bottle of Pinot Gris chilling in the refrigerator. But don't pour it all. They'll need some of it for dinner."

Mrs. Cohen tried to distract everyone by commenting on how nice the dining room table looked when it was set for a special meal. Mr. Cohen, however, was not about to be jollied out of his irritation.

"What in the world are these?" he asked, picking up a small cat-shaped bowl from one of the place settings. "If this is the size of the plates you're serving us for dinner, I'm not staying, Sarah. This thing's not big enough to hold a White Castle burger."

"Silly! That's an olive oil server for dipping your French baguette. Aren't they cute? We picked them up in Charleston on our honeymoon, right after we got this handwoven sweetgrass breadbasket. I've been dying for a chance to use them both."

"Since when do we have to dip our bread in olive oil? I'll have butter on mine, thank you."

"Not in my house. Olive oil clears your arteries; butter clogs them." With a tightly controlled smile on her face, Sarah picked up the bottle of olive oil and poured a dollop into Mr. Cohen's bowl. "You can have some fresh ground pepper in that if you like," she offered, handing him the pepper grinder. "It always makes me sneeze, but you might like the oil a little spicier."

She headed for the kitchen, motioning for David to

follow her. She filled two bowls with her vegetarian stew, sprinkled the tops with lemon zest, and handed them to David. "Here. Go feed your parents. Maybe if we fill your father's mouth, he'll quit grumbling. I'll be right behind you with our bowls."

Despite its inauspicious start, the meal was a success. Sarah started to relax when Mr. Cohen asked for a second bowl. And when she served fresh berries surrounding small scoops of lemon sorbet for dessert, she didn't even have to wait for compliments. "The perfect final touch," Mrs. Cohen remarked, and her husband nodded.

A little later, settled into the living room with coffee, Mr. Cohen returned to his former grouchy mood. "Can you believe some of the comments people made to me? Everybody has a horror story to share, even if it predicts the listener is about to keel over."

"People don't always think before they speak. The lady who said you'd be dead within a year if you retired—she wasn't thinking of you at all. I know she was remembering that her husband died within weeks of his retirement."

"Well, I wish they would keep their memories to themselves. And I'm not as kind as you are, David. Did you hear the guy who asked if he could have my Titans season tickets if I died? He sounded eager enough to push me off the viaduct abutment."

"Now you are exaggerating. He probably couldn't think of anything else the two of you had in common."

"Maybe so, but it felt like a whole lot of people were waiting for me to retire, although I can't see that it's anyone else's business."

"It sounds like fear to me," Sarah commented. "People look up to you. If you retire, it reminds them that the same thing is going to happen to them. They were hoping you'd say you were never going to retire so they could quit worrying about their retirement."

"You children can quit making excuses. You're probably salivating at the very thought of pushing me aside."

"That's not true, dad. I've told you before. I don't want to inherit the law practice suddenly. I want time to spend with you—to watch how you handle problem clients or deadbeats, to understand your unspoken agreements with the junior partners, to get used to the rhythms of the office before I have to run it on my own."

"How long can that take? You're already running things right now while I've been recuperating."

"But you're the missing element. I've been learning a bit about the firm this past couple of weeks, but I'm not seeing your personal touch on matters. That's going to take time, and I won't be free to be the 'fly on the wall' until after the November 2012 election. That's more than a year away. So, I'm not hoping you will retire. I'm counting on having you around for a long time."

"Speaking of that election, are you going to run for another term as an unaffiliated candidate? Or are you ready to admit the district attorney needs the backing of the Democratic party?"

"I'm not going to run at all, dad. I've had enough of a job that demands I please everyone all of the time. It can't be done. I want to follow the guidance of my conscience, and I'm ready to admit that I can do that best as a private lawyer, not a public servant. I will finish out my term of office because I promised the voters I would do so. And after that, I will need to refresh my law studies—maybe take one of those evening courses that help candidates pass the bar. And then—then we'll have to see where matters stand."

Sarah struggled to conceal her surprise at hearing David

declare his intention to leave the district attorney's office. It was a topic he had been avoiding while she debated her career options. Now it was out in the open, and there could be no more avoidance of this issue or the other decisions that lay in wait for them.

CHAPTER 19

Decisions, Decisions

End of August 2011

Thunder and lightning awakened them the next morning. David rolled onto his stomach and pulled the pillow over his ears. "Not fair! Not fair at all. One morning a week I get to turn off the alarm and sleep in. And what do I get but flashing lightning and rumbling thunder—enough to send the cats leaping from their perches to dash across the bed."

"Don't blame them. They're just scared, that's all."

"Humph! Scared enough for Delilah to sink her sharp little claws into my shoulder blade. I'm probably bleeding to death as I lie here."

"Well, try not to bleed on the sheets, OK? I don't want to spend the day doing laundry."

"What time is it, anyhow?"

"A little after seven."

"Seven? That's still the middle of the night on a Saturday."

"Oh, do shut up, David. You're keeping me awake."

The weather was no better when they awakened for a second time around ten.

"It looks like we're in for an all-day deluge," Sarah said. "I vote we declare it a pajama day, light the fireplace in the den, turn the TV to the old movie channel, and settle for two meals—brunch and supper."

"I was planning to take us out for breakfast this morning, but your plan sounds better, provided you have something delicious in mind for that brunch."

"How about an omelet? I have extra spinach, fresh mushrooms, and white cheddar cheese. And to go with it, fresh berries and hot biscuits topped with peppered gravy."

"Oh, you sweet-tongued rascal! Sold. And what's on offer for supper?"

"Whatever you decide to come up with, my love. After last night's triumph, I deserve a break."

"You do, indeed. But speaking of last night, we need to sit down and talk about what happened."

"Not until I have had that omelet and at least two cups of coffee."

Not even a gourmet breakfast could postpone the discussion forever. Sarah procrastinated for a few minutes by removing the dishes, but issues that separated them still hovered in the air.

"So, when did you decide you were not going to run for district attorney again?" She asked the question with her back turned because she did not want to see the expression on his face.

"I have been considering it for several months, but I didn't want to say anything until I had made up my mind."

"That's not how we decided to settle our differences. I might remind you of a discussion we had on the way home from Charleston. You gave me a long lecture about how, now that we were married, we had to start behaving like a 'we' instead of as two individuals. I had dropped my plans with the South Carolina archives without discussing it with you, and you had cut our honeymoon short because of the whistleblower's demands. In both cases, you said, we should have been able to discuss the issues as a couple and make a joint decision."

"I remember, but ..."

"So how is this different?"

"It's different because it's my job—one I had before we were married—and you don't have any idea how miserable that job sometimes makes me."

"Which suggests that we should have been discussing those problems a long time ago."

"I don't agree, Sarah. We also promised to keep our work problems separate from our home life, and that has been good for both of us."

"I thought so too, but you've been miserable and I haven't realized it. I can't change what has happened in the past, but we can start afresh from this time forward. What is it about the DA's office that leaves you so unhappy?"

"The job sounds important, but I cannot change things in any meaningful way. I stand halfway between the police and the legal profession, but I have no power over either one. Take our current case as an example.

"Brendan O'Malley is getting ready to sue Galyean Motors for selling him a defective car. His son and the girl he dated died in an accident caused by failing brakes on the new car. Richard Galyean claims he is simply the retailer. As a seller, he says, he bears no responsibility for any error in the manufacturing process. The police have focused much atten-tion on the warranty that comes with a car when it leaves the factory. They are also looking into the responsibility of the dealer's mechanics who check each new car to make sure all systems are working.

"I suggested to our prosecutor that something might have happened to the car between the factory and the dealership. I also wanted the police investigators to look into the people who stand to gain the most by manipulating the manufacturer's suggested retail price. So far as I can tell, they have done neither. As the legal representative of the people of Birch Falls, I am not required to tell O'Malley's lawyers or the police what I have recommended to their opposing investigators. As a result, I fear that both the prosecutor and the defense will miss a crucial clue."

"And what might that be?"

"The weather. I don't have access to the precise dates affecting the case. However, I do know that the car in question was built in Japan and delivered to New Orleans via one of those huge cargo ships. There could have been storms at sea or hurricanes in the Gulf of Mexico that caused damage to the cargo."

"And you can't step in?"

"No. I sit above the fray, watching both sides making mistakes and swallowing my tongue to keep from interfering. That's not how I want to spend my working years, Sarah. I want to be in the middle of the fight, not watching from the sidelines."

"I understand, although I'm not sure the voters will. And what about your father? What does he think about your decision? Could you tell from his reaction last night?"

"I thought he knew about my decision, but he didn't act as if he remembered. He was holding the line on any talk about his retirement, especially in front of us. He's back in his 'I'm going to live forever' position. Somehow, he thinks that allows me to do as I please, although it does nothing of the sort."

"So, what do you think he wants?"

"I know what he wants—a new firm name on the door reading 'Cohen and Sons.'"

"Sons? He only has one."

"He's using the plural in the sense of 'Sons of the Confederacy,' of which he is also a member. The 'Sons' refers to all male descendants, i.e., sons, grandsons, great-grandsons, etc."

"Well, then, he already has you and his grandson, Benny."

"Ah, but Benny is not a Cohen, and that makes all the difference. The last thing my father wants is a sign that reads 'Cohen and Steinmark.'"

"But he can't have a Cohen grandson unless you and I ..."

"Exactly, and he doesn't want to hurt your feelings or make you feel guilty for not being able to give him what he wants."

"Can't you just tell him ...?"

"Tell him what? That we're thinking about it? That would be a lie, and I try never to lie to him."

"You can tell him that we plan to think about it."

"And how lame is that? No, Sarah, we can't keep putting the discussion on hold. We owe it to our parents to be honest about it. Either we are going to look into one of the alternate ways we can become parents, or we can give them a flat refusal instead of keeping them dangling."

"All right. Why don't you say what you're thinking—that I'm the one who keeps avoiding the issue."

"No, we're both guilty. Look at us right now. What are we doing? We're talking about talking, not discussing the problem."

"OK. We've had three suggestions—fostering, surrogacy, or adoption. Which one should we consider first?"

"I don't want to take in foster children. It's too random, too temporary, and doesn't solve the naming problem anyhow. Will and Julia have probably had fewer problems than most because they knew Ronnie before they took him in, but even so ..."

"How are things going on that score? Is Ronnie still fighting Will over every step?"

"They have settled down some. Will convinced Ronnie to write to the Olympic track coach at Colorado Springs, asking for advice about starting serious Olympic training. Of course, what Ronnie didn't know was that Will and the coach are long-time friends. Anyhow, Ronnie received a lengthy answer, advising him to talk to his local track coach about setting up a training schedule. He also encouraged him to attend next summer's Olympics or at least watch the televised coverage. So, the whole family is now planning to go to London in June. And Ronnie has agreed not to pursue a spot on the 2016 team until he turns sixteen."

"Sounds fair."

"Fair, yes, but looking at it from a foster parent's point of view, it simply puts a closing date on their arrangement. I understand Ronnie has already pulled a couple of rebellions based on his knowledge that he'll be moving on within a couple of years."

"I want more permanence than that. If I'm going to be a mother, I want to raise the child from infancy. But I don't like the idea of using a surrogate, either. That adds a third party to the family dynamic, and I'm not comfortable with the potential for conflict."

"Then adoption is our only choice, I guess. Do you have any objections to that process?"

"I don't know enough about the requirements, but that sort of information will come as we move through the process. It's just that ..."

"What?"

"This is going to sound selfish, but I don't have time right now to take the first steps. We're already involved with the promotions we've promised to do—the internet postings and the debut of the stuffed Elijah. Meanwhile, Hannah and I have only until the end of September to finish the Hanukkah layouts. I should note that Rosh Hashana interrupts everything on September 29, and then we're into High Holy Days, with twice-a-day prayers, and your mother's big plans for two family dinners—one on Rosh Hashana and the other on Yom Kippur. I'm less than halfway into the nunnery book, so I can't afford to take any more time away from that research.

"The holiday season looms ahead, and we're already committed to traveling to New York with the Birch Falls High School Band over Thanksgiving. The Hanukkah book release is on Black Friday, followed by bookstore talks and signings. And, of course, the holidays themselves. I can't begin to think of something as momentous as adoption until after the first of the year."

"Fair enough, if that's a firm commitment. Is it one we can share with our prospective grandparents?"

Sarah drew a deep breath. "It is."

CHAPTER 20

Rosh Hashana

September 29, 2011

"Could someone hold the door for me, please? After spending all day cooking, I'd rather not dump these dishes on the sidewalk." Hannah balanced a large flat baking dish plus a wooden salad bowl, steadying both with her chin while she waited for Jacob to catch up.

Sarah scurried to push the screen open and take the wooden salad bowl. "You have been busy, haven't you? What all did your mother ask you to bring?"

"It's just a couple of side dishes—a salad of cucumbers and corn and some *tzimmes*."

"I've always wondered what *tzimmes* meant. It sounds so exotic."

"It's just roasted carrots topped with some sweet fruit. The Middle Eastern name makes it sound more exotic than it is. Let's get these into the kitchen and let somebody else worry about serving them. How's your day been?"

"I'm sure you know. Your mother has kept me busy all

afternoon learning how to turn brisket into a sweet dish. I've never seen a Rosh Hashana dinner from the inside before. That's one of the difficulties—or blessings, perhaps—of having your father be a popular rabbi. Someone always invited us for dinner, so my mother never had to cook all these fancy dishes."

"I'm sure Sheila Leibowicz will agree with you. Mother said she seemed to be both delighted and relieved that we invited them to join us. Sheila has had to cook this meal for years, but I don't think she ever really enjoyed doing so. This year she's baking the challah, but then she does about ten loaves a week, so it's not a major undertaking for her."

"I enjoyed her Rosh Hashanah dinners, but David attended only under threats of pain and suffering."

"David will be grateful if you never learn the fine art of adding sugar to everything to make sure the coming year is full of sweetness. He has always hated this meal no matter where we ate it because everything tasted the same."

"I'm on his side, I think. But I'll be taking careful notes all evening to use in the next Elijah book. How's *Hanukkah* coming along, by the way?"

"It's finished, in the mail, all tightly packaged, weather-proofed, and insured up to the limit. I kept a copy for you to see, but I didn't think tonight was the right time to reveal it."

"Are you pleased with it?"

"It's wonderful! Having those photos of Elijah meeting Delilah made it easy to do the sketches. Of course, I was there to see the real encounter, so I knew which drawings would have the strongest appeal."

A few minutes later, a blast of sound made everyone cringe. "Here comes the rabbi with his shofar. He was practicing it at the men's prayer breakfast earlier, and several listeners were threatening to steal it to shut him up."

"What's the meaning behind that racket, rabbi?" Sarah asked. "I never heard of a shofar in New York."

"Well, like so many of our traditions, there are alternative versions of the story. Currently, most experts would tell you that to blow the shofar, one must first draw in a huge breath, which symbolizes correcting our faults, and then blow it all out through the horn, which stands for helping others. In other words, 'Fix yourself first before criticizing others.' But the more ancient versions say the sound was a warning signal of an enemy attack. It had to be loud enough to carry from village to village. Today, it reminds us that danger is never far away."

"You got that right," Leonard Cohen grumbled as he made his way to the kitchen. "You just warned the women in the kitchen of your arrival."

"I never realized there was much meaning to this holiday, except that it was the first day of the Jewish calendar year, and that we had sugary things to eat to make the new year sweet," David said. "So, now I'm confused. What does the warning of an enemy attack have to do with a sweet new year?"

"What you're missing is a concept the ancient Romans personified as the god Janus, who had two faces—one looking forward, and the other looking backward. In other words, we can hope for good things in the future, but we must never forget the terrible things that have happened in the past. Rosh Hashanah celebrations must include both.

"This day is the first of the High Holy Days leading up to Yom Kippur—certain days in which we are given a chance to apologize for our past mistakes and hurtful actions. In our prayers, we ask for the wisdom to understand and correct our past errors. We seek the courage to think about those we may have hurt, no matter whether the injury was intentional or the result of ignorance. And then we must seek forgiveness.

"But there is another side to this as well. It is not enough to hope for sweetness in the future. We must also do what we can to make our lives better. For example, you might ask yourself what you would like to do if you could be certain it would turn out well. And then you must find the courage to give it a try. Or perhaps there is a decision you've been avoiding. This is the time to decide."

Sarah cringed as the words touched a nerve. "As the daughter of a rabbi, I knew most of this—the special prayers at the synagogue, the festive dinner, the apologies, the resolutions—but in my reading I came across the mention of a tradition I had never heard of. It was called 'tash-something.'"

"Aha! Tashlich, perhaps? It's a fine old tradition, one I'm sad we seem to have forgotten. As a child, I loved the drama of it."

"But what is it?"

"It represents the casting away of one's sins. You find a body of flowing water. It doesn't have to be a river or an ocean. It could be as small as the miniature funnel that forms when you empty a sink full of water. Then you take a piece of bread, mentally confess your mistakes, wrap them in the bread, and cast it away over the water, so that the water, the bread, and the errors all flow away together."

Young Benny had been listening to this conversation without comment, but this idea excited him. "Can we do that, Dad? Can we? We have a river. And lots of bread. I saw Mrs. Leibowicz come in with a huge loaf of challah."

Jacob glanced at the rabbi for guidance but saw nothing but an amused twinkle in his eye. "Not tonight, son. It's getting too dark to see where we'd be going. But how about right after lunch tomorrow? I know a small creek behind the Hideaway Inn up in the hills east of here. We could have lunch there, whoever wants to come along, and then we can walk up through the woods to Miller's Creek."

"Rabbi? Uncle David? Aunt Sarah? Do you guys want to join us? Maybe we can make it a family tradition again."

Mrs. Cohen spoke from the kitchen doorway. "Do we need another family tradition? Eating isn't enough?"

"Eating is never enough. Is dinner ready?

"Almost. But I want to know what I missed just now."

"A revival of tashlich. Did you have any plans for tomorrow's lunch?"

"Only that I don't intend to cook it."

"Well, then, how does lunch at the Hideaway sound, followed by a short walk in the woods?"

"Wonderful!"

As the family settled around the dinner table, Hannah turned to her mother. "I thought you were going to cook a turkey this year?"

"I was, but I couldn't figure out how to make it sweet. And I briefly thought about baking a pecan pie until I remembered Sarah is allergic to nuts. So, it's the same old menu, except for the sides you brought."

"Pecan pie wouldn't do for Rosh Hashana anyhow," the rabbi pointed out. "Nuts are one of the few foods we are forbidden to eat on this day."

"Why? What's wrong with a nut?"

"There's some disagreement there, but most say it's because the word 'nut' contain the same Hebrew letters as the word 'sin.'"

"What are the other banned foods?"

"Vinegar, for one, because it's so bitter."

Jacob frowned at Hannah. "What about this salad?"

"I used lemon juice in the dressing. And we're eating corn and cucumbers, not lettuce because it is considered a bitter herb at Passover."

"I can think of one more—horseradish. It's possible to eat brisket without horseradish, but you'll not find gefilte fish on the menu because it needs a lot of horseradish to disguise the disgusting taste of rotten fish."

"I'm still confused about this turkey thing," Sheila said. "Why would you even think of turkey in September?"

"Because David and Sarah may not be here for Thanksgiving, and I thought ..."

"Visiting the big NYC, are you?"

"Yes, but not for the reason you think," David said. "Do you remember a case we tried last summer accusing Tommy Yeager, the Used Car King, of bribery and embezzlement? He was trying to buy a football player to improve the local high school's lineup, which is also illegal. I had a fine time in court telling upstanding citizens that if they could afford $500 to buy a quarterback, they could afford another $500 to send a band member to march in the Macy's parade. We raised so much money, the whole band is traveling for free. And in gratitude, the principal has invited Sarah and me to travel on the bus with the band and sit in the grandstand to greet them as they pass."

"A bus full of teenagers for eight hours? Do you have any idea what you would be letting yourselves in for?"

"I do," Sarah laughed. "I was a band member back in the day—I played the flute. I can endure a hundred verses about beer bottles, but I do dread bathroom stops. Someone always gets left behind."

Sarah tried to smile, but the corners of her mouth wouldn't cooperate. She drew a deep breath and tapped her wine glass for attention. "We've been bouncing from one topic to another, but David and I have an announcement that is appropriate for this day. Remember the things the rabbi said we should be doing? One of them was to think about a decision we've been putting off."

"And that would be …?"

"We're going to start the process of adopting a child. The classes all prospective parents must take will start in November, and we'll be sitting in the front row."

A moment of silence followed, and then everyone spoke at once.

"How wonderful!"

"We've been praying for that."

"How long will it take?"

"Where do you have to go?"

"Boy or girl?"

"An infant or an older child?"

David held up his hands to stop the barrage of questions. "At this point, we don't know much about what will happen, but we'll need your support and your patience. We'll keep you informed as we move through the process. We do know one thing, though. It's going to be an exciting year."

CHAPTER 21

Sext—The Fourth Hour

From the journal of Mary Frances McMurtry, later known as Sister Francesca, and now, by the grace of God, as Mother Francesca, Mother Superior of this Convent of Our Lady St. Walburga:

Spring 1858

The canonical hour of Sext arrives at noon. The sisters have been working for six hours. They are tired and hungry, so we often skip the usual hymns and scriptures in favor of an edifying reading, such as the life of a saint. As the mother superior, I try to use this break as a time for a quick reassessment of what we are doing. We are well into the second decade of our foundation, and our missions have developed along with the changing years.

One example has to do with our home for expectant mothers and their dependent children. When I first agreed to take in a homeless and pregnant teenager, I had no idea that I was opening a floodgate for dozens of needy young women.

But it soon became obvious that there was more of a demand than our small guest quarters and infirmary could handle.

What caused that growing need? Some may point fingers and accuse pregnant girls of gross immorality. I cannot do that. I understand how the pressures of our society have split our country into factions—pro-slavery and abolitionist. Neither side is likely to change, and the two cannot continue to exist side by side. Violence rages. Just look at the example of Bloody Kansas and the growing talk of arming the slaves to rise against their masters. Young men on both sides are arming themselves and forming militia units, preparing for the inevitable war. Many of those boys will not be coming home. Who can blame the young for seeking temporary oblivion from a crisis they did not create and cannot solve?

So, I do my part. The result? We built the Maternity Home and Orphanage behind the church and within easy reach of our Chapter House. And as time has passed, we have developed certain rules and regulations to ease the pressure on our charitable resources.

First, we require any healthy young woman to take on chores within the convent. Some work in the kitchen, others in the laundry or gardens.

We also limit the number of days a mother may remain at the Maternity House after giving birth. Normally this amounts to no more than two weeks. In that time, the mother must decide whether or not she and her baby can return to her family or if she has another way to provide for the child. If she cannot support the child, we ask that she sign over custody to the nunnery, with stated permission for us to put the child up for adoption.

Over time, it has become customary for adoptive parents to pay back the expenses incurred by the convent to support the children until they join their new families. Of course, there is no set fee for such support, and the amount adoptive families can afford varies widely. Over time, however, these gifts have repaid our efforts nicely.

Throughout this process, I have had much to learn. I, who was determined to keep our convent cloistered, discovered that my nunnery was subject to the same rules of society as the surrounding community. As I tried to structure our policies to reflect our Christian beliefs, I found that the rules were already written into the laws of the land.

One example occurred recently. Mr. Ralph Innsley, editor and publisher of the local newspaper, came to see me one day shortly after Gretchen Butcher had given birth. He explained that he and his wife had been trying to start a family, but she had suffered multiple miscarriages. The doctor had advised that they seek another way to build a family. His offer was clear. They wanted to adopt Gretchen's baby girl.

I had to refuse his offer, generous though it was. It sounded like a reasonable solution to the Butchers' family argument, but it violated one of the basic tenets that the courts had established. In any adoption, every effort must be made to keep the paths of a child and her birth mother from ever crossing. Adoptions take place across state lines or over great distances. No birth mother with carrot-red hair and a freckled nose should ever spot a baby with the same color hair and the same freckled nose and wonder if that was her child. The rules were reasonable and designed to protect the best interests of all concerned.

Mr. Innsley was not happy, but he finally agreed to take his search for an adoptable child to an orphanage in another state. So, all should be well. Why, then, do I feel so uncomfortable about the whole arrangement of adoption? Lately, I have come to believe that the answer has to do with the peculiar institution of slavery practiced within our state and our neighbors to the south.

Several weeks ago, the citizens of Birch Falls awakened to discover their town had been plastered with flyers announcing Middle Tennessee's Largest Slave Auction. The proceedings would be held in the empty lot next to the law offices of Jonathan Poindexter, who described himself as a lawyer, a plantation owner, a cotton broker, and an auctioneer.

Because I had never seen a slave auction, I resolved to attend. After all, I reasoned, with a lawyer in charge, how bad could it be? The answer? Bad! The slaves were crammed together into a corral-like area, and to my horror, I could see they were chained together by manacles around their ankles —men and women, palsied old folks, and tiny children. All they had in common were their chains and their skin color.

A tiny lad who claimed to be six years old was one of the first to be offered. Poindexter announced he should bring a high price because he could be trained as a house servant. And indeed, the bidding was enthusiastic. But when he sold for fifty dollars, he started to cry "Mammy!" and a woman struggled to break loose from the crowd. Still chained, she managed to fall to her knees at Poindexter's feet. She begged to be sold along with her son, promising to help train him to be whatever his new owner wanted.

The auctioneer kicked her away and cracked a whip across the boy's shoulders. "Stop that whining, pickaninny!" he shouted, and the boy cringed in terror. I wanted to cradle him in my arms. Instead, I walked away, but I couldn't leave that image behind.

The following Sunday afternoon, the Jones family from Knoxville came to the nunnery to claim the child they were adopting. Here's the description I put in my journal:

Baby Esther went to her adoptive home today, joining the Jones family of three small boys. Mrs. Jones loves her sons, of course, but she longed for a little girl who could grow up to help around the house. As they left—everyone beaming, except for a wailing baby who did not understand who these people were— Mr. Jones passed me a roll of worn and tattered bills, which turned out to be over one hundred dollars. They had been saving their money for a long time to get their little girl, and it bothered me to accept the money.

There's so much wrong with this transaction, starting with the reason Mrs. Jones wants a little girl: 'someone to help around the house.' I asked myself a crucial question: How does this differ from what goes on downtown at the local slave market? Money changes hands, and a human being passes from one household to another. Are we not selling these babies? No one asks exactly what it has cost us to support the baby from birth to adoption. The amount often appears to depend on the attractiveness of the child. And that feels wrong to me!

What's different? Well, one's black, while the other is white. And a white girl is worth twice as much as a black boy, even if both of them are destined to work as household help. It's wrong. I know it. And I have done nothing about it. I am ashamed. My solution regarding the money is also wrong-headed. I'm squirreling it away until God lets me know it's all right to spend it. How silly can I be?

Elsewhere I wrote about the devil sitting on one of my shoulders and an angel sitting on the other. When I read that passage now, I realize that I thought I was someone special —that devils and angels would fight over my soul. What I failed to realize was that I was describing the human condition. We all have two sides to our characters. What sets a few of us apart is not whether we have an angel or a devil, but which one we listen to.

Am I sorry I decided to take in the homeless waifs the sheriff dropped on our doorstep? No. There was only one decent reaction to that, and I did it. Could I have stopped the process after I accepted one? No. I fear I am unable to judge the worth of others, let alone that of an unborn child. Am I wrong to let families adopt our unwanted orphans, left behind by mothers who are trying to reclaim their lives? No. In every case, I am on the side of the angels, even if I fall short of their wisdom.

If there is a child who needs a home, I will try to find one for him. If a child needs love, I will offer mine. And if I can play a role in creating a happy family, I will do so without regard to cost or outcome. This is the mission I feel calling to me. And at prayers during Sext, I will offer my acceptance of that mission. We must continue.

My actions regarding the slave auctions, however, fall short. I watched and I walked away. Did I think that little boy needed to be with his mother? Of course, he did. But I didn't say it. I didn't offer to buy them both. The devil on my shoulder says I can't change a society founded on slavery. Maybe not. Perhaps the coming war (and war is coming, to be sure) will accomplish what I failed to do. But I am still ashamed. I could have made a difference.

CHAPTER 22

Jewish Children's Home

October 5-10, 2011

Sarah had spent most of the week reading and pondering the mother superior's private musings about adoption. It must have been unfamiliar ground for a nun, Sarah realized. Nuns don't usually think much about adoptions. But in this case, the whole convent had been drawn into the effort to help unwed mothers with nowhere else to turn. For the past ten years, they had held the hands of women fighting labor pains, taught babies how to suckle, and encouraged the bonds between mother and child. They had voted to build a maternity house, with a separate wing for the nursery and housing for the children whose mothers could not keep them. Sarah marveled at their ability to love the new orphans and yet send them off to their new families without a backward glance. The mother superior, however, struggled with her role, and Sarah was beginning to understand the issues that troubled her.

She was staring out the window, lost in thought when the phone rang.

"Hello?"

"It's Bea Randolph, Mrs. Cohen. From Child Services? We met the night of that horrendous accident outside your house."

"Of course. I remember you well. I might not have survived that night of childcare if it hadn't been for your help. So, please, call me Sarah. What can I do for you?"

"I was just glancing through our 2011 calendar schedules and saw your name. You and your husband are registered to start adoptive parenting classes in mid-October. I was so excited for you, I just had to call. It occurred to me that you might find it helpful to tour the Jewish Children's Home in Nashville before these classes start."

"Why is that?"

"Well, you are Jewish, aren't you?"

"Yes, we are, but that shouldn't have any effect on our ability to become parents, should it?"

"Quite the contrary. Oh, dear, I'm not making myself clear, am I? That's what happens when I get excited. Look, under normal circumstances, the people who try to match children with suitable parents will draw suggestions from all over the state. We don't get many Jewish children, but when we do, they usually come with a request from the birth mother that her Jewish child be placed only with a Jewish family.

"So, in your case, they will first check with the Nashville office of Jewish Family Services to see if there is a Jewish child who might be a good candidate for you and Mr. Cohen. Only if there is no viable match will they move on to consider other available babies within the state. The result, you need to understand, is that you could be fast-tracked to get your child. Or it could take much longer than normal. You can help with the process if you make your wishes clear from the beginning. And to do that, you need to understand how we operate.

"Anyhow, I have to drive to Nashville next Monday, the tenth, to take care of some paperwork. I thought you might like to ride along. You can visit with the staff and the children while I work, and we'll be back home by dinnertime. What do you say?"

"I say yes. I think I mentioned to you that I've been granted a year's break from teaching to write a book about the early history of the land on which the university stands. It's an incredible opportunity, of course, but the sameness of every day leaves me cross-eyed. I can use a break!"

Monday turned out to be one of those rare days that people wish could last forever. The world was bathed in sunlight so clear it put a sharp edge on every view. At the same time, the air had a crispness to it—composed of drying leaves, smoky bonfires, the scent of ripe apples, and cool breezes that promised colder weather to come. Sarah and Bea rode in silence for a while, content to soak up the beauty of the Smoky Mountains. But as the landscape flattened out, Sarah sat up straighter, as if she had just reached a decision.

"So, tell me about this Jewish Children's Home we're going to visit. I tried to look it up on the internet but couldn't find any mention of it."

"That's because helping with adoptions is just a small part of what we do. We're heavily involved in other legal matters as well. Unless you have come face to face with some of the areas of conflict between Jewish law and civil regulations, you might not realize how much of the Talmud contradicts the Constitution of the United States. One example has to do with abortions. The passage of Roe versus Wade was necessary to give American women the right to terminate a dangerous or unwanted pregnancy in its early stages. But according to Jewish law, a woman has not only a right but also an obligation to end a pregnancy at any time, right up to the moment of birth if she feels it necessary. The American legal system protects the rights of an unborn child if there is a heartbeat. The Jewish law says those rights come only with the first breath after the actual birth."

"I hadn't realized that difference even existed. Are there similar problems with adoptions?"

"Oh, absolutely, and they are even more complicated, thanks to the various degrees to which different congregations observe the prohibitions of the Talmud. There's a whole body of legal discussion over the bloodline that makes a Jew a Jew. Jewish identity is matrilineal, as you probably know; that is, it can only be conveyed by a birth mother. A child born to a Jewish father and a Christian mother is not—and in Orthodox communities can never be—a Jew. A Reformed community allows fairly easy ways to convey Jewishness to someone not born into the matrilineal line. And Conservative communities dance around the issue, depending on how liberal they are.

"All agree, however, that it is impossible to break or exchange one bloodline for another, so technically, adoption —as most Americans think of it—is impossible because the biological parents of a child cannot be separated from that child."

"But Jewish adoptions do occur. You said yourself that our religion would not hinder our efforts to adopt a child."

"They won't, under most circumstances. But this is why we need to start the discussions early. Problems arise when adoptive parents assume their children will use the father's last name."

"Of course, they will. That's an easy one."

"No, it's not, because, in Jewish law, surnames are patrilineal. For girls, that may not matter too much because girls eventually take their husbands' names. But a little boy cannot legally drop his birth father's name and assume the last name of an adoptive father because that name defines his position within the faith. The Cohens, for example, are part of a priestly lineage with special obligations regarding the Torah. Orthodox families are particularly strict about the matter."

"I'm cringing because this could become an issue in our family. David's father has been urging us to ask for a male child because he wants to have a grandson to carry on his Cohen name. Their family attends a pretty laid-back Conservative congregation; they prefer not to raise controversial issues if they can be avoided. My father, however, is a well-known rabbi who toes the Orthodox line in many cases. If a real problem crops up, he might oppose our choices."

"The usual way of handling the matter is to let the adopted child use the name of his adoptive father at school, at play, in college, and even on his diplomas. But on religious documents and when the issue involves family obligations, like saying Kaddish for a birth parent, the child must use his patrilineal name.

"You academic folks do something similar. You separate your personal and professional lives. At the university and with your students, you still use the title Dr. Chomsky, don't you?"

"Yes, but when I attend a political affair as the wife of the duly-elected district attorney, I introduce myself as Mrs. Cohen, which is now my legal name."

"Different situations; similar solutions."

"That makes sense, although I had no idea that anything in my religion conflicted with American laws. Is there more?"

"Undoubtedly, but let's not poke at those sleeping puppies. As we assure our clients, our lawyers are trained to find the answers, so you don't have to. That's what Jewish Family Services is all about."

As she spoke, Bea was pulling into a leaf-covered driveway leading to groomed lawns and spacious brick buildings that looked more like a colonial neighborhood than institutional office space. "This is where you will start your tour. I'll come in with you to introduce you to our superintendent, Dr. Adams, and she will take over from there. You can plan on having lunch with whatever age group you prefer, although I'd recommend the fourth to sixth graders Their idea of a joke can be pretty crude, but lunch will be less messy than with the young ones. I'll meet you back here around four and we'll head back to Birch Falls."

The superintendent turned out to be a sophisticated woman in her forties. She wore a tailored but feminine navy suit with a frilly pearl-gray blouse and sensible low-heeled shoes. Silver hoop earrings, a platinum wedding ring set with tiny diamonds, and a multi-function watch completed her outfit.

"I'm Dr. Elizabeth Adams, head housemother around here. My doctorate is an academic degree, by the way, not a medical one. I've been looking forward to your visit. We're quite proud of our facilities, and I hope you'll end your visit with a new appreciation of what an orphanage has to offer."

"So, tell me more about the children in your care. How many are there?"

"The numbers change every day, but we average around ninety to a hundred."

"All waiting to be adopted?"

"No. Every story is different. We accept all children under the age of eighteen. But on their eighteenth birthdays—just like foster children—they are considered adults and must move out of adoptive care. For some of our residents, that is problematic, while others plan for their next moves. Take our Joseph as an example. He's seventeen and finishing his last year in high school. He was an only child; his parents died in a boating accident two years ago. Once he has his diploma and he turns eighteen, he plans to enlist in the Army. That will give him a roof over his head, his meals, his clothing, and his occupational training. Eventually, he will parlay that military experience into college credits and be on his way to a productive life.

"Other situations are more complicated. One family of five children, ranging in age from three to fifteen, refuses to be split up. And the chances of finding a home ready to take on five are slim. In a bizarre reversal of roles, the oldest girl may turn eighteen, declare her adulthood, and then adopt her siblings. We're not sure she will be able to handle that, but it's a possibility. And then there are a few residents with physical problems that need to be addressed before we can saddle new parents with high medical costs. As I said, each child is different. But you'll be able to see that for yourself."

"What about schooling?"

"Our preschool and kindergarten children live in this building. As you'll see, we've designed the layout to be as much like a real home as possible. You're standing in our living room. Just on the other side of that partition, there's a family room with musical equipment, a TV, and games. The windows and doors open onto a playground for use in good weather. I keep my desk in a corner over here where it won't look too official. Each child has a private sleeping cubicle, and they share bathroom space with several others. There's also a family kitchen with dining facilities for those who can feed themselves.

"The other wing is equipped as you might find in any well-run day-care center—cribs and nap-mats, as ages dictate, instructive play areas, and gentle caregivers for feedings and diaper changing. Our staffing includes several trained early-childhood educators who can guide the children's learning experiences through kindergarten. As they grow, the children move to the next house, which has a fully-accredited elementary school. We've found that in grade school, children are more comfortable in a private classroom, where there are no room mothers, and their classmates share their orphan status instead of making fun of it.

"Starting with junior high, however, that adolescent desire to declare one's independence takes over, and classmates with families often look on our orphans with envy. We follow their lead and allow older children to attend regular public schools through high school graduation. Children with special needs may need separate accommodation, but we deal with that problem only as it arises."

"I'm surprised at how quiet everything is."

"Well, it's nap time for most of these little guys. They'll be awake soon and clamoring for lunch. Perhaps we should start your tour with the grade-level classrooms next door."

CHAPTER 23

A Couple of Little Terrorists

October 10, 2011

It was a reasonable plan: let sleeping babies sleep. Dr. Adams had forgotten one small detail—that among those sleeping innocents lurked a set of twins who were overdue for a little attention. As she and Sarah started toward the front door, a loud crash echoed from behind one of the closed baby cubicles. This was followed by a rhythmic thumping against a wall, and then two voices raised in screams, the words unclear but the meaning no longer in doubt.

"Here we go. The twins are at it again."

"Twins? Just two, making all that noise?"

"Not just any two. We have a tiny terrorist group—two sweet-looking cherubs, hell-bent on making life miserable for anyone who dares ignore their wishes. Here come their faithful servants now." Two nurses rushed by, one carrying bottles, the other a pile of diapers.

Dr. Adams peeked in the doorway. "Have they broken anything that matters?"

"A small lamp, but it can be put back together."

An unmistakable baby giggle followed that announcement. Dr. Adams shook her head and blocked the doorway as Sarah tried to catch a glimpse of the troublemakers. "We try not to encourage them by catering to their little tantrums. The nurses will meet their immediate physical needs—bottles and diapers—but no visitors or other distractions until they settle down."

One of the nurses shut the cubicle door as Dr. Adams tried to apologize. "This duo is giving us our first lessons on how to deal with twins. We've never had a set before, so what they do surprises us every day. Neither baby will sleep unless their cribs touch so that the twins can reach each other. And just as the textbook on newborns predicted, they have developed a private language, which they may well have spoken in the womb. It's called cryptophasia, and it defies all our attempts to understand it. But the babies chatter away in it, and we know they are planning their next bit of mayhem."

"Maybe their new parents will be ..."

"If we're ever lucky enough to find someone to take them. Twins are notoriously hard to place, and you're hearing a demonstration of why that is so. Most new adopters are already worried about handling a new baby. Try offering them a matching set, both of whom are screaming their lungs out. We're lucky if the prospective parents hang around long enough to see the other children."

Sarah looked puzzled. "I understand what you're saying, but did you mention that this was your first experience with twins? Perhaps the others weren't as ornery. I know there was another set here earlier in the summer. Someone must have adopted them."

"No, these are the only twins we've ever had, and they've been here ever since they were born. At one time, we thought we had found a home for them, but the parents died in an unfortunate accident, and ... Why are you looking at me with that funny expression?"

"Were they killed in a car crash in Birch Falls?"

"Yes. How would you know ...?"

"I think the accident happened in my front yard. My husband and I managed to rescue two babies from the back seat of a wrecked vehicle, and they spent the night with us until your people could come and pick them up. Is it possible that these are the same children?"

"They must be. We've all heard that story about the young couple who rescued the twins."

"And they've been here ever since then—institutionalized, no family, no one to love them or comfort them? Do they have names?"

"No, not yet. We try to leave that choice up to the adopting parents."

"So how do you refer to them? "He and She? Hey, Kids? Guys? Baby One and Baby Two?"

"We call them The Twins, but you are making it sound uncaring. We do make every effort to give the children the love they are missing."

"I'm sure you do, but ..."

"But it's no substitute for a mother and father. I know, all too well. I was an orphan from the age of six months until a lovely family adopted me when I was a petulant and overweight twelve-year-old. I still think of them as my only family, but they had huge obstacles to overcome before I was willing to believe that their affections were sincere. I had learned the harsh lessons of the orphanage before I was able to understand how emotionally damaged I was."

"Then you should see why ... Please. Let me visit them. I know they won't remember me, but maybe they will feel something of my connection to them."

Dr. Adams shrugged and stepped away from the door she had been blocking. Sarah stepped into the small room, leaving the door open behind her. She spoke in a whisper to capture the little girl's attention. "Good morning, my lovelies. You won't recognize me, but I've known you forever. And look how you've both grown since the last time we met."

Her gentleness caught both children by surprise, and they hesitated in the middle of the tantrum they were staging. The little girl was the larger and stronger of the two. At ten months, she was already standing on her own and walking from one end of the crib to the other with only an occasional touch of the railing. The boy could pull himself upright by grasping the side of the crib, but when he let go of that support, he sat down with a thud. As Sarah observed their interaction, she noted that the little girl had two teddy bears in her crib—one blue and the other pink. The little boy, his face screwed into a belligerent pout, had not a single toy within his reach.

"You took your brother's bear, didn't you?" she asked the girl, who responded by tightly clutching the blue bear. "You need to share." Sarah picked up the pink bear with one hand and stretched out the other to receive the stolen toy. "Let's trade."

The little girl may not have understood the words, but she recognized the gesture. Reluctantly, she offered Sarah the blue bear and reached for the pink one. "Nicely played," Sarah commented with a gentle smile as she completed the trade and handed the stolen bear to its rightful owner.

"Everyone happy now?" The boy grinned at her. "That's how you deal with your sister, my friend. She'll always want whatever she doesn't have."

Dr. Adams had been watching the interaction with approval. "You were using hand gestures to accompany your words, weren't you?"

"I suppose I was. I've been used to communicating with my deaf grandmother. She never learned official American Sign Language, but her gestures were clear, and I picked them up from her."

"I was interested to see the children react to you that way. We're already starting them on ASL, not because they are deaf but in the hope that it will prove a transition from their cryptophagia to standard English. They are due for a lesson right now, so ..."

"I was hoping to spend some time with them—maybe taking them for a walk or ..."

"As I said, they have a pre-language lesson now, followed by lunch. But perhaps after that ... they have a double stroller you could use to walk around the grounds."

"Wonderful!"

The children were restless when their nurses strapped them into the stroller, and they struggled to turn around to see who was pushing them along the sidewalk. Sarah tried chatting as they made their way toward a stand of oak trees, but neither child paid much attention until Sarah parked the stroller on a bit of mossy turf under the trees themselves. She pulled on the brake so that they wouldn't roll away. Then she sat on the ground in front of the stroller and looked around for objects the twins could handle—an oak leaf, an acorn, a dandelion gone to fuzzy seed.

Plant life lost its appeal, however, when a squirrel showed up. His bright eyes studied the children for a potential threat, but Sarah signaled for them to be silent. Once again, gestures worked where words failed. The children froze in place, staring back at the fuzzy-tailed animal. After a few more seconds, the squirrel reared onto his hind legs, eliciting a giggle from the little girl. It was enough to set the tableau in motion. The squirrel gathered some small twigs, holding them in his teeth as he ran to a nearby oak tree, flicked his tail, and scurried up to a low-hanging branch. From there, the little acrobat leaped for a dark spot on the tree trunk and seemed to disappear. Both children whined with disapproval until Sarah explained, showing them a circle with her fingers and then gesturing a movement toward the center of the hole.

"Wait," she told them, using her silent finger again. In a few moments, the squirrel popped back out of his hole, ran down the trunk, and sped across the grass. "Wait again," she cautioned, and soon the squirrel was back, carrying more twigs up the tree and into his hidey-hole.

This time she used her cupped hands to suggest a nest and then used a sleeping gesture to illustrate his hibernation during the coming cold weather. The children nodded. On the squirrel's next trip, he appeared with cheeks bulging. At the base of the tree, he gathered a couple more acorns, stuffed them into his cheeks, and delivered the pile of them to his new nest.

The boy used a food gesture to indicate he understood the purpose of the acorns, and Sarah nodded her approval. Then, once again, the little girl showed that she was a step or two ahead of her brother. Twisting her mouth around, she tried to mimic Sarah's pronunciation of 'squirrel.' What emerged was something like 'uruh,' but it was a budding word. And to Sarah, author of children's books, it translated into a suggestion of a new book, "Earl the Squirrel."

Not to be outdone this time, the boy, too, tried to add a word—'ook.' For a moment, Sarah was puzzled; then light dawned. "Cookie? You want to give the squirrel a cookie?"

He nodded. She looked around helplessly, failing to find anything that resembled a cookie. "I'm sorry. I don't have a cookie. But maybe we can come back tomorrow and bring him one. What do you think?"

Both children nodded. They chattered between themselves on the way back to the preschool building.

Sarah turned the twins over to their nurses and let Dr. Adams show her the rest of the Children's Home campus.

She had hoped to spend most of her time with the grade schoolers, but she found them depressing. They were all neatly dressed, although they were not required to wear uniforms as the public schoolers were. They appeared to be listening in their classes, reading, taking notes, or discussing the question of the day. But something was missing. They were going through the motions doing and saying all the right things but without a trace of enthusiasm. The school was simply the way one got through the day.

The older children, of course, were still at off-campus schools. The junior high group returned first, followed by a straggling group of high schoolers who had been attending club meetings or sporting practice. The resident children were polite. They spoke when spoken to and then moved on. They were, however, not interested in visiting adopters, nor was Sarah particularly interested in the older orphans.

By the end of the tour, Sarah had made up her mind. She would rescue the twins from the institution before the institution broke their high spirits. She was waiting at the door when Bea Randolph returned to pick her up.

"I'm not going back with you," Sarah explained. "If you'll drop me at that Red Door Inn down the road, I'll book a room for the night. I want my husband to join me here tomorrow. There are details he needs to hear firsthand, not from me. And then we need to hold a family conference. I'm grateful that you invited me to come with you, but you've managed to unleash the mother tiger in me. I need to get started on this adoption business now."

"You've met the twins, I take it."

"I have."

"And your mind is made up."

"As you know it would be."

"Correction: as I hoped it would be. But you had to decide on your own, without my pressure."

Sarah's next step was to call David and convince him to come to Nashville in the morning. He was surprised, but he knew Sarah well enough not to argue with her. "I'll be there by nine," he promised, "but in the interval, I want you to think carefully about what you're doing. I only ask that you be sure of your decision."

"I will, I promise. Oh, and David, if you can, would you bring a package of cookies with you—something mild, like the vanilla wafers we use in banana puddings?"

CHAPTER 24

Preparing for Parenthood

October 11, 2011

Sarah spent most of the night worrying about how David would react to the twins. She tossed the covers off and fluffed her pillow a dozen times, not because she was uncomfortable but because so many questions nagged at her. She nibbled at the cold items at the buffet breakfast provided by the inn, her stomach too nervous to handle their offerings of scrambled eggs and biscuit gravy. Would the children charm him as they had charmed her, or would they reject him as an interloper? When at last his car pulled into the parking lot, she threw herself into her husband's arms, crying with joy and apprehension at the same time.

"What's happening, love? I can't tell whether you're crying because you're happy to see me or because you have bad news."

"I'm just relieved you're here. I need you."

"Talk to me, Sarah! Tell me what's going on."

"Oh, David. I've found them, and they're beautiful. We clicked immediately, and I just knew ..."

"You found—who?"

"The twins. Our twins. The babies we sat up with all night."

"After the accident?"

"Yes. They're still here. No one has tried to adopt them, and they've just been waiting for ... for something or someone ... They hold hands and chatter away to each other, but they've never had parents. They don't even have names. They're just little creatures, waiting for someone to love them and make them a family."

"Whoa! Slow down! You've been here less than a day. You know better than to jump headfirst into a decision."

"That's why I need you—to confirm what my heart is telling me. Because I also know when HaShem is sending me a message. When that car wrapped itself around that oak tree, something told me to check for survivors, and there they were. I had been told I couldn't have babies of my own, but suddenly there were two, dropped into my lap. I sent them away, but they've been waiting ever since, and now HaShem is giving me another chance. They were the first— and only—children I saw when I arrived here. They might as well have been holding up a sign that said, 'Here We Are Again.'"

"Oh, Sarah. Are you sure they are even the same children? It's been months. They must have changed a great deal."

"I am sure. The nurses confirmed it."

'But you said they don't even have names."

"They don't. Everyone just calls them 'The Twins' as if they ..."

"Oy vey! You've named them, haven't you? Sarah, ... you

can't just walk in here and claim them, you know. It's not your place to pick their names."

"Whatever I call them has to be better than having no names at all. It gives them an identity for the first time. Dr. Adams—she runs this place—says they are still 'pre-verbal and pre-memory' so they won't remember, but it helps them for the moment. It tells them they are two separate individuals, not a single unit. And they need that. It's an important developmental step."

"I'm losing this battle, I realize. OK. What are their 'names for this moment?'"

"Jeremy and Jillian."

"Jerry and Jill. Nicely biblical, if you make it Jeremiah, but not overtly Jewish."

"I thought so, too." Sarah grinned for the first time as she recognized that David was weakening. "Come and meet them."

Sarah led the way to the twins' cubicle. "Good morning, Jillian! And how are you, Jeremy? I've brought you another new friend. This is David, and he's going to spend the day with us."

Under his breath, David murmured, "I'm relieved that you're not calling us Mom and Dad, at least not yet."

Sarah sent him a brief glare and then twisted it into a smile that told him to watch his step. She turned back to the twins, using signs to ask if they had had breakfast. When they nodded in unison, she gave them a quick clapping sign and then reached for Jeremy. "In that case, we have permission to take you into the playroom for a little while." She handed the little boy off to David and hoisted Jillian onto her hip. "Let's see what we can find to play with."

With the children happily deposited in front of a pile of building bricks, she gave David another glare and dropped gracefully onto the carpet with the children. David moved slowly onto his knees and helped himself to a couple of blocks. "I'm glad to see these are foam rubber, not carved wood like mine were when I was a kid."

"Me, too. At least with these, they can't brain one another. Whoops! You do have to watch out for flying objects, however," she said as Jeremy hurled a red cube at his sister.

When the building blocks had outworn their appeal, Sarah directed the children's attention to a couple of wheeled hobby horses. Jillian hopped right on and began to propel herself across the floor, while Jeremy settled for crawling on his knees and pushing his horse in front of him.

"Is she that much more advanced than he is?" David asked as he compared the two.

"The nurse tells me that's quite normal. Little girls start in life with better motor skills and more advanced physical development, which may keep the little boys from hurting them. It's not until adolescence that the boys suddenly spurt upward, growing noticeably taller and stronger as they take on a protective stance over their sisters."

"Seems reasonable to me."

"What I find unfair," Sarah laughed, "is that the boy has a full head of glorious curls, while his sister's hair is straight as a stick."

"Oh, we can fix that. You give Jillian a permanent, and I'll take Jeremy for a buzz cut."

"Now you're doing it, David. They're not ours yet, remember."

The day passed quickly as the Cohens learned about bottles, diaper changes, and nap times. By mid-afternoon, it was time for another walk, and the children chattered happily as David pushed the stroller. Sarah led them back to the grove of oak trees where they had met yesterday's squirrel.

To everyone's delight, the squirrel was still busily stocking his hollow oak tree for winter. "Uruh, uruh," Jillian squealed, causing the squirrel to freeze momentarily before he returned to his chores.

"I thought you said the twins were pre-verbal. That sounded like a basic 'squirrel' call to me," David said.

"It was, but you recognized it because you also had the visual image of a squirrel in front of you. That's part of the theory of using sign language with them, too. That's why it's called 'pre-verbal,' not 'non-verbal.' It's one step closer to building a spoken vocabulary. And you'll be pleased to see that Jeremy is also making good progress at this stuff. Did you bring the vanilla wafers?"

"I have a pocket full of them."

"Show one to Jeremy."

"Ook, ook."

That's right, love. It's a cookie." Jeremy demonstrated his understanding by crunching away at the cookie. Jillian grabbed one but did not try the word. And Sarah startled herself by saying, "Let's give the 'uruh' an 'ook.' She placed the wafer on the ground in front of them and gave the silent sign, which both children understood. All four held their breath as the squirrel tiptoed closer, grabbed the cookie, and dashed for his tree.

"I hope he eats it now. If he tries to keep it for winter, it'll just be a soggy wad."

When the children showed signs of dropping off to sleep, they returned to the nursery. The twins went down to naps without a fuss, and Sarah and David headed for Dr. Adams' office.

"You've had a successful day, I understand. Have you enjoyed yourselves?"

"Oh, very much so. The twins have been delightful—not a sign of the fighting we saw yesterday."

"I would think not. They've had your full attention all day and have enjoyed themselves just as you have. You look like a perfect match to me."

Sarah gasped. "Does that mean ...?"

"Now, don't get your hopes up too high. You still have a lot of hurdles to leap. What I meant was that a preliminary comparison of your physical and educational levels shows a good match. And you've enjoyed one another's company. But there are still requirements we cannot pass over. You'll both need background checks. We'll be doing interviews with your family, friends, neighbors, and employers. If there are skeletons in your closets, you can expect to have them dragged about. We'll need to see your financial statements, a credit report, and a check of police records. We'll start those immediately.

"You will begin your parenting classes next week, I understand. Those involve basic child care, first aid training, and the hated 24-hour mechanical baby test. In that one, you'll be given a doll programmed to fuss about dirty diapers, cry when hungry, and thrash about when bored. If you ignore a cry or put the doll down before it goes to sleep, your instructor will be notified of your failure. And just to make your lives interesting, since you are considering twins, you'll get two dolls, and their schedules will not correspond.

"The final step will be some group therapy, during which you will be encouraged to discuss your worries, your fears, and your doubts with other prospective parents. If you're not sure about your decisions, this will be the place where you can admit any hesitancy you are experiencing.

"When you have passed all of those barriers, there comes a six-month trial adoption. The children will be placed with you for those six months without any guarantees about permanency. Social workers may drop in on you at any time. The children will undergo close medical supervision to make sure they are getting adequate nutrition and mental stimulation, and that they have no ongoing physical problems. To make your situation even harder, both children will have to get good reports. There will be no question of separating them if one develops a problem."

"We understand."

"And you still think you are ready to forge ahead?"

"We are." It was David who answered for both of them, and Sarah sighed in relief.

As they started the drive to Birch Falls, the couple remained silent, both of them trying to process the day's experiences. Sarah stared out the side window, and David concentrated on the early evening Nashville traffic. But as they left the city behind, Sarah sighed.

"Are we making a huge mistake, David? Have we committed ourselves to a dream that can't possibly come true?"

"What makes you think that?"

"I'm just imagining all the things that could go wrong. The financial statements the doctor mentioned involve an issue we haven't discussed recently. It's probably not the best time for you to be planning to quit your job as district attorney and go out on your own as a lawyer."

"I wouldn't make a move like that if I thought we couldn't afford it. Besides, the election isn't until 2012. That gives us a year to get the adoption thing settled."

"OK, so I'm looking for trouble unnecessarily. But I don't want us to get blindsided by issues we haven't discussed. The parenting classes and the 24-hour dolls scare me, but what worries me even more are the interviews and the restrictions our synagogue may enforce."

"We didn't talk a great deal about our Jewish identity. Do you know more than the basics Dr. Adams explained?"

"I'm afraid so. There are some real deal breakers in the mix. She hinted that we have skeletons in the family closet, and from what Bea Randolph told me, we may face opposition even from within our families."

"Oh, come on. They would never ..."

"Talmudic scholars would not hesitate to point out a violation, and knowing my father, he would listen to them."

"We don't have anything to worry about. If you're thinking of that little police record I have for throwing stones over a roof and breaking some skylights, you can relax. It's not a religious violation."

"No, but being a Cohen is."

"What?"

"Do you even know what your name stands for?"

"I guess not, so you're going to have to explain what you're talking about."

"All right. I'm a little shaky on the details, but here goes. In modern Judaism, there are three tribes left from the original twelve tribes mentioned in the Torah—the Kohens, the Levites, and the Israelis. The Kohen tribe claims patrilineal descent from Aaron, the brother of Moses, and as such, they have inherited certain priestly responsibilities. For example, they are always the first to be called upon to read from the Torah in the synagogue. They must never allow the legal use of their name by someone not born into the tribe—an adopted child, for example."

"But they told us there are ways around that. Jeremy would go to his *bar mitzvah* as Jeremiah Shapiro, using his Israelite birth father's name and he would be obligated to sit Kaddish for his birth father. In his professional life, however, he could use the name, Jeremy S. Cohen. As long as he does not use the name to claim priestly privilege, most people will just hear it as a surname."

"That's true. But it gets worse, my love. Someone born into the Cohen tribe is forbidden to marry a divorced woman." She swallowed the tears beginning to form behind her eyes. "According to Talmudic law, our marriage must be annulled as illegal; if not, you lose your rights to perform any priestly function your name entitles you to."

"I don't exercise any priestly function now; in fact, my job as a gun-toting policeman also disqualified me as a Cohen, although that was the least of my father's worries. And as for your teen-aged transgressions, your elopement and subsequent divorce occurred when you were seventeen —below the legal age to manage your affairs. So, legally, they don't count, either."

"Spoken like a lawyer. But that doesn't mean that someone won't challenge our fitness as adopting parents. And the agency doesn't have to have legal grounds for declaring us unfit. They can just say, 'No.'"

"Sarah, look at me. You said you felt that HaShem was

sending you a message about your responsibility for the twins. If that is so, he won't let other mere mortals interfere with his divine plan. Now, relax."

"Why are you pulling over?"

"There's a scenic overlook here. But I stopped because I don't trust myself to drive while I say what I need to say. This afternoon, while you were playing with the children, I was watching you. And I realized that you had never looked as beautiful as you did in that setting—not even at our wedding, lovely though you were. Today there was an aura about you, an inner light that encircled you and the twins. My last doubt disappeared at that moment. We are meant to be their parents, and nothing—no rule or regulation—will ever change that."

CHAPTER 25

Riding the Whirlwind

October-November 2011

"Sarah? Wake up, sweetheart. We're almost home."

She yawned, stretched, and grinned. "Would you believe me if I said I was only resting my eyes?"

"Of course, I'd believe you. But I'd note that your eyes make strange noises when you rest them."

"I don't snore."

"Right. Got it. What about eating? It's too late to think about cooking once we get home. Where would you like to stop?"

"I don't want to go anywhere we might see someone we know. I want to keep this snuggly feeling private for as long as possible. And I don't want to tell anyone about the twins —not even our families—until we're one hundred percent sure they are going to be ours."

"We can keep reminding nosey people that it's a long process and we won't know anything for sure until it happens. That's an easy stance to take because it happens to be true. We dare not get our hopes up too high."

"I won't tell, but you can't stop me from believing. Now, as for dinner—how about that new pizza place ... Garibaldi's ... the one that's been advertising you can call ahead and pick up your pizza in fifteen minutes?"

"Sounds good. Got your cell phone handy?"

If Sarah and David had hoped to keep their adoption news a secret, their plans were quickly banished. Within hours, interviewers began contacting their families and friends. And soon thereafter, their phones began to ring. Everyone had questions. Their parents found the intrusions upsetting. "Why are they asking these things?" they wanted to know. "Are they suspicious about you? Does it mean they are looking for reasons to reject you? What do you want us to tell them?"

Among their friends, the interviews stirred curiosity. "You're adopting! Why didn't you tell us? We just had a visit from Social Services, asking how long we had known you and whether or not we thought you'd make good parents. We told them how great you are, but it was hard to tell how much they believed. They had odd questions, too. Did we know how you met? How long had you known each other before you got married? When did you decide to buy your house? Had you made plans for a nursery before you moved in? Some of what they wanted to know seemed normal, and other questions were off the wall. Hope we said the right things. Now tell us what's happening. They asked about multiples. Are you considering asking for twins?"

When the interviewers visited the neighbors, the questions focused on other issues. "How often do the Cohens throw wild parties? We've heard stories about one night when they woke the entire neighborhood."

"Oh, that was the night Mr. Cohen won his election as district attorney," one neighbor explained. "His supporters came out to tell him he'd won in a landslide, and he gave them a little speech about his views on equal justice. The neighbors were all up because we wanted to hear what he had to say. It was a celebration, not a wild party. They are usually friendly but quiet."

David found these interviews more upsetting than Sarah did. He was used to asking such questions, not being the target of the investigation, and he said as little as possible when friends asked for details. Sarah, in contrast, sometimes welcomed curious friends because they gave her a chance to talk about what had become her favorite topic. She also found it reassuring that so many of their friends supported their plans. Both of them worried, however, that someone might accidentally give the interviewers an erroneous impression. Often, they knew, a person's answer depended on the wording of the question.

"Do David and Sarah both work long hours at their jobs?" There was no right answer. If the interviewee remarked that they often did not get home until late in the evening, the interviewer might follow up with a question about how much time they would have to spend with the children. If someone remarked that they usually arrived home in plenty of time to cook together or relax in the yard before dinner, the next question might have to do with whether either of them would do well in their careers.

Parenting classes began on the next Monday night in October, and the Cohens were relieved to learn that their classmates' worries were similar, no matter who was involved. "It's just another one of those rites of passage," one man said. "They have to ask something, but they don't expect to discover that one of us is a raging maniac. I suspect we all came through that exam with flying colors."

As the holidays approached, time passed in a blur. David's office was now fully engaged in preparation for the liability trial concerning the failed brakes on a new car. Unhappy with both sides, David had assigned investigators to trace the history of the wrecked car from the time it passed off the assembly line until Brandon O'Malley drove it away from Richard Gallean's dealership. Records showed several gaps as the car passed from its Japanese manufacturer to the cargo liner delivering the car to a dealership in Austin, Texas. The dealership records also failed to show how the car moved from Austin to Alvarado, a small town north of there. The car then disappeared from everyone's inventory until it turned up again months later at Gallean's dealership in Birch Falls.

"What happened during those missing months?" David demanded. "Read the newspapers. See what was going on in Texas. Something affected the sales of cars during that time frame. Find it."

A university student doing his internship in the DA's office was the first to spot a clue. "There was a hurricane that summer—or rather, more like a tropical storm when it moved inland. Tropical Storm Hermine dropped over a foot of rain in just a few hours and flooded much of the downtown business district of Alvarado, Texas. The local paper says there were over a hundred calls for high water rescues during that period."

"Was the car dealership flooded? Go there. Ask questions. Talk to people on the street. Someone will remember. And if new cars were involved, the law requires all repairs to be reported and attached to the manufacturer's list price. If that car's brakes sustained unreported water damage, we can make a case of criminal liability." David's nose began to twitch at the suggestion of fraud, and he spent long hours researching brake damage.

Meanwhile, Sarah spent her days in the library archives where she could legitimately hush anyone who wanted to ask her about their adoption efforts. By the end of October, she was working her way through the journals that covered the 1860s—a period that was her favorite time frame. As her understanding of the nunnery and how it functioned increased, she developed a deeper level of compassion for Sister Francesca and her challenges as the mother superior. She discovered she was seeing the Civil War from a perspective she had never fully considered. Comfortable at last with her subject matter, Sarah let her words flow easily through these central chapters. For the first time, she could say with confidence that she would finish this book by spring.

The parenting classes filled their evenings until November third, with sessions every Monday, Tuesday, and Thursday evening. One prospective father had complained about the frequency of the meetings until the instructor put him firmly in his place. "Mr. Higgins, three hours of class, three nights a week, for three weeks, amounts to twenty-seven hours out of your month. If you cannot make time for these sessions, how do you propose to raise a child, whose needs will outweigh your own for twenty-four hours a day, 365 days a year, for the next eighteen years? Have you considered getting a cat?"

The parenting classes challenged different people in different ways. The 24-hour mechanical baby test, for example, required the parent to remain in physical contact with the doll for the entire 24-hour period. They had to respond to all needs, such as feeding, changing, and comforting; the doll signaled a need for attention by crying, getting progressively louder until the need was met. The exercise was easier for Sarah than for David because she had done it once before in a high school home economics class. She had learned her lessons well. This time around, she simply put the doll into a sling that draped across her chest. In a pocket, she carried a supply of pacifiers that switched off the crying. David, however, had to resort to hiring one of his clerks to babysit while he made court appearances.

During the second week, the classes addressed emergency measures—knowing what to do and how to do it. The 24-hour dolls became patients who suffered from choking, broken bones, burns, drowning, high fevers, and nausea. Now Sarah was the one who was challenged to rise to the occasion, while David remained calm and confident. As part of his police training, he had been through this course every year and had taught classes on artificial respiration. At one point, he interrupted the instructor, saying, "Excuse me, Miss Winkler, but I believe you just broke that baby's ribs."

The third week centered on group therapy, where they were encouraged to admit their fears, plans, and hopes. For some couples, this is where the doubts began to come out. But for Sarah and David, there were only dreams of family life and a touch of impatience.

For Sarah, there was one bad moment. A young woman admitted that her mother-in-law had warned her about taking on the responsibilities of motherhood while she was working full-time as a paralegal. "She says I'll have to choose —that I can't have both motherhood and career."

Sarah cringed and then shrugged it off. "That's silly," she said. "Someone once told me the same thing, but I don't believe it for a moment. Mothers always have time for their children, no matter what their other responsibilities are. Look at the old folks, your grandparents, for example. I'll bet those women worked harder as farmers' wives than you do in your legal office. And they didn't get time off, either. The cows had to be milked every day, no matter what." Sarah was proud of her answer to the general issue of "having it all." In the car going home, she broached her other concerns.

"I think we've still got a lot to learn about managing our time before we add the complications of parenthood."

"I thought we'd been doing well lately," David said.

"Maybe so, but we've made a hash out of Thanksgiving week. Have you thought about the logistics? First, we have two sets of parents hoping the weather makes it possible for us to join them for Thanksgiving dinner. Your folks want a blizzard to keep us here, and mine want warm sunshine to speed our travels. And the truth is, the weather won't matter. There are not enough hours in the day to let us travel between Tennessee and New York that week. We've promised to join the band for the Thanksgiving parade, but think about the bus schedule. We'll need to make the trip Tuesday or Tuesday night to give the kids time to settle in and rehearse before the parade. And then we've promised them a whole sight-seeing day after Thanksgiving, which means we don't get home until late on Saturday. So, your parents' holiday plans for us are impossible, and if my mother wants to cook a turkey on Thursday, we'll be eating late that night."

"That's OK. Midnight suppers can be fun, and we don't have to do touristy things with the kids on Friday. We can sleep in late while they visit the UN or ride the ferry to the Statue of Liberty."

"Uh-huh. And what's happening back in Tennessee on Friday while we're being slug-a-beds?"

David shrugged. Then a realization hit him. "Oh, no, that's Black Friday and the release date for your new book, *Elijah and the Hanukkah Gift*."

"Exactly. And your sister has already promised that we will bring Elijah and Delilah to the Barnes and Noble Bookstore in Cookeville, where they are planning an early open house for Black Friday, which they are calling Black (Cat) Friday. And then we're scheduled to make appearances at three smaller bookstores in Birch Falls."

"And you're not willing to let Hannah take the cats to those crowds of kitty fans."

"Certainly not. She can't handle Elijah when he gets in one of his moods. And we have no idea how Delilah will behave. No, we'll have to scratch my parents' Thanksgiving dinner and fly back to Nashville Thursday evening. Maybe your mother can save some leftovers for us."

"You're right. It's a mess, no matter which way we turn."

"So, maybe I should stay home and let you handle the school kids. I had nothing to do with that whole story anyhow. They only invited me as a courtesy toward your wife."

"And I only accepted the invitation because it was a way for me to let you see your parents over the holidays. No, Sarah, I think we will have to cancel the New York trip. The high school folks don't need us, but Hannah and the cats do."

"Maybe that's the broader answer. From now on, we can't just do what we want. When we face a situation in which we can't have it all, we have to think about where we are most needed. And once we have a family, the children's needs will come first."

CHAPTER 26

None—The Fifth Hour

From the journal of Mary Frances McMurtry, later known as Sister Francesca, and now, by the grace of God, as Mother Francesca, Mother Superior of this Convent of Our Lady St. Walburga:

1866

The canonical hour of None occurs around 3:00 PM. marking the hour of Jesus's death on the cross. Those of us observing the hours look forward to the end of the day's work and the promise of rest. It is good, therefore, that we pause in our efforts and examine what we have accomplished while there is still time to finish what we have started. We should ask whether we have succeeded in our efforts or failed to accomplish what we set out to do.

As I sit here in my hidden cubicle, I find myself looking back over the past few years—the war years. When we sisters came to Birch Falls, we intended to create a Christian haven where religious women could find shelter and peace to pursue their relationship with Jesus and with God. There are moments when I think we have accomplished that. But more often, we have been drawn into the world and its problems. We began as a cloistered community and expanded to a maternity home and orphanage. Our charitable efforts grew with every passing year, but the war years have brought demands we could never have anticipated.

I admit we didn't notice the impact at first, although southern state after state joined the Confederacy after January 1861. I don't even remember being disturbed when Tennessee joined their ranks on June 8th. But when Union forces overran Nashville on February 25, 1862, forcing a mass evacuation of that city, we began to worry about our safety here at the foot of the Smoky Mountains. Still, I hoped something good would come out of this violence.

We held a private service of gratitude on January 1, 1863, when the Emancipation Proclamation put a legal end to slavery. I remembered the little boy and his mother from my first slave auction, and I prayed they would somehow be reunited. It was not until much later that I began to realize how ill-prepared the former slaves were for freedom that failed to provide job training, education, and the necessities of life. If someone should ask me now how much the proclamation accomplished, my answer would have to be, 'Very little.'

It was not only former slaves who suffered during the war years. Orphans, young widows, and bereaved parents and grandparents all found themselves abandoned and impoverished as, in battle after battle, they lost the men upon whom they had depended. Each major confrontation brought new reports of deaths, grievous injuries, and missing soldiers. The Battle of Gettysburg in July 1863 alone produced a tally of seven thousand known to have been killed outright, thirty-three thousand wounded, and ten thousand missing. But even those figures could scarcely have prepared us for the impact of losing a million and a half young men—an entire generation—wiped out in four years.

Looking back now, I realize I had not expected the war to affect us. The conflict was between northern abolitionists and southern slave owners, I thought. The fighting would occur in northern places like Gettysburg or along the coast of South Carolina—surely not in the sleepy hills of Tennessee. But in the fall of 1863, that assumption collapsed as the fighting raged through Tennessee from Knoxville to Chattanooga, and the northern forces tightened their control of vital rail lines along the Tennessee-Georgia border. In Nashville, Union hospitals sprang up to handle nearly 25,000 wounded soldiers from the Battle of Chickamauga, and Union forces entrenched themselves at Knoxville, Lookout Mountain, and Chattanooga. Tennesseans were in the middle of the action instead of safely hidden away in the mountains.

Here at St. Walburga's nunnery, we were nervous. The fighting was miles away, but rumors flew even faster than bullets. I am ashamed to admit my weakness as I listened to horror stories of marauding Union soldiers. In my private office, I worried about the treasure chest I had hidden beneath my worktable. It contained cash payments, property deeds, and bequests from adopting parents and those who needed shelter for their elderly relatives. In one of those weak-kneed bargains with God that we all make when we put too much value on the goods of this world, I had allowed our convent to become wealthy—a shameful fall from our vows of poverty. I had promised myself (and God) that I would not use the money until I knew it was for a worthy cause. But now the money seemed to be in jeopardy, and I could not bear to think of Union soldiers seizing it and sharing our wealth. My solution? I called in a couple of trustworthy nuns and ordered them to secure the chest in the crypt, disguising it as one of the funereal monuments or caskets for the blessed dead.

Meanwhile, our tiny community of some thirty-five women struggled against overwhelming odds to alleviate the mental, emotional, and physical suffering that surrounded us. And on and on it went. In September 1864, General Sherman led his well-organized Union forces from Nashville to Atlanta, leaving a wide swath of destruction. They took control of Atlanta, held it through mid-November, and then set the city on fire, leaving little behind them.

Sherman had organized his men into four divisions, each following a slightly different path and foraging for supplies as they went. Their passage from Atlanta to Savannah and 'the sea' left behind only destruction and invited the surrender of Georgians who now understood the war was hopeless. When the Yankee forces turned north in early 1865, following the coast to South Carolina and then into North Carolina, we worried again. But Sherman was no longer interested in Tennessee. It had been little more than a jumping-off point. Now he headed for Virginia and an end to the war.

A few difficult events followed. The surrender at Appomattox on April 8, 1865, was a sad occasion. Despite the evils of warfare, despite the deaths and destruction, most Confederate soldiers believed in their cause. Their reaction to having lost the war was despair, not defiance.

Then, of course, came the assassination of Lincoln just one week later. For most people, the huge casualty numbers were impossible to comprehend, while the murder of one good man who believed in his country was almost too much to bear. We were a solemn and silent group the evening he died. When we looked back at None to discover what we might have accomplished that day, we could only shake our heads in denial.

One final event was yet to come. Pulaski, Tennessee, is a small town located directly south of Nashville near the Alabama border. Nothing of importance ever happened there, except on Christmas Eve, 1865. On that fifth anniversary of South Carolina's secession from the United States, a small group of angry men—haters of former slaves, Republicans, and the federal government as a whole—came together to defend their most cherished prejudices. They were destined to become part of the larger Ku Klux Klan, terrorists who are still spreading murder and mayhem in the South, even as more reasonable men struggle to reconstruct the unity and guiding principles of this country. I watch these miscreants in fear and pray that we are strong enough to control them.

But what more can we say of None? The damage caused during the war years was—and is—immeasurable. There were a few inventions and improvements—ironclad warships and rifled artillery changed the nature of warfare, although perhaps not for the better. For civilians, dress patterns, roller skates, and celluloid film provided a bit of distraction, and medical treatment slowly began to improve with the acceptance of Lister's germ theory.

Several books caught the public's attention: *Alice in Wonderland, Crime and Punishment, Das Kapital,* and *War and Peace* gave the intellectuals some questions to ponder, and for would-be-writers, the invention of the typewriter came shortly after the war. For others, mail-order catalogs provided some moments of escape.

Small inventions improved everyday life: milk bottles, machine-produced sewing machine needles, rolled measuring tapes, earmuffs, and washing machines delighted housewives. And for cooks, there were key-opened cans, tabasco sauce, bottled horseradish, margarine, and ice cream sodas. No great inventions, perhaps, but enough to reassure us that some people were still thinking.

But what of us, the nuns of St. Walburga? As we paused at the end of the war to re-evaluate the war years, we faced a test, our moment on the cross when we might proclaim, "It is finished." But nothing was finished in the aftermath of such a traumatic conflict. The wounds still bled and the scars still itched. Lovely plantation homes had been reduced to rubble. Families waited for their soldiers to come home, although those homecomings were frequently painful. Brothers had fought on opposite sides. Men broken by the horrors of death and destruction suffered from nightmares and debilitating fear. The wounded survivors left the army hospitals without the ability to cope with their injuries. How does a man with no arms feed himself? And who will take on the thankless task of caring for the elderly who had been abandoned by their families? Our work had just begun.

Earlier in my tenure as mother superior, I had authorized the building of a school and orphanage to care for the lost children who found their way to our door. Now, as I surveyed our convent, I saw another empty plot of ground that could be filled. At our weekly chapter meeting, I proposed a long-term care facility for severely wounded soldiers and elderly orphans with no family to care for them in their last days.

"With the addition of six or seven experienced nuns from

nursing orders," I proposed, "we can do our part to reverse some of the local suffering caused by the war."

"Where will we put another building?"

"There's an open spot between the refectory and the veterinary school. The windows will face the orphanage and the playground between the two buildings. I think the residents of the nursing home will enjoy hearing the laughter of children. The old and the young often inspire one another."

"Why are we always the ones who have to do the work?" asked Sister Priscilla, one of the younger nuns. "When do we get to rest?"

"My dear sister, you are forgetting the central tenet of our founder, St. Benedict: '*Laborare est orare*—To work is to pray.'"

"Yes, ma'am."

"How will we pay for more construction?" Sister Benedicta asked. "Are you planning to tap into your treasure chest at last?"

"No. With the depredations of local terrorists, I have no intention of calling their attention to a large sum of money. We will follow our usual pattern of fund-raising—appeals to the local congregation through novenas and earned indulgences, requests for support from the diocese and archdiocese, fund-raising affairs, a Christmas bazaar—along with volunteer help. If we put our minds and prayers to it, we can get it done.

"When Jesus faced His ninth hour on the cross, He said, 'It is finished.' And for Him, it was. His work here on earth was complete. But for poor mortal souls, our work is never finished. We may rest at Vespers, but we will still have much to do. Our None is over but not our mission. It's time to go back to work."

CHAPTER 27

Parents-in-Waiting

Monday, Nov. 14, 2011

"Our work is never finished." Sarah read that statement for the second time and slammed the journal closed. Across the archival workroom, several heads came up at the startling sound in the otherwise silent library. "Sorry," she mouthed as her assistant researcher raised a questioning eyebrow.

"Problems with what you're reading?"

"Not really, but sometimes the mother superior seems to be talking directly to me, and I'm frustrated that I can't argue with her." Sarah shrugged, a motion that translated itself into a shiver and ran down her spine. Then she stood, flashed her fingers to indicate she was taking a twenty-minute break, and headed for the outer hall.

From the library steps, she looked across the cloister gardens and saw a familiar figure coming toward her. "Julia!" she called.

"Sarah! Hi! I'm waddling over to the Grub Hub for coffee. Do you have time to join me? We haven't talked in ages."

"Of course, I do. How are you feeling? You're … what? Eight months along?"

"Eight and a half by my count, and the doctor says any day now. But Maddie Rae doesn't seem to be in a hurry to join this crazy world."

"You've finally chosen her name?"

"Madelaine, for my grandmother who raised me, and Rae, for Bert's mother's side of the family."

"I love it, particularly with a built-in nickname. And look at you. You're glowing."

"It's the black skin—I don't wrinkle as fast as you pale-faces. And speaking of pale faces, you're looking a bit frazzled. Are you OK? It will be good for you to get out of the archives for a while when you go to New York. We plan to watch the Macy's Parade on Thanksgiving to see the local band. Maybe we'll even spot you and David."

"We've decided not to go. There are just too many things happening here, and we had second thoughts about those long bus rides."

"So, what all is happening here?"

"Well, our new book about Hanukkah will come out on Black Friday, and Elijah makes his first book signing appearance in Crossville. I have to admit he is none too pleased. When I brought home the first sample of the stuffed Elijah, he took one look at his stuffed image and hissed at it. I could imagine his critique: 'I'm not that fat, and my eyes are greener than that.'"

"Well, you can tell His Highness that I saw a picture of the stuffed version and recognized him right away. I intend to buy one for Maddie Rae, too, along with the book. I know she won't need it for a while, but I want to be ready."

"Speaking of being ready—we are on edge, waiting for the phone to ring."

"A phone call? From whom?"

"The Jewish Children's Home in Nashville."

"Does that mean ... Sarah, are you waiting for an adoption?"

"Looks like it. We've passed all the interviews and coursework. It's just a matter of them getting all the paperwork together. And then we'll get the call to come to pick them up."

"Them? Wait! Are you ...?"

Sarah grinned at her friend's inability to phrase the questions about news she had not expected. "Yes. We're adopting twins. Do you remember the car crash back in June and the two babies we rescued from the back seat?"

"The same ones?"

"Isn't that amazing? I went to visit the orphanage, and the twins were the first ones I met. I was shocked that they were still there, but the nurses said most people are afraid to adopt twins. But for me, it seemed like it was meant to be. I called David and had him come to Nashville the next day. As I told him, I felt as if HaShem dropped them into my lap not once, but twice. I got the message, and so did David. We never hesitated. So in a few days or weeks, Jillian and Jeremy Cohen will join our family."

"Wow! What changes we will all be facing. And just think. In a couple of years, our kids will be playmates."

"We can hope. Every time someone makes a statement like that, I cringe and cross my fingers, because we're not done yet."

"But I thought you said ..."

"The next step is six months of a trial adoption, although I object to the term trial. How could anyone take these two angelic children home with them, keep them for six months, and then return them? What would that do to the children, right at an age where they are prone to separation anxiety? But the adoption agency is hard-nosed on this point. The chances are slim, but they want the option of taking the children back if there are problems with the adoption."

"I can't believe they would do that without a good reason."

"David says not to worry. We should proceed as planned. Buy new baby/youth furnishings for their room. Plan to give them separate rooms at age six as they start school. Enjoy each day and don't worry about being turned down. The important thing is to love these kids with all our hearts. The other problems will solve themselves."

"It's good advice."

"I hope he's right. But for now, I have to get back to work. The mother superior keeps reminding me I have a book to finish."

For the prospective parents, the early November days dragged, although they were busy enough. During the weekdays, Sarah followed her usual pattern of library research in the mornings and drafting her book chapters in the afternoons. Her home-cooked meals welcomed David each evening. And early bedtimes meant she could lose herself in a few pages of frivolous reading before she dropped into a heavy slumber.

David was still investigating the 2010 hurricane season in Texas, believing a tropical storm might have contributed to brake failure in a deadly car crash. He became a familiar noon visitor to the local library's newspaper collection, eating a sandwich while he read weather reports. Then, if he was not needed in court, he spent his late afternoons at his father's law office. Mr. Cohen had not yet returned to work and was relying more and more on David to keep his clients happy. But for both David and Sarah, keeping busy did not mean they forgot why they were keeping busy. They were simply filling the hours while they waited to be told they were parents at last.

The long-awaited phone call came on Monday afternoon. Sarah clutched the phone as if it might scurry away from her while she scrambled to find a calendar.

"You want us there on Thursday, the 17th, and we'll get the children on Friday. Is that correct? No. It's not a problem. I just wanted to be sure I had the dates correct. It's perfect. It gives us a clear weekend to figure out our schedules."

She heard a chuckle in the background before the official voice resumed its instructions. "Yes, we have a double stroller and can bring it. And we're to... what? OK. That sounds like a final exam. No, no, it's fine. You can tell Dr. Adams that we will meet her in her office at 2:00 on Thursday."

Sarah was still shaking as she punched David's private cell phone number. "Clear your desk. We're on our way. The secretary from the Jewish Children's Home just called with instructions. We are to meet Dr.Adams at 2:00 this Thursday, the 17th. We'll spend some time with the children and meet with the board to sign the paperwork. Then they want us to check into the Red Door Motel, requesting two cribs. We're also to take the children out for dinner at a local family-friendly restaurant where they will get highchairs and we can order finger foods for them."

She held the phone away from her ear while listening to David sputter. He did not like to be told what to do, she knew, and these instructions were not going to suit him. "Yes, dear, I understand that in the time it will take, we could be driving home. But this is the way they want to do things. It's pretty obvious. They're going to have people watching us to see how we handle those first few steps."

"That doesn't make me feel better."

"Maybe not, but if we mess up, I'll be happy to know there's someone around to help out."

"How could we mess up?"

"Oh, I don't know. We just have to feed them and keep them from choking or disturbing the other customers. And then we get to take them to a motel room and put them into unfamiliar cribs. People in neighboring rooms will expect to go to sleep without their neighbors wailing their heads off. What could go wrong?"

"Cut it out, Sarah. It will all work out. This is what we've been waiting for, right?"

Despite Sarah's worries, the afternoon they spent at the Jewish Children's Home went smoothly. The twins had been engaged in their usual squabbles, but they settled down immediately when the nurses opened the door to their cubicle and invited Sarah and David to go in by themselves. Jillian had looked up curiously and then grinned. "Uruh?" she asked.

Sarah clapped her hands in delight. "She remembers us. That was her word for squirrel."

David nodded, too. "So much for Dr. Adams' theory about them being pre-memory. It's a good sign, although I'm not sure how useful the word 'squirrel' is going to be in the next few days. We probably ought to start with 'Mama,' 'Dada,' and 'cat.'

Sarah laughed; then her eyes narrowed as she watched her new daughter. "Say 'Mama.'" She repeated the sound several times, using a hugging gesture to indicate the word applied to her.

"Mamamamamam," Jillian responded.

"Mama." Sarah spoke with a distinct pause after the word. This time she gestured by patting herself on the cheek as she said the word. Jillian frowned with concentration and touched her own cheek.

Sarah smiled but shook her head. She reached for the little girl, who responded by lifting her arms to be picked up. Holding her in her left arm, Sarah took the child's hand and patted her cheek. "This is Mama," she repeated. "Mama."

David had been watching the procedure carefully. Now he stepped in to try his luck. "Dada, Dada." And after several tries, he succeeded in hearing his little girl call him, "Dada."

Sarah had been about to say something congratulatory when she looked over David's shoulder and saw little Jeremy sitting quietly in a corner of his crib, his thumb in the side of his mouth. "Poor baby," she murmured. "He's so quiet and shy. We're going to have to help him assert himself in the face of his sister's more outgoing personality."

She reached across the side of Jeremy's crib and held out both hands to him. "Come to Mama. I have secrets to tell you. Tonight, we're going to stay in a hotel room and have dinner in a restaurant. Those will be new experiences for you. And tomorrow you and your sister are going to move into our house as part of our family. You will have a big room and toys and two cats to cuddle and a pretty yard to play in next summer. Best of all, we will be there to take care of you until you're all grown up."

"Mama?" Jeremy buried his face in her shoulder as if to make sure she was not going to leave him again. She held him tightly to reassure him, and then shifted him to one hip. "Come on. Let's go see if the nurses have finished packing your things."

The move to the hotel and the short trip to the restaurant were remarkably easy. The children were wide-eyed and speechless with excitement. They stared around the dining room and wriggled in their raised chairs—so unlike the metal highchairs they had used in the kitchen of the orphanage. The waitress fussed over them and brought them sippy cups of juice. Their dinners arrived on trays divided into several sections, each one displaying a colorful choice of tasty snacks, all chopped into finger-sized pieces. They sampled scrambled eggs, flakes of salmon, mashed sweet potatoes, peas, and shredded chicken. Dessert included pieces of fresh raspberries and slices of ripe bananas.

Only one incident marred the experience. Between dinner and dessert, Jeremy developed an attack of hiccups. At first, he giggled, but as the spasms continued, he began to fuss. Jillian made matters worse by laughing at him.

Sarah tried offering him sips of water, but they didn't help. David tried scaring him, but that didn't help either.

"Now what do we do?" Sarah whispered.

"Beats me. We never covered hiccups in my first aid courses. I don't think they're fatal, though."

At last, a motherly woman approached their table. "I don't mean to interfere, but I couldn't help noticing your little problem here. Are you by any chance brand new parents?"

"It shows, doesn't it? We're adopting these two little angels, and this is our first night with them. Do you by any chance know how to cure hiccups?"

"Scaring him was not a bad idea. You need to get his mind off what's going on. Water seldom works because it's too boring. At home, I'd probably feed him a teaspoon of peanut butter. But in a restaurant setting like this, the best solution I know is sugar." She glanced around their table and pounced on a packet of sugar crystals lying next to David's iced tea. "Here. Feed him about half a teaspoon of sugar."

Jeremy first jerked his head away from the spoon as another hiccup hit him, but then he took a mouthful of the sugar and looked surprised. He smacked his lips, grinned, and opened his mouth for more. The hiccups disappeared.

"Thank you," Sarah said, squeezing the woman's hand.

"That was nothing. You'll catch on soon enough. We should be the ones thanking you for caring enough to take these two beautiful children into your home. May they be a blessing to you."

CHAPTER 28

One Day at a Time

Saturday, November 19, 2011

The twins were so tired from their new experiences that they fell asleep in the car on the way back to the motel. One by one, David carried them in and placed them in their cribs, while Sarah did the overnight diaper changes.

"That was easy," David commented, holding up his hand for a silent high-five. "Every night should go so smoothly."

"In your dreams! Enjoy this night. It may never happen again."

In the morning the Cohens awoke to the chattering of two small voices. The words were indistinguishable, but it was clear that the twins understood each other. And from the smiles on their faces, the subject matter seemed to please them.

"That must be the cryptophasia that Dr. Adams was telling me about. It's a unique language they developed in the womb."

"Will we ever be able to understand it?"

"No, probably not. It's more likely that as they learn to speak English, they will forget the crypto language themselves. That's unfortunate, though. Breaking their code might help explain the development of human language."

"Perhaps we could secretly record them before they forget."

"Maybe. But I suspect we're going to be busy enough learning to sign and teaching them our language rather than learning theirs."

"How do you say breakfast in sign language?"

"You simplify—meals, food, the process of eating—they all use the same sign of two fingers moving from table to mouth."

"Well, let's announce that breakfast is served and go to the lobby to see what is on offer."

Once again, the children were fascinated by the newness of a hotel lobby with a full spread of breakfast foods. They pointed eagerly from one item to another, and Sarah did her best to comply with their orders. She added some orange juice to their sippy cups and filled two small bowls with dry puffed cereal. She chopped some scrambled eggs into finger foods on a separate plate and added some banana slices. From her plate, she picked a couple of bites of soft biscuits with white gravy and some chopped pancakes with syrup.

David watched the food preparation with an indulgent smile at his wife's skills, but he also picked up another important clue about twins. "Look, Sarah. They're both plunging into the scrambled eggs because they've had them before. But with the new foods, their tastes are quite different. Jeremy is chowing down on the pancakes and syrup, while Jillian is fascinated by the biscuits and gravy. One likes sweet; the other wants savory. That says something about their different personalities, doesn't it?"

After breakfast, the family returned to the Jewish Children's Home to load up the children's clothes, toys, and their favorite shelf-stable baby foods. The nurses came to the car with them to say farewell, give the children their final hugs, and wish the family good luck. Then the Cohens were off, headed for Birch Falls and new lives as a family of four.

The children slept for almost the entire trip. "What great little travelers they are," David whispered. "When we want them to go to sleep, all we will have to do is load them into their car seats and drive around the block. Out like little lights, both of them."

The peaceful drive ended abruptly as they turned into their cul-de-sac because in the driveway were two cars. "My parents and Hannah's family," David sighed. "Should I just keep driving?"

"No. Much as I might wish they had given us time to get home and settled, I understand why they are here. They are grandparents, and they've been anticipating this first meeting just as we were a couple of days ago."

As they pulled into the driveway, the waiting family members rushed to meet the car. Their cries of "Welcome home!" were enough to wake the children and frighten them as well. And by the time their doting grandparents pulled open the car doors, Jeremy and Jillian were wailing at the top of their lungs.

"Poor little things," Mrs. Cohen wailed along with them. "They must have been miserable strapped into those tiny seats."

"They..." Sarah started to correct her but swallowed her words when David frowned at her.

"I think they are just overwhelmed by so many big

people, but if you'll give us room to get them out of the car, they may be happier."

"Oh, let me help. Grandma's hugs are always welcome."

Sarah clutched little Jillian even tighter and turned away from her mother-in-law. "Even a grandma will be scary until they get to know you. If you want to help, bring one of those boxes of baby food into the kitchen for me."

David caught the message and lifted Jeremy away from the next pair of reaching hands. "Did we leave the playpen set up in the living room?" he asked. "The kiddos can settle down there while we finish unloading the car."

"Jacob and I rechecked all the baby furniture last night to be sure it was ready. But the last time I saw the playpen, it had two cats in it." Mr. Cohen cocked his eyebrow, making it clear he did not approve of mixing babies and cats.

Sarah had been prepared to yell at Elijah, but instead, she laughed as the cat took one look at the babies and leaped for the safety of the stairs. "The children and cats will have to get to know one another, too. But this little wiggle worm already has a thing for animals."

"Uruh?" Jillian struggled to get down.

"No, love, that wasn't a squirrel. It was a cat. Can you say cat?

"Uruh," she insisted.

With the children safely deposited in the playpen and the cats under the bed, the family made short work of bringing in the rest of the boxes from the orphanage. "They have you well supplied," Hannah commented. "I picked up lunch for all of us on my way over here, but I didn't know what to get for the children. It's been a while since I needed to feed a baby."

"No problem. There's a big container of finger foods in that cooler. Let's see what you brought for us. Once we have our lunch on the table, we can move the children to their highchairs and give them enough finger food to keep them busy and well-fed."

Hannah laughed. "It's finger food for us as well. Those long packages are submarine sandwiches from Jerry's Subs. And somewhere around here, there's a big bag of potato chips and a gallon of lemonade. It's picnic time for everyone, even Daddy, who has been being diligent about his Mediterranean diet. I figured I could get away with giving him an Italian sub."

"Sounds wonderful. And we can probably do penance for the potato chips at supper."

"Ah, yes, supper. Mother took care of that, and you don't have to open the fridge to guess what's inside."

The two young women rolled their eyes at each other as they spoke in unison: "Tuna noodle casserole and tossed salad. Welcome to the Cohen family traditions, little guys."

After lunch, the twins were ready for another nap, and their new parents would have gladly joined them. The grandparents, however, had other plans, and so did Hannah.

"Sarah, while you have some downtime, I need your help with the Elijah book. It goes to press Monday morning unless we spot corrections in the proof copy. After that, it will be too late to change even a punctuation mark. But I'm so tired of staring at those pages that everything looks wrong. Can you please curl up with the proof copy and look for hidden errors?"

"I can try, but I'll warn you my brain feels like mush. I want to see the proofs, though. I never got a chance to look at some of the finished pages. I'll take it back to my home office, where I can keep one ear tuned to catch the sounds of trouble coming from the twins' room. I need to learn how to do that from now on."

"At least it will give you an excuse to avoid Dad's plans for the afternoon. One of his golfing buddies suggested that the adults should get down on the floor and try to see the house from the babies' viewpoint. That's supposed to help us spot the attractive nuisances. So don't be surprised if you come downstairs and find us all on our hands and knees."

Sarah emerged an hour later to report only two small errors in the Elijah proofs. Unfortunately, the other family members had spent that hour discovering many small hazards around the house.

"Where's David?" Sarah asked Hannah

"Off to Home Depot to buy safety plugs for all your electric outlets."

"And Mother Cohen?"

"In the kitchen, moving all the breakables to upper shelves where little fingers can't reach them."

"But I had already arranged my cupboards the way I wanted them."

"That was during your B.C. days—Before Children."

"And your father—what in the world is he doing to the door to my laundry room?"

"He's installing a cat flap, so Elijah and Delilah can get to their food bowls and litter boxes without leaving the door open to invite babies to sample what's on offer."

"Ew-w-w-w-w."

"Yep. You can't argue with that one. It will be up to you to teach the cats to use the flap, however. There's also a list of future projects on the kitchen counter. It starts with checking your houseplants to make sure their foliage is not poisonous. And the most complicated tasks include bolting the heavy pieces of furniture to the walls."

"Like what?"

"I gather chests of drawers are the biggest threat—anything with drawers that can be pulled out and climbed upon. Free-standing bookshelves are another danger, along with heavy objects like a television or computer. The list goes on and on. Luckily, you have lots of volunteer help, although it means people underfoot while you're trying to help the children adjust to a new environment."

"Maybe most of these projects can be finished by tomorrow, so that when Monday comes ..."

Hannah laughed at the thought. "You're forgetting ... this is Thanksgiving week. You guys made a wise choice when you bailed out of the band trip to New York, but it's still going to be chaos around here. David tells me he has closed the DA's office for the whole week, but Daddy refuses to follow suit. He's planning on having David at the law office, and I'll bet you thought he'd be here to help you."

"He'd better be here. I'm going to need him."

"Well, I can come help now and then, although Mother expects me to help with Thanksgiving dinner, too. You are planning to be there, aren't you?"

"I don't know. I want to get the children on a schedule as soon as possible, and that doesn't include a huge family dinner and football games."

"But my parents have made all sorts of changes—it's supposed to be a surprise for you, but they have created a grandbaby nursery with cribs for naps and highchairs to share dinnertime."

"Oh, no! They didn't have to spend that kind of money. They shouldn't have ..."

"They didn't. The synagogue maintains a 'grandparents'

closet' where they can borrow baby furniture and then return it or exchange it as the kids grow. But there's not going to be a way for you to weasel out of the family tradition, my dear. And then ..." Hannah grimaced and paused, pretending to put away the lunch leftovers.

"Spill it. What else have I forgotten?"

"Black Friday, and the formal book release in Crossville. We need you there. I promised that Elijah would be there, and you know no one can handle him but you. And then three local bookstores want at least brief appearances. I'm sorry to dump this all on you, but we didn't expect twins to arrive at the same time as the new books."

Sarah gave in because she lacked the energy to protest. "I'll manage. I'm not sure how, but it's only one day at a time, isn't it?"

CHAPTER 29

Be Careful What You Wish For

November 24 - 28, 2011

The Cohen family's Thanksgiving dinner had gone off without a hitch. The twins were wide-eyed at their grandmother's dining room table, over-flowing with platters of new and fascinating foods. As it turned out, many of those foods were ideally suited to a baby's taste. They loved the mashed potatoes and gravy, but once they sampled the mashed sweet potatoes with marsh-mallows, the gravy was less appealing. The turkey stuffing, too, had strong appeal. Sarah had picked through a spoonful to remove the onions, celery, and giblets, leaving just the savory soft bread. Jillian enjoyed several bites, just as she had with the earlier biscuits and gravy. Jeremy, however, was happy to stick with marshmallows. Sarah had also worried about nap time at the grandparents' house, but the twins seemed to have decided that any crib was cozy when they were sleepy. David was a little disappointed when his new son slept through his first football game, but Sarah was grateful for the reprieve.

Black Friday's trip to Crossville had been more complicated. The cat joined the twins in the back seat, and his miserable wailing conflicted with the twins' natural inclination to sleep in a moving car. Elijah hated his cat carrier when someone was not pushing him or offering him tasty tidbits. He hated the moving car. He hated everything about being dragged from one setting to another. The cat meowed, the babies fussed, and David clenched his jaw and tried to ignore them all. Sarah fidgeted with her need to plan an introductory talk at the bookstore. At one point, she turned to the back seat and delivered a cat-oriented lecture.

"Elijah, hush. You've done this before, and you know you love being the center of attention. This isn't a trip to the vet. You have a new book, whether or not you realize it, so sit up and look proud. And be quiet!" A hiccup caught Sarah's attention. She glanced at the twins and then took a second look. They stared at her with wide eyes, tears running down their cheeks and lips trembling.

"It's OK. I'm not angry at you. I was yelling at the cat because he was yowling back here. I'm sorry if I scared you. Please don't cry." Sniffles and reluctant nods signaled their efforts to understand. Jillian leaned forward in her car seat, her hand reaching out to touch Sarah's shoulder.

"Mama."

"Oh, dear. Now I'm going to cry. We'll all be a mess before we arrive."

The bookstore opening, however, was hugely successful and took Sarah's mind off the twins for the first time. Hannah had approved an additional marketing gimmick as a surprise for Sarah. For the next thirty days, each new copy of *The Hanukkah Gift* came with a tiny stuffed kitten—white fur, blue eyes, a dark gray patch between its ears, and a dark gray tail—at just three inches tall, it was a miniature Delilah. Book sales boomed, and most buyers also bought a stuffed Elijah to complete the set.

"The kittens are adorable, but how did you manage to get them finished in time?"

"That's a trade secret, but it involves an over-run order of 500 white kittens designed to cash in on the Beanie Baby fad. I told the supplier we'd take them, but only if they dyed the head patches and tails to keep them from looking like our copycat author's version of Elijah. I had to buy them outright, but you watch. With only 500 available nation-wide, the kittens will become a collector's item. I'm holding enough of them back to recoup our expenses."

"I love them! And by the time our third book comes out next fall, our real Delilah will be full-grown and can pose for her adult version. Hannah, you're a genius!"

The appeal of the new book and its fuzzy accomplices brought in record profits. The excitement of their young customers fed Sarah's and Hannah's enthusiasm, and they scarcely noticed how tired they were. Even Elijah perked up and showed off for the children who visited him in his carrier. Poor David, however, was not enjoying his role as a babysitter, pushing the twins' stroller back and forth outside the bookstore. Eventually, he gave up and took them inside the store, where they joined the customers jostling for places in line to buy the books. Jeremy didn't much like the crowds, but Jillian chose this moment to recognize that fuzzy black animal in a stroller like her own.

"C-ca," she said. It was a soft sound, but Sarah heard her and grinned at the addition of another word in the twin's vocabulary. On a whim, Sarah picked up the little girl and sat her on the bookstore counter, where she patted the stuffed animals and repeated her new word: 'ca.' She proved to be an excellent salesgirl.

By the time Thanksgiving Week drew to a close, however, Sarah was nearly ready to collapse. She and David begged the family and friends to give them one whole day to spend with just the twins. "We've been dragging them hither and yon," she explained to her mother-in-law. "They've been good sports about behaving themselves, but they also need to find out what their daily lives are going to entail."

The new family spent Sunday quietly, away from crowds and bustling fans. The twins seemed to understand the need for downtime and played quietly with each other. At one point they developed their version of a peekaboo game—one on each side of a dining room chair, looking around the front and then the back of the chair and mirroring each other's movements. Giggles echoed through the quiet house. Sarah and David worked in tandem, each lifting or carrying a twin as they moved through a reasonable schedule of mealtimes, naps, bath play, and cuddle breaks. For those quiet moments, all was well.

And then it was Monday morning. David went back to work, forgetting the twins' car seats were still in his rear seat. He found the bustle of court business to be energizing, and he took a deep breath, noting that the air smelled of leather-bound law books, not baby powder. His office staff welcomed his return and happily filled his desk with memos, telephone messages, and a calendar full of court dates. His primary investigator wore a huge smile as he waited his turn to report some good news about the merchandising history of that wrecked car. He ate lunch at

Isolde's with fellow lawyers and marveled at how quickly the workday passed.

At home, however, Sarah was overwhelmed. She had wakened to the wails of two angry babies who were wet and hungry. Still in her pajamas, she had managed to change both babies, only to note that the drawer of clean diapers was nearly empty. She grabbed the overflowing diaper pail and headed for the laundry, where she discovered one of the cats had left a puddle on the floor outside the utility room door instead of using their litter box.

"So much for the clever little cat flap," she mumbled. "If it weren't for my in-laws, that door wouldn't have been closed. And for that matter, I wouldn't be dragging around a pail of dirty diapers if my mother-in-law had not made me feel guilty for considering using Pampers instead of cloth. I notice neither of them is around while I have to clean up the messes."

Breakfast posed another set of challenges. No matter which baby she picked up first, the other one screamed in protest. She carried Jeremy downstairs to the playpen and handed him a small bottle of milk to keep him occupied. Then she hurried back upstairs for Jillian, who was bouncing her crib against the wall.

Two high chairs awaited at the table, but when she put Jillian in one and turned her back to get Jeremy, Jillian tried to crawl out of the chair. Sarah caught her before she fell, but they had a struggle over fastening the lap belt. Then Jeremy, upset by the fuss, regurgitated his milk, managing to get most of it on Sarah rather than himself. And Jillian expressed her displeasure by dumping her bowl of baby oatmeal on the floor.

Sarah slumped into a chair, overcome for the moment by sheer frustration. "It reminds me of a Dr. Seuss line: 'The mess is so big and so deep and so tall. I cannot clean it up. I can do nothing at all.'"

Attracted by the noises coming from the table, Elijah the Cat chose that moment to appear in the dining room. He sniffed curiously at the overturned oatmeal bowl and settled in to have his breakfast. Sarah shouted at him without thinking: "Elijah! Stop it! Leave it alone!"

The cat ignored her. "Oh, go ahead. Clean it all up. Please, do. Just be sure to lick up every drop so I don't have to mop the floor for a third time this morning."

Elijah did as he was told, but when Delilah the kitten showed up to help him finish, he turned on her with an uncharacteristic snarl.

"Don't the two of you start fighting just because the twins do it," Sarah warned. "I can dump your furry little butts outside, remember."

David chose that moment to call and check on her. "Hi, love. How's it going?"

"Don't ask!"

"Tough morning already? If you need to, you could always take the kids over to Mom's for a while. I'm sure she'd be happy to babysit."

"And just how would I do that? If you take a look at your parking lot, you'll see that the infant seats are still in your car."

"Oops. Sorry. I'll take care of that right after dinner."

"You expect dinner?"

"Well ... I'll help."

"Sure, you will."

"Sarah ..."

"I'm sorry, but it's crazy around here. The house is a wreck. I'm still in pajamas, which reek of spit-up. The twins are threatening to beat each other to a pulp. The cats are hissing and snarling. The phone keeps ringing. The paperboy wants his weekly payment. The lawn guy says the mower is out of gas. Three politicians want my vote in the upcoming run-off primary, and some woman is worried that my car warranty will expire. I don't want to talk to you because I don't want to talk to anyone. I just want a little downtime. And if you ask me how my book is coming, I will surely kill you. Just come home on time, OK?"

CHAPTER 30

How Can I Help You?

Tuesday, November 29, 2011

Sarah promised herself she would have a better day on Tuesday. She set the alarm for a half hour earlier and laid out old clothes she could jump into quickly —sneakers, jeans, and a sweatshirt. In the kitchen, she prepped the coffee maker and selected non-perishable breakfast items. She took pleasure in defying her father-in-law's instructions by propping open the laundry room door to allow the cats free access. She filled their bowls with dry cat food. On her way to bed, she started a dryer load of diapers but turned the signal buzzer off.

Her intentions were good, and she had her household under control—at least those annoyances she could control. But David started to snore almost as soon as the light went out. A baby dropped a teddy bear and screamed for help in retrieving it. The phone rang with the wrong number. Somewhere downstairs, a cat gagged and coughed up a hairball.

And outside an unpredicted thunder shower filled the bedroom window with lightning flashes. Sarah pulled a blanket over her head and curled into a ball of misery.

Still, she woke to feel fairly rested. She splashed her face with cold water and ran a comb through her hair before tiptoeing past the nursery. She even avoided stepping on the hairball at the bottom of the stairs as she headed for the kitchen and a much-needed cup of coffee before starting to prepare a healthy breakfast.

When David appeared in the kitchen doorway with a baby in each arm, she grinned at him. This was the family portrait she had dreamed of. And all would have been well if at that moment a saucepan of poached eggs had not chosen to boil over on the stove. She yanked the pan from the burner, grabbed a towel to keep the spilled water from over-flowing onto the floor, and tried to ignore a small wisp of smoke rising from the toaster.

At the same moment, David discovered that while he held a baby in each arm, he could not get a hand loose to place either one of them in a highchair.

"Sarah, take one of these kids, would you, please?"

"The toast is burning. Put the twins in the playpen. I have my hands full."

"Me, too."

"What do we do now?"

"We eat cereal. Hope you like Cheerios."

"What a crazy start to the day! Do we have any milk?"

"I have no idea. Look in the fridge."

"I'm still trying to get Jillian to sit down. Why does she insist on standing up?"

"Knock her feet out from under her."

"David!"

'OK, do it gently."

"Bribery is kinder," Sarah chuckled as she handed the little girl a sippy cup.

"Encouraging her to take bribes may lead her to a life of crime."

"I'll take my chances."

Their eyes met across the table. and they exchanged grins. This was family life in all its messiness, and they were enjoying the byplay. If Sarah wished David did not have to leave for work in a few minutes, she would not have admitted it. For the moment, it was enough that they were all together.

The doorbell rang, breaking the spell. The visitor was Sheila Leibowicz, the rabbi's wife, bringing a picnic basket and a pair of helping hands. With a cheerful "Good morning," Sheila bustled straight to the kitchen, pausing only long enough to drop a kiss on the forehead of each of the twins. Then she began to extract goodies from the basket, naming them as they came out.

"I brought a few bagels still warm from the oven. I wasn't sure how you'd prefer them, so there's some cream cheese and jam, but also some lox, chicken liver spread, and chopped onion. Oh, and a shaker of 'Everything but the Bagel' seasonings. Also, some lovely red grapes and an extra thermos of coffee.

"For the babies, some tiny satsuma oranges—seedless and easy to peel. If you cut those segments into little pieces, they make great finger food. And they have a bag of baby breakfast cookies, which are mostly rolled oats, mashed bananas, and applesauce."

Sarah meant to say, 'Thank You," but when she opened her mouth, her tears overflowed. "I'm sorry. I don't know what to say. I can't tell you how much this means right now. We're managing, but I spilled the eggs and burned the toast, and ..."

"You're a new mom. You're allowed to do all those things. Sit down and eat. I'll have your kitchen put back together in no time. Let's start by getting rid of the burned toast crumbs so you can use the toaster for your bagel." She flipped the toaster, snapped off the bottom tray, and brushed out the evidence of the morning's disaster.

Sarah shook her head as she watched. "I never knew that bottom plate came off."

"There's always something new to learn," Sheila laughed. "You aren't the only the only woman to burn the toast in the morning."

"I've got to get to court," David said. "Are you ladies sufficiently in control here?" He grabbed half a bagel, smeared it with cream cheese, topped it with a few slivers of lox, and headed out the door.

Sheila watched him leave and then commented. "That's one great husband, Sarah. You're lucky to have him."

"I know—even if he isn't a great deal of help around the house."

"What man is? You need a woman who can handle the household affairs for you."

"I know I do. I've checked the college's job center and put up a notice asking for babysitters in the mornings or afternoons, but there have been no responses."

"Ah. You don't want a college student. They're too busy and too unreliable. You need one of my young women."

"Your young women? I don't understand."

"Hasn't David told you about the training center our Women's Interfaith Group runs? I was sure he would have mentioned it to you. He called me yesterday afternoon to see if we had someone available because you needed help."

"I don't know. Maybe he did. My mind is just mush these days with so much going on—the babies, Thanksgiving dinner, the upcoming holidays, the new book ..."

"It's OK. Here's the short version. We have a center for young women who find themselves in need of support and employment. Some are runaways, some have been abused, and others are just 18-year-olds who have outgrown the foster care system. We teach them basic life skills and then train them for a variety of caregiving occupations like companions for the elderly, emergency house cleaners, assistants after a rehab facility, or mother's helpers. They get classroom lectures first, followed by practical experience and supervised internships. Then they move on to six months of work experience, after which they can apply for a state-issued caregiver's certificate.

"When David called yesterday, I had just finished interviewing a young woman who is ready to start her six-month trial experience as a mother's helper. I took the liberty of asking her to come over here this morning at ten to meet you and the children and discuss a possible job offer. I hope you don't mind."

"No, of course not, although I wish David had mentioned it to me. I'll be happy to talk to her. A mother's helper is exactly what I need."

When the doorbell rang again, Sarah answered it. She expected to see a typical teenager, so she was surprised to find an attractive young woman—neatly dressed, with hair caught up in a bun, and a face devoid of makeup.

"Good morning! Are you Mrs. Cohen? I'm Janice, a mother's helper. I understand you have your hands a bit full these days. Perhaps I can help you."

"Perhaps you can. Come in, won't you?"

Janice glanced into the kitchen and waved. "Hi, Mrs. Leibowicz. Thanks for the directions. They were easy to follow." She looked at the table and clapped her hands in delight. "Twins! How exciting. Tell me, who's who?"

"The little girl is Jillian and the little boy with all the curls is Jeremy. They are eleven months old and just beginning to walk. They have a couple of words, but so far, they're better at sign language than the spoken word."

"Fascinating. Do they also have a twin language they use with each other?"

"They do, although I can't distinguish the sounds."

"So, do you use American Sign Language with them? I ask because, when I was growing up, the little girl next door was deaf. I learned ASL along with her, although I only remember the action signs. I was never much good with the alphabet although I suppose that won't matter with babies who aren't ready to spell."

Elijah chose that moment to walk into the kitchen. Janice caught her breath. "What a beautiful cat!" She turned to the twins and spread her fingers on either side of her nose to make whiskers—the sign for cat.

Jillian cocked her head and looked puzzled. "Uruh," she said.

Sarah explained. "Uruh is her word for squirrel. A squirrel in the yard at the orphanage was the first animal she recognized, so now she calls every little animal a squirrel."

"She'll learn."

"Around here, she will need to," Sheila added. "Elijah is quite a famous cat, and he won't take kindly to being called a squirrel."

"Wait! Elijah? The famous cat from *Elijah, the Passover Guest*?"

"You know the book?"

"Of course. In the first family I worked for, the children wanted to read that book every night at bedtime. I can repeat it almost word for word."

Janice was as fascinated with the cat and the book's author as she was with the children. "You wrote the book? Wow! You must have made a fortune on it."

"No, not really."

"But you will. Elijah's popularity is still growing."

Sarah found the girl's enthusiasm a bit unsettling, but she blamed it on her over-active imagination.

"Oh, please, Mrs. Cohen. Tell me I can come work with the twins—and the cat."

"When can you start?"

"How about now?"

Sheila smiled with satisfaction at her matchmaking. "I'm going to get out of here and leave the two of you to put the house back together. Sarah, there will be some paperwork to be filled out, but since David will have to sign the consent forms, too, I'll drop by again this evening to get those signatures. If that's all right, I'll be here around seven."

Janice, meanwhile, was in the kitchen. Methodically, she checked the cupboards and the refrigerator to see what was available and where the various foods were stored. She chose lunch entrees for the babies and then began to assemble ingredients for Sarah's lunch.

"I thought you might need some comfort food," she said. "How does a cup of tomato soup sound, along with a grilled cheese sandwich?"

"Heavenly."

"Good. Suits me, too. In the meantime, why don't you take a soothing bath and relax a little? I'll run a bubble bath for you when I take the babies upstairs to get dressed. Oh, one question. Where do you keep the Pampers?"

"I don't use them. My mother-in-law gave me a long lecture on how many trees it takes to diaper a baby with Pampers for two years."

"What did she have to say about how much water it takes to wash cloth diapers for two years? And what about the pollution from detergents? Not a peep out of her on those costs, I'll bet. Nor is she the one washing, drying, and folding the cloth diapers. I have a big box of Pampers in the car. I'll go get them for you. What's more important—the life of a tree or your sanity?"

After lunch, Janice started a load of laundry and sent Sarah to her office to get caught up with email. She prepared a casserole of pasta primavera in Alfredo sauce and stored it in the fridge for dinner. "Pop it in the oven for thirty minutes," she instructed, and Sarah responded with "Yes, ma'am." Then she gave the house a quick straightening, vacuumed the living room, and dusted the flat surfaces. At four o'clock, she carried the twins down to their playpen and brought the mail in from the box out by the road.

"I'm through for the day," she announced, "but I'll be back first thing in the morning. What time do you get up?"

"Around six."

"All right. I'll be here by 6:30. Let's try for breakfast at seven. How do you and Mr. Cohen like your eggs—sunny side up or well done? I assume you don't eat bacon or sausage, but I could make grits or hash browns to go with the eggs. Which would you prefer?"

When Sarah described her new reality to David that evening, she commented, "It's like having a genie in a bottle. I wish for something, and she makes it happen. She's a miracle."

"Well, just keep in mind that she doesn't live in a glass bottle. As I remember, she used to live in a cardboard box at the side of a Chinese restaurant."

"What?" Sarah stared at him, befuddled. Slowly, the light came on. "Janice Highsmith? The Girl on the Porch?"

"The same."

CHAPTER 31

Having It All

December 2011

The first three weeks of December passed in a blur. At the Cohen house, Sarah continued to believe that she had let a genie out of her bottle. Janice, the mother's helper, had a seemingly unending repertoire of delicious meals to offer the family. In the mornings, her menu featured various egg dishes or blueberry pancakes or French toast with powdered sugar, and on cold mornings, big steaming bowls of oatmeal. In the evenings, the table featured casseroles, stews, and soups to warm the family's hearts as well as their stomachs. The children fared equally well, dining on pared-down and simplified versions of their parents' meals.

After a couple of days, Sarah gave up trying to tell Janice what needed to be done around the house The young woman was nearly always one step ahead. If Sarah suggested it was time to change the bedding, Janice was likely to say, "Yes, I know. The old sheets are already in the washer." Thus relieved of responsibility for housework, Sarah permitted herself to disappear for a couple of hours each morning and afternoon to work on the history of the Convent of St.Walburga. And if she happened to need a citation from the archival collections, her editorial assistant, Jean Pendergast, was more than happy to bring the needed book to the house. The manuscript's word count increased with every day that passed.

The new Elijah book continued to draw attention from both Jewish and Christian parents who were looking for a way to explain Hanukkah celebrations to their children. Now that Benny was back in school, Hannah visited book clubs and civic organizations during the week, thus further freeing Sarah to concentrate on her work as a writer. Even Hannah's husband Jacob, who usually kept his distance from his wife's projects, became involved, taking over the entries for Elijah's website and *Faces* page. In exchange, Sarah and David, accompanied by Elijah and the twins, spent Saturdays and sometimes Sunday afternoons visiting major bookstores and putting on library programs for both children and their parents. Sales multiplied. The stuffed Elijahs were becoming the 'Toy of the Year' and by mid-month, the entire supply of tiny Delilah kittens had been exhausted.

"When the holidays are over," Sarah promised, "we're all going out for the biggest steak dinners we can find."

Hannah agreed. "We certainly will have earned that, and the publishers can pay the bill. When they tally their sales figures for December, we may qualify as their star authors."

As the holidays approached, two other events brightened Sarah's days. The first began with a phone call from Julia

Winthrop on a Wednesday, asking if she could drop by that afternoon.

"I always have time to see you, Julia, but are you sure about being out and about? You must be close to delivery."

"I admit, I'm waddling. But I have some college news for you that you must see in person. I should be there around 3:30."

When the doorbell rang, Sarah embraced her friend and paid no attention to the vehicle in the driveway. "Now, what's so important it couldn't wait until your baby arrived?"

"Our church ladies threw me a baby shower while you were in Nashville. Honestly, it was a horror show—all pink cookies and punch, silly games, and useless gifts. It made me realize you were going to need a shower, too, but I refused to subject you to that kind of 1950s silliness.

"Then Beth Wilkinson came up with a brilliant idea. She proposed a literature shower. She asked the children's librarian at Barnes and Noble to prepare a list of the best-loved children's books of all time—everything from *Pat the Bunny* to *Harry Potter*. We invited our attendees to go to the bookstore, pick their favorite from the available list, sign the book with a message for the children, and deliver it to us via the department chair's office. The word got around, and we soon had people asking to join in. Even the cleaning lady asked to buy *Pat the Bunny*. Some of our other attendees bought whole sets of titles. We ended up with over a hundred books—a nice start to your children's library."

"A hundred books?"

"Yep. Kevin and Gabe are waiting out in the driveway. Kevin insisted we move the books out of his office, so they loaded them into Gabe's pickup. That's why we had to do this today. Can we let them in?"

This year's Hanukkah celebration, stretching from December 20th to the 28th, nicely coincided with Christmas. At the college, classes and exams were over and the library archives closed from December 23rd to January 2nd, forcing Sarah to take a break in her research. At City Hall, the courts were in recess. The Police Department, of course, had to gear up in anticipation of a few people who would carry their holiday celebrations to excess. But for the District Attorney's office and local law firms, litigants tabled their negotiations and postponed their arguments. Colored lights decorated nearly every available tree, and candles flickered on windowsills. Occasionally, a dusting of snow tossed a soft blanket over Birch Falls and reminded everyone to put their worries to rest for a few days.

The elder Cohens took charge of the family's holiday plans. Most of the relatives had not yet met the twins, so Leonard Cohen invited all the cousins to the family's Hannukah gatherings. Miriam agreed to do the cooking for the first four days and enlisted the women on her side of the family to help with early preparations each day. Sarah and David had only two responsibilities. First, they had to show up each day before sundown with neatly dressed twins. Then they needed to keep them from destroying the menorah before the candles could be lit. The children were suitably distracted when visiting cousins gave them small Hanukkah presents. They didn't even seem to object when they were bustled to their cribs upstairs before their grandmother served a dinner heavy on fried foods and sweets.

There were conflicts, of course. A few of the older relatives had nosy questions about the adoption process. Others questioned the appropriateness of the twins' names.

Their full names—Jeremiah Mikael and Jillian Devorah—had a slight Biblical derivation, but their everyday nick-names—Jeremy and Jill—were not overwhelmingly Jewish. When the issue arose for the third time, David came close to losing his patience. "Would you have preferred Mordicai and Bathsheeba," he asked. Sarah kicked him under the table and smiled at her in-laws. She knew she would even-tually have to deal with the same questions from her own family.

The Chomsky grandparents had also wanted to claim the twins for Hanukkah. The solution, at least temporarily, was an invitation for them to come to Tennessee and spend the holidays with Sarah and David. Sarah had pointed out that in Birch Falls, they wouldn't have to share their twins' time with all of the Chomsky relatives. She also promised to bring her family to New York City for a Passover reunion. The current plan, assuming the weather cooperated, was for the Chomskys to fly into Nashville on Christmas morning and stay until the end of the month.

As the beginning of Hanukkah came closer, Sarah broached the question of time off for Janice. "When Hanukkah begins on the 20th, we will be very involved with David's parents at their house. There won't be much for you to do here. If you'd like to take a few days to visit your family, we'll be fine."

"Visit my family? Hah! I don't ever remember them cele-brating Christmas. We didn't even have a tree. I quit believing in Santa Claus around the age of four. My mother's idea of a celebration was simply to have another drink. My father was usually off somewhere doing whatever he needed to do to get his hands on his next snort of cocaine. That's why I'm here, remember? To get away from all of that."

"Yes, I remember you telling us about them. I just

thought perhaps now that you're an adult, your relationship with your family might improve."

"Not a chance. The problem was not that I was a rebellious teenager. The problem was that I was the only adult in the family from the time I was a child. No, no, if I won't be in the way, I'd rather stay here on the job helping out when I can. I can at least fix breakfast, make beds, take out the garbage, and feed the cats. Besides, I'm really curious about Hanukkah. I'd like to be a fly on the wall and watch how you celebrate."

"Well, then, why don't we just consider you a member of the family? You'll be welcome to join in whenever you feel comfortable doing so. You can even come along with us to visit David's parents. I'm sure Mrs. Cohen would be happy to have you."

"No. That's going too far. But I'll be available if and when you need me."

Janice's instincts proved correct. The Chomskys arrived on Christmas morning, and they were thrilled to meet their new grandchildren. They did, however, make a lot of extra work around the house. Janice found more than enough chores to fill her vacation days.

It was not until the last day of Hanukkah that Sarah and her mother finally found time to sit down and have a mother-daughter talk over a cup of tea.

"Motherhood agrees with you," Mrs. Chomsky remarked. "You're glowing. And the children's attachment to you is obvious. How lucky you all are to have found each other."

"You're right, but I am convinced there was much more to it than luck. From the moment I laid eyes on the twins for the second time, I knew they were meant to be my children. I told David that day that HaShem had dropped them into my lap twice. I had no intention of asking him to do it a third time. I got the message."

"I'm so happy for you. I've always known you'd be a wonderful mother."

"Well, there have been times when I doubted that. I still doubt it, if the truth is known."

"Sarah! How can you ...?"

"There's still an issue of trying to have it all. I'm not teaching this year, so I'm free to be home whenever I'm needed. I'll have to go back to the classroom in August, though, and I'm not sure I can juggle taking care of two children here and a hundred or more older children passing through my classes."

Sarah's mother saw it as an appropriate question for Hanukkah. "That's what Hanukkah is all about, isn't it? Succeeding, despite facing the impossible? So, where did your idea come from—the one that says you can't have it all?"

"It came from a woman who spent her life teaching in the classics department at Columbia. The year I was on the job market at AHA, we were also interviewing candidates for our ancient world history position. One of the applicants was a middle-aged woman, and Dr. Hall pointed her out to me one evening in the hotel restaurant. "We'll never hire her. Just look at her over there, having dinner with her husband and teenage son. Imagine bringing your whole family to your interview! Poor oblivious creature. Someone needs to tell her that sooner or later she will have to choose between a family and a career. No woman can handle both full-time responsibilities. You can't have it all."

"And you believed her? You should have talked to your advisor about it."

"I did, and Dr. Kaplan explained why she believed as she did. He was a new professor when she came up for tenure in the early 1980s, so he witnessed her crisis. She was dating a young man at the time, and the committee asked her outright if she planned to marry him. When she admitted that they were engaged, they gave her an ultimatum—marriage or tenure. She chose her career and returned the fellow's ring."

"Did she ever marry?"

"No. She accepted the ultimatum, although Dr. Kaplan said she hated teaching."

"How sad."

"Her story gets even sadder. She had never been to Europe and had never seen the Mediterranean or the cities she taught about. Because she was a single woman, she knew she had to save her money for retirement. She had her career, and she had her savings, but when she finally retired, she decided to make up for lost ground. It was time she got a taste of having it all, she told her colleagues.

"She planned a trip to Rome and Athens, financing it by applying for a job as a tourist guide in the cities she knew well from reading about them. She looked forward to spending her time with eager tourists who shared her love of the ancient world. The job, as you might imagine, kept her on her feet, climbing up and down hills and ancient buildings all day long. At age 65, she found it exhausting. The porter found her dead in her hotel room three days after her arrival.

"Dr. Kaplan said it was the general opinion around the department that the end of her life proved the statement by which she had lived her life. She didn't get to have it all."

"May her life be a blessing to her students. But it is one of the saddest stories I have ever heard. Surely, daughter, you do not believe her example is one to follow."

Sarah sighed. "Well, the first day with the twins was a disaster. I still can't handle it all without Janice's help. Right now, I can be a wife, a mother, and a writer, but what will happen when I have to return to the classroom? I dread discovering that I have over-reached my limit."

"I'm going to hope David's support is enough to help. He can give you the confidence your Dr. Hall did not seem to have."

"On the contrary, Ima. David, too, has come to realize her view is valid. He is doing well as the district attorney, but he is aware that he will eventually have to take over the family law firm. And he knows there is a conflict of interest. He cannot do both. So, yes, mother. We have both accepted the pronouncement, which means we will be forever conflicted."

CHAPTER 32

Choices

December 29, 2011

"Let's talk about Professor Hall a bit more," Mrs. Chomsky suggested the next afternoon. "From your description, it sounds like she and I are almost the same age. If she retired in 2005 at the age of sixty-five, she was born in 1940. So was I. World War II was waging in Europe, although the United States remained neutral until the end of 1941. Our pre-school memories, however, preserve the images of war—the attack on Pearl Harbor, the enlistment of young men going off to fight the enemy, rationing, blackout curtains, newsreels full of bomb footage, air raid warnings, the ominous appearance of gold stars that appeared in windows to indicate the family had lost a son in battle.

"After the war, our world faced major adjustments. While a whole generation of young American men—nearly a half million in all—had died or suffered permanent physical disabilities, many others came home to resume their lives.

The women who had waited for their return had filled their war years by assuming unfamiliar responsibilities. They had worked in factories, run small businesses, and cared for aging parents. Then, at the end of the war, they needed to step back to make room for the returning soldiers who had lost years of education and work experience. A new generation—the baby boomers—required thousands of those women to return to roles as wives and mothers. The new realities required new gender rules, and women felt those changes as sharply as men did.

"Do you remember an old quiz show that offered contestants a chance to choose one of three doors? At my high school graduation, my female classmates asked each other, 'What are you going to be? A teacher? A nurse? Or are you getting married?' Those were our three doors. After ten or fifteen years of changes, they were still a woman's only acceptable choices. We didn't get to think about being doctors, pilots, scientists, weather predictors, lawyers, or stockbrokers. We didn't get to choose—we knew we couldn't have it all. So maybe I can understand Dr. Hall better than you can.

"Now think about the woman whose application was rejected because she was traveling with a husband and a teenage son. She was fairly close to the baby boomer age group, wasn't she—certainly closer to my age than to yours? To a woman who grew up during the war years, she must have seemed to be violating all the rules. You internalized that pronouncement about having it all, but it was not meant for you. Whether she realized it or not, Dr. Hall was talking about herself as well as that woman—and me—and all the others like us. I chose motherhood and never regretted it. But sometimes in the middle of the night, I wonder what else I might have done with my life if I had chosen a different door.

"That's what makes me so excited about the promise of your generation. You can open every door, and many of you go after that wider goal. Not everyone does, of course, and that's all right, too. But look at yourself—a professor, a wife, a mother, a writer. You have found a way to do everything you want to do. You already have several open doors, and you use them well."

"Do I? The odds are against me, I think. I'm pretty overwhelmed, especially when I think about returning to the classroom. Can I still write lectures that entertain students while they learn? Will I give a star performance after being up all night with a sick child? And what about when the children start school? Will their school hours conflict with my schedule? Can I find time to go to a teacher conference or chaperone a field trip? Without a mother's helper to support me, I'm sure I'm going to be lost."

"Janice is not just a crutch for you to lean on, Sarah. She's a necessity."

"You never had one. As I remember my childhood, you didn't even like using a babysitter now and then."

"No, I never needed a mother's helper. I had nothing else to do. But you ... you have juggler's pins flying through the air. You need a catcher, so you have found one. When you go back to the classroom, the twins will be old enough to go to the college nursery—another necessary tool. You'll keep doing everything you do so well."

"I understand what you're saying, but I still hear that voice telling me I can't have it all. It may mean something different to me than it does to you. For my generation, the problem may be that we have too many choices. And in my case, I have this feeling that if I face three doors, I have to open all three. And then there will be more doors waiting to be opened. Let me give you an example.

"I passed my third-year review, but that's not the end of the challenge the academic world has in store for me. Now I have to earn tenure and promotion to associate professor at the end of my fifth year at the university. Will I be finished then? No. After tenure, they can't fire me without cause. But there's a final promotion waiting out there, this time to a full professorship. I'll have ten more years to accomplish that, but it will require another book beyond whatever I've done in the first five years."

"Is the full professorship that important?"

"Maybe not, but without it, I can't retire with the title of Professor Emerita and remain listed as a member of the permanent faculty. And without Emerita status, I revert to being no one but Mrs. Cohen. No more academic confer-ences, no more published articles, no more books handled by university presses. End of career."

"There's no alternative?"

"Well, it's possible to become a department chair with just an associate professorship. That's the path our current chair has chosen for himself. But then, he's a man; he has less to prove."

"Nevertheless, it sounds like a worthy goal."

"Yes, but the full professorship comes with more goals to shoot for—the possibility of becoming the academic dean, and then maybe a vice president, or the president of the college ... You see how it continues to grow?"

"I'm tired just thinking about it! I'm sure you'll make the right choices along the way. But you must not compare your-self to my generation. You ought to look at those who are your contemporaries. How are they managing?"

"The ones I know are as confused as I am. Let's start with

Julia and Will because you've met them. She is a prize-winning historian and one of the best lecturers I have ever heard. But when she and Will decided to start a family, she timed her pregnancy to coincide with a sabbatical leave. She wanted both motherhood and professorship, but she deliberately chose to keep them separate, at least for the first year or so.

"Julia went into labor two days before Christmas. We got a call from Will the next morning. 'Little Maddie Rae is here, and she has all the usual appendages,' he reported. 'She weighs seven pounds and has a great pair of lungs. In other words, she's perfect.' Julia understands the motherhood half of the bargain. We'll have to wait to see how she manages when the second half of her responsibility comes due.

"Julia and Will are also dedicated to fostering Ronnie, a fourteen-year-old boy whose parents virtually abandoned him. Julia adores him. She's been helping him see the new baby as a responsibility, not a rival—all of which is good—but Will feels some resentment about sharing Ronnie's attention.

"It also doesn't help that Ronnie is pushing to try out for the Olympic running team, and Will won't let him. Will wants to be the perfect father for Ronnie, but he correctly understands it is too early for Ronnie to compete—and at this stage, the disappointment might discourage him forever. So he can't give Ronnie what he wants. And his offer to take the family to London for the 2012 Olympics feels like salt in a wound to Ronnie because he will be a spectator, not a competitor. As for Julia, she wants to treat both her children equally, but they are going to be too far apart in age to see each other as companions. Julia is also irritated with Will, who seems to be so focused on Ronnie that he forgets about the baby. They all want a perfect family but are not close to getting it. Is this exactly what Julia feared would happen? And is she maybe helping to make the trouble? I don't know, and neither does she. She's ambitious and confident about her career, but less certain when it comes to her family.

"We are also close friends with a dating couple at the university. Lyle Agaretti is in the biology department, where he's investigating the medicinal and hallucinogenic properties of mushrooms. Beth Wilkerson teaches Victorian literature in the English department. They are both great fun away from campus, but the career question looms over them, too. Lyle thinks the only important studies are in the sciences. He makes fun of the liberal arts and doesn't take Beth seriously as a scholar. What's worse is that Beth is beginning to accept his view. I think she would like to get married, even though she knows he would never see her job as equal to his career. He is already eating away at her self-confidence.

"Then there is the dilemma faced by Gabriel Ramirez and Maria Hernandez. He's a first-year history professor, and Maria is a brilliant student. They are attracted to one another by their Hispanic backgrounds, despite the differences in their ages and positions at the college. As a graduating senior, she is applying for a White House Fellowship for next year. She is highly qualified, and Gabe has pledged to support her application.

"The problem there is that Gabe has decided he will quit his job and follow her if she goes to Washington. Maria clearly understands that Gabe's presence in DC would be so smothering as to destroy her chances at a political activist career. While she loves him, she needs to leave him behind or give up her dream. She cannot have them both. As for Gabe, he is beginning to realize that it would be a huge mistake to quit his job. He can't have it both ways, either.

"The issue of two-career families seems to plague many of my older students. Chad Overstreet and Olivia Cartwright have not yet married, but they are living together. They both work for Cartwright Industries, but last year, Olivia inherited the company from her father. Chad runs the charitable foundation behind the company and is their public relations representative. Now she's the boss and he works for her—a reversal of society's rules. Can they both accept the uncharacteristic business rules and have a traditional romantic relationship? Maybe not. She can't walk into their apartment and shed her authority like a raincoat. And he can't give up the romantic dominance he maintains at home to say, 'Yes, ma'am' at the factory.

"Neither Emily Pottersfield nor her partner Farah Mahmud was happy with their decision to move to Tennessee. They were both accustomed to the bustle of big-city life and found our rural atmosphere boring. But their problem, like so many others, was that they had very different needs. Emily wanted to be an academic; she needed that ivory tower. Farah needed the stimulus of the artsy world in a big city. So now, Emily has decided to quit her job and follow Farah back to London. But will that work any better? I doubt it."

"So, are all your friends involved in troubled relationships?" Mrs. Chomsky asked.

"Well, no. Several are single and focused on their individual goals. Ramona Bishop is still convinced that there is a vertical labyrinth hidden in the outdoor amphitheater on campus—despite much evidence that such a thing has never existed anywhere. Matt keeps postponing his move to Knoxville to do his doctoral work in classics because he can't bear the thought of selling his gay bar. And Jean Pendergast has just offered to pick up an adjunct slot at the university to fill in for Emily's departure—although that means not taking a full-time job in her husband's school.

"All three would vigorously deny having any conflicting motives. But they all seem to be settling for becoming less than they could be. And maybe that's what scares me the most. Our lives offer us multiple doors and then start locking them again. I see us reaching the end of our lives drowning in disappointment because we failed to be all we could have been."

"That sounds a lot like the description of my middle-of-the-night musings." Mrs. Chomsky said.

"It does, indeed. So maybe the choices of our generations are not so far apart after all."

CHAPTER 33

Vespers—The Sixth Hour

F*rom the journal of Jenny May Foster, later known as Sister Genevieve Marie, and now, by the grace of God, as Mother Genevieve, Mother Superior of this Convent of Our Lady St. Walburga:*

August 1918

I always think of myself as Sister Genevieve Marie. I have never quite accepted my role as Mother Superior of St. Walburga's Nunnery, although I have held that title for forty-two years. I am extremely good at managing numbers, but not so skilled when it comes to people. I don't make small talk with anyone, nor do I have any real friends among the nuns over whom I preside. I even hate small duties like this one—calling attention to the time and urging my sisters to fulfill their religious obligations.

I cringed inside even as I spoke the standard warning. "Come, sisters. Put down your tools and make your way to the chapel while it's still light enough to see your path.

Sunset will come soon, even though it still feels like summer. It's nearly time for Vespers, and we must not be late."

On this particular day, I knew I would be called upon to report two items of heartbreaking news as part of my prayer for God's intervention in the world at large. In France, allied troops are wrapping up the Second Battle of the Marne. Although our forces have won, it appears that over 137,000 men from the United States, England, France, Italy, and Siam have been killed or wounded in France during the last two weeks. Such a victory is not news that any Christian should welcome. Nor do I have any idea of how to justify the killing of one's fellow Christians in the name of peace. I have only the words of President Woodrow Wilson to quote: "a war to end all wars" that will "make the world safe for democracy."

But the news about the current pandemic is even worse. Medical authorities now estimate that before this pandemic of influenza runs its course in 1918-1919, over 25 million people will have died worldwide. I cannot wrap my mind around such numbers. Nor can I offer any comfort to those who have lost loved ones. And so, on this crucial day, I hesitated in the doorway of the Chapter House and prayed for guidance. When I lifted my head from prayer, one of the younger sisters approached me.

"Is there something special about Vespers today, Mother Genevieve? My prayer book describes the hour of Vespers, or Evening Prayer, as a time to give thanks for the closing day—to be grateful for the specific gifts of the day—the warmth of the sun, the gentle morning shower that softened the ground, the first harvest of fruits and vegetables. The Psalmists call upon us to sing the praises of God for his generosity, and the priest urges us to pray for God's continued assistance during the days to come. But we pray those prayers every day and at every hour, do we not?"

"We do, indeed, my child, but during these days, we are in special need of His guidance."

"Why is that?"

"Because no one has ever told us how to pray about a war or an uncontrollable pandemic."

~

Whenever I look out over our cloister gardens and wonder at their beauty, pride in our success fills my heart. Our first six sisters arrived here in 1843 to face a bare plot of ground, a ramshackle barn, and a well. What they built with God's help during the following 75 years is nothing short of a miracle. The success of St. Walburga's Nunnery is a great gift, and no one needs to remind me of God's astonishing generosity.

We share the blessings of our cloister area. Several of my sisters helped to design the flower beds and nurture the plants. Sister Clementine, our trained nurse, spent hours expanding the herb garden to include medicinal plants. All of us, I suspect, have turned to the cloister for comfort in times of stress. And there is a great solace to be found in our protecting walls and buildings. The church, reception hall, refectory, and chapter house enclose our lives and help us center our thoughts and prayers on doing the will of God.

Without looking, I can also picture the back quadrangle of our convent. Those structures reflect our vocations. An orphanage now joins a hospital area with its original maternity house. The central area has become a playground for our children and an exercise area for hospital patients. Facing the orphanage is our protective home for the elderly. To my growing pleasure, the old folks and the children love one another and often share their free time.

Behind these residential buildings and forming the rear boundary of our convent grounds lies our agricultural area. A solid barn houses a menagerie of helpers that work for us—cows, sheep, and goats giving milk for the dairy, chickens leaving their eggs for our breakfasts, and horses plowing our fields and delivering supplies. Local women come often to tend our vegetable gardens and the fruit orchard and help us preserve the crops that feed us all winter long. Scattered all through the grounds, our dogs protect us, and the cats keep the mice under control.

We have created an amazing place of worship, love, and charity, but now it is complete. And in the Vespers service at the end of the day's work, we must remember to be properly grateful after this long effort. This is what I have been commemorating during recent Vespers.

But now that the war news has started reaching our local news with more regularity, I remember there is more to Vespers than gratitude. As we read and listen to the Canticle of Mary in Luke 1:46–55, Mary reminds us that God favors the lowly among us and rejects those who have risen to high places--reason enough to forswear any pride we take in our accomplishments.

> *My soul magnifies the Lord,*
> *and my spirit rejoices in God my Savior,*
> *for he has looked with favor on the lowliness of his servant.*
> *Surely, from now on all generations will call me blessed,*
> *for the Mighty One has done great things for me,*
> *and holy is his name.*

Her verses also remind us that God often oversees a reversal of human fortunes. We will take time to reflect on how the mighty are brought low while the lowly soar on the wings of angels.

> *He has brought down the powerful from their thrones,*
> *and lifted up the lowly:*
> *he has filled the hungry with good things,*
> *and sent the rich away empty.*

And finally, we will acknowledge the fulfillment of an Old Testament promise made to Abraham by God—that his people shall make a great nation and that great blessing shall descend upon them. It comes in Gen. 12:1-3:

> *Now Yahweh said to Abraham,*
> *"Go from your country and your kindred and your father's house*
> *to the land that I will show you.*
> *And I will make of you a great nation,*
> *and I will bless you and make your name great*
> *so that you will be a blessing.*
> *I will bless those who bless you,*
> *and him who dishonors you I will curse,*
> *and in you, all the families of the earth shall be blessed."*

With all these thoughts swirling in my head, I joined my sisters for daily Vesper service with mixed emotions. One part of me took great comfort in Mary's *Magnificat*, whose words reminded me to follow Mary's inspiration: "My soul doth magnify the Lord." Meanwhile, a nagging voice in the back of my mind kept reminding me that today's world was different and would require something new from me. I must speak to my sisters of war and then pray for God's intercession in the affairs of the world. But here, too, the words of Mary reminded me that the Lord still keeps his promises to Abraham and his people forever. The intercessory prayer I offer must convey a message of hope. That will allow us to finish our devotions with The Lord's Prayer and a final blessing: Go in Peace.

Easy enough to say; difficult to accept. I see my sisters struggling. For many, the news that America was joining in the fight that has been tearing Europe apart came as a shock. From the beginning, I could read their fears: "My brother! My father! My cousins! My uncles!" They had trusted the barrier of a great ocean between us and the warring factions to keep their families safe here in America. But now their young men have boarded ships and dashed headlong into danger. There is bravery—or perhaps bravado —in their war cry:

Tell them the Yanks are coming,
The Yanks are coming,
And we won't go home
Till it's over, over there.

The fears of loved ones left behind echoed as the ships sailed off. They had to face the reality that not every Yank who plunged headlong into the conflict would return safely. Some would suffer debilitating physical injuries from terrifying new weapons. Others would bear permanent mental and emotional scarring. And some would disappear into unmarked graves. How can anyone go in peace while men die in war?

Is it any wonder that I have never enjoyed serving as mother superior over our convent? The problems overwhelm me, and the solutions seem far away. On this day, before

Vespers, I sought consolation for myself and for my sisters in the words of one who walked this same path centuries ago.

Julian of Norwich, England's first anchoress, was born in 1342. As any historian will testify, the fourteenth century was a dark period, full of wars, dynastic quarrels, failed crops, a changing climate, and fast-spreading disease. In 1337, war broke out between the Plantagenet royal family of England and the Valois line on the French throne. Inter-marriages complicated the relationships between the two families and resulted in what has become known in later generations as the Hundred Years' War.

The English use of cannons at the Battle of Crécy in 1346 began to change the nature of European warfare, making the killing of one's enemy a less personal act. Death by cannon-ball was violent, of course, but the shooter did not have to look his enemy in the eye as did the swordsman.

Bubonic plague had been traveling along trade routes for years, killing as many as a third of those who lived in cities. In 1348, when Julian was only six years old, the disease leaped the channel to England and caused periodic outbreaks for the next twenty or twenty-five years.

Just as our nuns now feel threatened by World War I and influenza, so Julian's generation struggled with the Hundred Years' War and the plague. And when I compare the two periods—six hundred years apart—I see them asking the same question. Why is God letting these terrible things happen? Perhaps Julian's solution will help my nuns just as she guided the parishioners of Norwich in the fourteenth century.

When Julian was just thirty, she came down with a grave

illness. Was it plague? No one was sure, but the disease was so severe she did not expect to recover. As she struggled to accept her fate, she experienced a series of dreams—or perhaps hallucinations or visions—in which God revealed sixteen messages to her. The promise for which she is best remembered is this one:

All shall be well,
And all shall be well,
And all manner of things shall be well,
For there is a force of nature
moving through the universe
that holds us fast
and will never let us go.

Julian recovered miraculously and became an anchoress living with her cat in a cell attached to the church in Norwich. And from there she wrote her famous book, *Revelations of Divine Love*, which attempted to explain how God could promise that "all would be well" when it was obvious that all was very bad, indeed.

Her explanation? "God is Love. No matter what seems to happen, God's Love will never let us go."

Perhaps that is the lesson my ladies need to learn. We will talk about it at dinner this evening.

CHAPTER 34
All Manner of Things

May 1, 2012

"I swear, Elijah! If you kick the food bowl over one more time, I will start feeding you on the back porch. And don't give me that pitiful look, cat. Eat it off the floor if you're hungry. I haven't time to sweep up after you."

"Whoa, Elijah! Sounds like you're in trouble with the head of the household. We have a family motto around here: 'When Mama ain't happy, ain't nobody happy.'"

David was watching his wife with mixed emotions. One part of him had to laugh at her anger with her favorite cat; the other was concerned about another early morning temper tantrum. "Bad night?" he asked.

"Not bad. Just too short. I stayed up past two o'clock to finish the final chapter of the nunnery book. I was so close to the end I couldn't bear to stop."

"You're finished?"

"Well, the first draft is finished although I haven't re-read those last few pages. They could be pure drivel. And it still needs a chapter covering the meaning of the seventh liturgical hour, Compline. But at the moment I'm not emotionally ready to handle that."

"It sounds to me like you need a break. Janice, can you stay through lunch today and take care of the twins so that Mrs. Cohen and I can get away for an hour or two?"

"Sure, Mr. Cohen. I usually just mess around on my lunch break anyhow. I'll be glad to take over here."

"David, I really shouldn't ..."

"Yes, my dear, you really should. Do what you like with your morning, but meet me in front of Isolde's at noon."

"Isolde's? For lunch? You know I can't resist going there. It's a date."

Once seated at their favorite banquette, David reached for Sarah's hands. "Hello there, Mrs. Cohen. It's been a long time since I've had you all to myself."

"I know. The last few months have kept me crazy busy, but things should settle down over the summer."

"I won't take that as a promise, but I do hope you remember this is an anniversary date for us."

"Anniversary? What...? Oh, it's May Day, isn't it? The day we first knew we had something special going on."

The waiter who approached their table was new, but he was closely followed by Chef Andre Ramón. "These are some of my favorite people. I'll take care of the Cohens personally, Jonah. Just bring them a bottle of sparkling water and a couple of iced glasses, please."

"I'm happy to see you here at lunchtime," he continued. "It'll give you a chance to sample another area of our new summer menu. We have a special today that you both might enjoy. It's a four-cheese soufflé, enhanced by chives, chopped spinach, and crispy bacon, or we can substitute soy-based bacon bits if you prefer. It comes with a loaf of crusty bread and a deconstructed fruit salad, with all the flavors of the season."

"That sounds perfect, Andre, so long as you throw in a couple of glasses of Sauvignon Blanc and let us dawdle the early afternoon away."

"Wine at noon, David?" Sarah looked doubtful.

"Why not? You need to relax. Now, tell me about the book. You used to complain about the unfamiliar rituals within the nunnery. Did the practices change over time? Or did you?"

"Of course, the language changed as the years passed, but the big change has been in my understanding. Once I began to see the mother superior as an ordinary human charged with enormous responsibility, my sympathy grew accordingly. These women taught me a great deal. They also helped me grow as a historian."

"How so?"

"In 1918, Sister Genevieve Marie was in charge. She had held the title of mother superior for forty-two years, but this was the most difficult year yet. The United States had just joined the allied forces in what became known as World War I, and American men were suffering great casualties. The world was also fighting an influenza pandemic that was killing thousands. The sisters of St. Walburga's nunnery were frightened and disheartened. Genevieve looked for a way to reassure them during Vespers, and she found it in the words of St. Julian of Norwich, a fourteenth-century anchoress.

"The fourteenth century was a dark period in England's history. Their country was at war with France in what became known as the Hundred Years' War. And when Julian was only six years old, bubonic plague jumped the English Channel and killed nearly a third of the population. You see the parallels?"

"Of course, but ..."

"When Julian was thirty, she fell seriously ill and did not expect to recover. We don't know if it was the plague, but it's quite possible. In any event, during her delirium, she had a series of visions or delusions. She claimed they were revelations from God, and when she miraculously recovered, she began to write a book about the divine messages she had received. Her most famous prediction declared, 'And all manner of things shall be well.' It finishes with

this:

> *There is a force of nature*
> *moving through the universe*
> *that holds us fast*
> *and will never let us go.*

That was exactly the message the nuns needed to hear. As did I."

"It reminds me of an often-quoted line from a poem called 'Desiderata':

> *And whether or not it is clear to you,*
> *no doubt the universe is unfolding*
> *as it should.*

"It's the same thought, isn't it, David? There's no mention of a specific religion—no Christianity, Judaism, or Zen Buddhism, for that matter—just the assertion that we are all a part of the universe.

"And I suspect the current crop of Catholic clergy will find it as moving as we do. Nicely done, my dear."

"Well, it's not quite the end of the book. It still needs a wrap-up chapter to cover Compline, the closing of the nunnery, and the sale of the property. But Julian's *Revelations* all point to the inevitability of that development."

"Fair enough. You'll know when you are ready. Now, what about Elijah #3?"

"You're referring to *Elijah and the High Holy Days*. At least, that's the temporary title, according to your sister. I'm still holding out for *Elijah's Fast* or *No Cat Should Go Hungry*. Whatever we decide to call it, we'll be ready to publish by late August.

"We have a pretty good handle on the contents, and Hannah is already producing sketches. We're also negotiating with the publisher to put a sound effects button on one page. Push it and you get a blast of the shofar. Rabbi Leibowicz has already volunteered to do the recording, but the publisher is worried that awful sound will alienate the parents who pay for the books."

"So, are you covering Rosh Hashana, the whole ten days of prayer and repentance, or just Yom Kippur?"

"The ten days, but only the highlights. We'll do your favorite sugar-loaded dinner celebration to welcome the new year. That's where we will include the shofar and a picture of Elijah hiding under the bed and covering his furry little ears.

"We'll describe the prayer days, and several pages will deal with Elijah's conscience as he remembers his sins—like the time he stole the lamb chop off the kitchen counter. Benny gets to add his discovery of Tashlich as he tries to explain how to demonstrate repentance. Elijah can't find a body of water, but he will repent and try to go to the synagogue for morning prayers. Did you know your mother is crocheting a little prayer shawl and matching yarmulke for Elijah to wear at book signings?"

"Oy Veh!"

"He'll join the fast, too, with Delilah saving a few tasty bites for him during the day."

"The story sounds wonderful."

"I think it will be, but we're going to stop there before we wear out our welcome. Now, tell me about what's happening at the courthouse. I know you've been busy, but you haven't said much about what you've been handling."

Over coffee, David launched his tale of discovery. "We've had our usual run of small-town disputes, family quarrels over inheritances, petty thefts, domestic disturbances, and teenage antics. But the case that resonates covers a three-state area.

"You may remember the terrible automobile accident that occurred two years ago. Two high school seniors were headed to their senior prom. The boy was driving his graduation present, a new Japanese sports car.

"It was hit and crushed by a large tractor driven by two farmers who were also killed when they were thrown from their seats by the impact. The boy's father, Brendan O'Malley, sued Galyeon Motors for selling a new car that had defective brakes. The O'Malley family hired the Cohen Law Firm to represent them. The case of O'Malley versus Galyeon then went to the police department because of the high death toll and the implications for others who might have bought similar cars.

"Negligence is hard to prove, and the dealer had paperwork showing this was a new car that had been thoroughly inspected. But something about the case bothered me. I assigned one of our young investigators to look for possible water damage during transport from Japan to Texas or from hurricanes in the area two years ago.

"He found probable cause to suspect water damage between September 6 and 9, 2010. Tropical storm Hermine made landfall in Mexico and moved across Texas, not as a hurricane but still strong enough to be a dangerous storm. In a small town about twenty-five miles northeast of Austin, a huge thunderstorm dumped sixteen inches of water on the town and hit vulnerable buildings with wind gusts from fifty to seventy miles per hour. When the clouds lifted, much of the downtown area was underwater. Sixty-eight homes were destroyed, and more than five hundred others suffered damage. One hundred people were trapped by the high floods and had to be rescued from rising waters.

"One of the hardest hit businesses was a local car dealership that handled the major Japanese models. In the days after the flood waters receded, several people took pictures of the car lot. They showed the cars standing in mud and draining water from open doors, hoods, and engine compartments. Our investigator asked for records of the repairs to those cars. He found none. Instead, the cars had been sold to a dealer in Alabama using the original invoices from Japan instead of repair orders. You-Pull-It Auto Parts turned out to be a glorified chop shop."

"What's a chop shop?"

"It's an illegal business. They buy cars with questionable ownership and cut them into non-identifiable pieces. Then they sell them as parts to people doing their own repairs. As you might imagine, the shop owner gets a great price break when he buys the cars and makes even more money when he sells the parts. The company was, in other words, a central clearing house for stolen automobiles.

"But in this case, they bought over one hundred flood-damaged new cars from various dealers in Texas. To give them credit, they did good work. They cleaned the cars, shampooed and dried the upholstery, painted over rust spots, and polished the engine compartment. Then they sold the cars to new car dealers in Tennessee, using the same new car certifications and bills of sale from Japan.

"And then, the Tennessee dealers sold the vehicles as brand new, once again using the original bills of sale. Every dealer through whose hands the cars passed got a terrific price break on the cost of the vehicle and then sold it at exorbitant new car prices. Everyone profited except, of course, the families of the two farmers, along with Patrick O'Malley and his girlfriend Melissa Higgins. All of them died because of the deliberate negligence of those who handled the cars after the flood. With that information, our investigator had a mechanic tear the wrecked sports car apart. He found holes in the brake lines caused by erosion from salt water picked up by the storm. Patrick must have seen the tractor coming and slammed on the brakes. Unfortunately, he no longer had any brakes."

"Wow! What's going to happen to everyone?"

"Well, the trials are still going on and will be tied up in civil courts for years. But already the three dealers—Buddy Jamison in Texas, Tom Highsmith in Alabama, and Richard Galyeon in Birch Falls have all been found guilty of gross negligence, fraud, falsification of VINs, and money laundering. They are going to prison for many years, each one in his state, and their businesses will be sold to help pay for civil charges of negligence, up to and including unintentional manslaughter."

"Wait. Thomas Highsmith in Alabama? Is he related to Janice? It's an unusual name and the right geographic area."

I don't think it's her father. This Mr. Highsmith has no previous criminal record, while Janice's father is a dedicated cocaine addict with a lengthy arrest record. He may, however, be an uncle or a cousin. I do not intend to ask her or even mention their names around her. She has split away from the family, and I do not want to interfere with that."

"I'm glad, but it sounds like you're still going to be tied up with these cases for quite some time."

"Yes, indeed, but dad's law firm is already reaping great rewards. not to mention the fact that it was his son who broke the case." For the first time, David grinned at the story.

"David, I'm so pleased for you. That should smooth your entry into the law firm."

"It will. So perhaps Julian was right. All manner of things shall be well."

CHAPTER 35

Summer Interlude

July 2012

When the phone rang, Sarah was chin-deep in research. She nodded to Janice to handle whoever was calling. She was not pleased, however, to overhear Janice's side of the conversation.

"Absolutely! I know she needs a break. Why don't you bring Maddie Rae and come over for lunch? I'll stir up something easy and yummy. The twins will be fascinated by the baby, and maybe you and Sarah can have time to relax. Great. See you around 11:30."

"Janice! Don't make plans for me without checking. I'm buried in this last chapter."

"That was Julia, and you haven't talked to her in weeks. I know you've been writing, but a break will do you good."

"But …"

"No buts! Part of my job is to keep you healthy, and that means seeing to it that you eat well, get enough rest, smile, and keep track of your friends."

"Okay, you've made your point, and lunch sounds delicious. I've been obsessing over this ending for too long. But if Julia and the baby don't go home by 2:30, you'll have to send them packing somehow."

"Sure. I'll stage a fire drill or bribe the twins to scream in unison."

Despite her protests, Sarah grinned at the first glimpse of her best friend. "Julia! I've missed you. And just look at that little sleeping angel. She's grown so much since those first days in the hospital nursery. Come in and get Maddie settled in the extra playpen. Janice is just finishing the twins' lunch, and then they'll be headed straight for nap time. Maybe we can keep all three of the babies asleep long enough to let us have lunch in peace."

"I hope you realize how lucky you are to have Janice here to help you. Aunt Flo has been staying with us ever since Maddie was born. She's good with the baby stuff, but I can't ask her to do the cooking or housework."

"I'm blessed, I know. And wait till you taste Janice's cooking! But I'm dying to hear about your trip to London. Did things work out the way Will hoped they would?"

"They did. Ronnie grumbled on the way to the airport, but once we got there, we learned that he had never been on a plane. The poor kid was terrified at first and then fascinated by the kinds of things we take for granted—tray tables, reclining seats, pretty flight attendants, complimentary pretzels, tiny bathrooms. It was really fun to watch his discoveries. He even loved the airline food and those little toiletry bags they gave us!"

"What about the Olympics?"

"Will's coaching friend recommended that we arrive in London the week before the opening so that Ronnie could observe some of what goes on behind the scenes. He visited the Olympic Village, met the American track and field team, and even worked out with the athletes. That was a real eye-opener for him. For the first time, he realized what Will meant when he said Ronnie was too young to participate. Teenagers grow so fast that the seventeen-year-olds seemed twice as big—and fast—as our little tenth-grader. By the time the competitions started, he was more than ready to join us in the stands rather than having to compete against the 'big guys.'

"We had to leave for home right after the opening ceremonies, but he was satisfied. And since we've been home, he's been glued to the television, watching every track event, keeping notes on track records, and checking out the younger competitors from other countries.

"The trip was a worthwhile investment, even if I didn't get to do the touristy stuff. While Ronnie and Will were meeting the athletes, Maddie and I stayed at the hotel, indulged in their full English breakfast every morning, stayed warm by the coal-burning fireplace in the reception hall, and watched the passing scenes outside the windows. It was lovely. I even learned to enjoy baked beans for breakfast."

"Ewww!" Janice poked her head into the living room. "Lunch is ready, ladies. No baked beans, thank goodness, but you will be having Spanish omelets and hot water cornbread. Enjoy!"

~

Julia leaned back in her chair. "My word! Do you folks eat like that all the time? That was delicious."

"Janice does do some yummy dishes—things I wouldn't attempt. I asked her once where she learned to cook, and she admitted that she had worked as a short-order cook at one of the big touristy pancake houses in Gatlinburg. I love watching her bounce around my kitchen, and I hold my breath every time she flips a fried egg in the air. The best part is that she cleans up as she goes along."

"And you get all this time to write. Lucky you! So, fill me in on your progress. I remember commenting that only you would be ambitious—or foolish—enough to plan to write three books at once. And that was before we knew about the twins!"

"Ah, but the two Elijah books did not involve that much work. Stories for young children's books almost always have a total of thirty-two pages, and that includes the inside covers. More than half of those pages have pictures rather than words, and word totals per page range from ten to fifty words. That works out to less than eight hundred words per book. How many two- or three-page papers did you whip out in a single night when you were in college?"

"But they have to be the right eight hundred words. That takes talent."

"No. That just takes practice. And with an imaginative illustrator, the pictures carry a heavier load. Anyway, we were already working on Elijah's High Holy Days book last spring. That was before our publisher put that project on hold because someone published a similar Elijah book. And the Hanukkah book centered on the night Elijah received his 'gift' of Delilah. Hannah had been there when the two of them met, and she had dozens of pictures from which to work. Truth be told, those books were my way to relax after a day in the archives. I never saw them as real writing, at least not the kind of work that a historical account demands. The nunnery book, however, ..."

"What about that?"

"... was a soul-searching, conscience-crushing, back-breaking, eye-straining, and brain-draining nightmare."

"That bad?"

"At times, yes. I had to research my way through my ignorance of Catholicism, and I frequently had to fight the temptation to judge the women of St. Walburga as if they were lapsed Jews. I learned a lot as they struggled with their crises of faith. I came to realize that—as different as we appeared to be—we faced similar fears and challenges. And sometimes that made writing even more difficult because I couldn't maintain my objectivity as a historian. I don't know if that makes sense, but ..."

"Give me an example."

"One mother superior was asked to take in a pregnant teenager who was living on the street. While I was reading about that episode, David and I stumbled upon a young vagrant living in a cardboard box behind a Chinese restaurant. We argued when David threw her in jail. I couldn't help but wonder how we should be helping people whose behavior has caused society to reject them. The nuns weren't sure, and neither was I—even when the girl on the porch turned out to be our Janice.

"At another point, the nun questioned whether it was ethical for St. Walburga's to accept payment from parents who adopted a child from the nunnery orphanage. She equated paid adoption and slavery. How can we justify buying human beings, she wondered? I read her soul-searching debate while David and I were trying to decide whether we were ready to adopt."

"Whoa!"

"Yeah! As a historian, I was used to reading factual accounts of verifiable events. The writers of the nunnery journals, however, were writing about the 'what-ifs' of history. They faced moral dilemmas and ethical questions for which their religious teachings had not prepared them. They struggled to find answers, and I struggled to understand their struggles."

"But you are finished?"

"Whatever 'finished' means. I have a manuscript—a first draft. Is it what the college wants? Is it what the diocesan authorities will approve? Who knows? All I know is that for the time being, I have gone as far as I can go. We'll send this version out to some beta readers and see what reactions it produces. In the meantime, I think it's going to be a relief to get back to the classroom for the fall semester, where I can feel in control."

"Famous last words!"

"I know, I know, but don't spoil my optimism. Have you been up to campus? What's happening in the department?"

"Quite a bit. I assume you've heard that Elizabeth resigned. Her partner received a job offer from the Victoria and Albert Museum, and they both leaped at the chance to return to London. So, Jean Pendergast will be using her adjunct appointment to take over courses on the French Revolution, the British Empire, and the Formation of Modern Europe.

"Our other Europeanists are also working on some new ventures. Kevin is due for a sabbatical, but he's going to settle for the spring semester and the following summer— giving him a break of about eight months total. This fall, he's teaching Early Greece, Rome, and Egypt—a transition into the Ancient World slot. Matt will come in as an adjunct to cover the Roman Empire in the spring. Ramona Bishop will slide into her preferred Medievalist position. And that pushes me back into Renaissance and Reformation, which I'm going to enjoy.

"As for you Americanists, Gabe has decided to stay with us and handle the Age of Exploration through Western Frontier, leaving you with almost all of Nineteenth-Century America. And Tom Etheridge will continue to handle the wars of the Twentieth Century. He's settled nicely into that niche. We have a balanced coverage, I think. We'll be hiring just one position—roughly, Nineteenth-Century Europe. Kevin will start the interview process for that at the Southern, and then I'll get to wrap it up in the spring while I'm Acting Chair."

"It all sounds logical, although I feel some questions coming on."

"Like what?"

"What happens to Jean's family life when she turns down her husband's permanent job offer so she can earn much less as a poverty-stricken adjunct? And Matt ... Is he ever going to make the big move to Knoxville and the doctoral program? And what's holding him here? Is it his profitable little bar, or the addition of that interesting new young woman in our master's program?

As for Gabe, I gather that Maria sent him home from D.C. I'm happy for us; we need him. And I'm happy for Maria; she didn't need a new husband to interfere with her appointment as a White House fellow. But what about Gabe himself? How badly is he going to flounder now that he's back in a job he was ready to quit for the woman he loved?"

"Interesting questions, all. But how many of them also apply to you, my friend? I get the distinct feeling that you're still struggling with your own tenure decisions."

"I am. Of course, I am. I promised the dean I would return to teaching for the 2012-13 school year. And I'm seriously considering postponing my tenure year until 2014-15. But I'm still not sure I can handle having it all—the teaching, the writing, the parenting. I don't know yet what door I want to choose when I grow up!"

CHAPTER 36

Where Have You Gone?

October 2012

Sarah had struggled with her emotions as she thought about returning to the classroom. On most days, she found the prospect exciting. She had never doubted her ability to connect with her students. Nor did she worry about the mastery of her subject. A classroom was her stage, and the students were her audience. She had an exciting gift of knowledge to offer them, and her enthusiasm bubbled over as she launched into each day's lecture. Each new topic delivered deeper analyses, along with a few memorable quotes. No one watched a clock. Her timing was instinctive, and the students were too busy keeping up with her flow of thought to think about the passage of time.

She had studied with some of the finest scholars in her field and absorbed their rhetorical tricks along with their factual statements. One of those lecturers was known for leaving a class in suspense. He had a favorite tale about a ship's captain who hid underwater in the South Carolina marshes and breathed through a hollow plant stem until his pursuers gave up and went away. Many of Sarah's lectures now ended with a signature wrap-up; "Would the plan work? You think about it, and we'll look at what happened the next time." Leaving a class wanting more had become part of her repertoire.

But, of course, like any good actor, she suffered from bouts of stage fright at the beginning of each semester. Each new student brought a potential challenge, and in the early days of each fall semester, Sarah found herself anticipating trouble. Cheerleaders and football players were the hardest to win over. She dreaded having an early morning class full of young women who were still busy combing their hair and touching up their makeup. But worse were the burly young fellows who interrupted her lecture about someone like George Washington with a protest that began with these familiar words: "That's not true. My tenth-grade history teacher was also my football coach; he knew everything about American history. If our first president had lied about chopping down that cherry tree, Coach would have told us so."

This year's return to the classroom, however, was different in another way, for this year, Sarah was a mother as well as a professor. That meant that there was always a portion of her attention that focused, not on the classroom but on the nursery downstairs where her twins were learning a rather harsh lesson about getting along with the rest of the world. True, the college nursery was staffed by experienced and trained personnel. Professors from the department of early childhood education made regular visits to the nursery, and their students put in long hours in practicum as they learned firsthand how to deal with fractious two-and three-year-olds.

Sarah's method of handling her dual role required that she keep an eye on the clock and stick to a rigid schedule. The Cohen family arrived at the nursery at 8:30 in the morning. That gave her just enough time to see the twins comfortably settled into an activity and then make her way to her classroom building where her 9:00 class awaited her. Assuming there were no emergency messages from the nursery, she then had the rest of the morning to deal with department business, class preparation, or writing projects.

At noon on days when she did not have an afternoon or evening class, she closed her office for the day, picked up the twins from the nursery, and headed home for a late lunch. By the time they arrived at the house, Janice, her mother's helper, had meal preparations underway. Once fed, the twins went down for a much-needed nap. Janice turned to housework, and Sarah had another period of personal time to complete her professorial duties. By the time the twins woke up from their naps, she was ready to take charge and spend some quality time with them. On Tuesdays and Thursdays, Sarah returned to campus around 4:30 PM to teach early evening classes, and on those days Janice stayed to care for the twins until David got home from work.

Sarah had a bout of nerves on her first day back as she thought about facing a new crop of students, but it disappeared as soon as she stood in front of the class. The faces were new but their attitudes—a mixture of curiosity, excitement, and apprehension—were all familiar. Her usual practice was to wait until the beginning of the class hour before entering the classroom, and she began talking as soon as the door closed behind her. If someone had asked her, she might have admitted that her entrance always felt to her as if she were walking onto a stage. The podium on which her lecture notes rested gave her a focus, and her performance was underway.

Within a week or so, the Cohen household had settled into the schedule that allowed the twins to enjoy their time in the nursery. Then Sarah could turn her full attention to the class at hand without feeling guilty. So, on that early October morning, she noticed nothing unusual about the day—not until she returned to the nursery to pick up the twins for lunch. Then things began to go wrong.

"Where are the twins? Off on a mini field trip?" she asked.

The student at the reception desk looked puzzled. "They went home for lunch ... Didn't they?"

'No, they didn't. That's why I'm here." Sarah's mind was still partially back in the classroom, and she felt a few moments of strong irritation at the delay. "Are they in a kind of Time Out for some imaginary two-year-old's infraction of the rules?"

"Of course not. They're always very well-behaved. You mustn't assume that they are in trouble. Our professor says that if you assume the worst, it makes children feel guilty for no reason at all. And that's when they start to misbehave."

The girl's know-it-all attitude and sneering tone of voice were beginning to wear on Sarah's nerves. Her voice went up several decibels. "Where are my kids?"

"Is there a problem here?" A supervisor appeared behind the young receptionist, but she reserved her glare for Sarah, the one who had raised her voice. "We try not to shout in here. It upsets the children."

"Well, at the moment I'm the one who's upset. I'm here

to pick up my twins, and they are nowhere in sight. What have you done with my kids?"

"You're Mrs. Cohen, aren't you?"

"I'm Doctor Chomsky on campus if you don't mind. But, yes, I'm here to pick up Jillian and Jeremy Cohen."

"Just a moment. I'll go get them."

She disappeared through a swinging door. In a few moments, the nursery manager came out. "Professor Chomsky? I'm so sorry about the misunderstanding. Your mother's helper—Janice, isn't it?—picked them up around mid-morning. She said you had a busy schedule and had asked her to help by taking them home early. She was saving you an extra trip later today."

The woman smiled tolerantly at Sarah and nodded to close the discussion. She turned and disappeared into the back room, leaving Sarah standing speechless at the registration desk. It took a few moments for her words to register; then panic set in.

Sarah fumbled with her phone, her shaking finger hunting for the fast-dial button that would call home. There was no answer. She tapped the cell number for her mother's helper. A disembodied voice informed her that the line was no longer in service. She touched the fast-dial button to summon her husband. The line was busy. She punched it again and again, finally breaking through to a ringtone. But the voice that answered was Stella, David's secretary.

"Sarah? That you? Mr. Cohen is taking a deposition. Can I help you?"

"No! I need David!"

"I'm sorry, dear. He asked not to be disturbed for anything short of life and death. I can slip him a message, however."

"The children! They're gone! Get him!"

"What do you mean by 'gone'? I'll understand you better if you slow down and quit shouting at me."

"Gone! As in disappeared! Missing! Abducted! I can't find them!"

"Where are they?"

"I don't know!" Sarah stopped and drew a deep breath as she tried to control the fear washing over her. "Stella, please. Just get him for me. He'll understand."

She listened as Stella summoned a clerk and sent her scurrying to the inner office, where a high-powered couple had come to hammer out the details of their divorce. "Miss Emory. Tell him it's an emergency. Here. Hand him his cell phone. It's his wife. She'll explain."

It seemed to be taking forever, but David's voice came through the line within a minute or two. "Sarah? I asked not to be disturbed. What is so important that ..."

"The twins! They're gone. I came down to the nursery as I always do, and they weren't there. The manager says Janice picked them up around ten with an elaborate story about how I had sent her. But I didn't!"

"Calm down, darling. I'm sure there is a logical explanation. They are probably at the house wondering where you are."

"No, they are not. I tried calling there. No answer. And Janice's cell phone is no longer in service."

"Odd. She probably didn't pay her bill. I'm sure it will turn out to be a simple misunderstanding."

"David, they've been gone for almost two hours. And I don't want to hear flimsy excuses. My children are missing, and no one had permission to take them out of here. Even if Janice has simply taken them to a park, I need to know where they are."

"All right. Don't yell at me. You head for the house, and

I'll meet you there. No, wait. That's not the best idea. You stay where you are until I can meet you there. I'm going to send a uniformed cop to the house to put the fear of God into Janice. I'll come to the campus nursery. I want to hear the staff's story for myself."

Sarah paced the waiting area outside the nursery door. She kept one eye on the parking lot outside and the other on the swinging doors that led to the playroom. Possible scenarios raced through her mind. Janice might have misunderstood something they had said this morning. Maybe she just took the twins for a treat, intending to bring them back before lunch. Perhaps they had had a flat tire or run out of gas. Maybe the preschool interns had confused the twins with two other children.

Those simple excuses interplayed with more serious versions. Had they been in an accident? Or, what did they know about Janice, after all? Perhaps she had been planning an abduction to get even for the time David had thrown her in jail. Maybe she was a hardened criminal, looking to make a quick buck. Or she might have acted under duress, forced by her felonious father to participate in a kidnapping.

Sarah was unsure whether to feel relieved or frightened when David entered the nursery door. He smiled, but the expression failed to reach his eyes, which darted from one side to the other.

"Any word?" he asked.

"No, nothing."

"My cop friend is on his way to the house. I've told him we'll meet him there. Leave your cell number with the girl at the desk, just in case they come back here."

"You don't expect that to happen, do you?"

"I'm suspending judgment. But hurry. I want to check out things at home."

On the short drive to the house, David tried to reassure her. "Janice loves those children. She wouldn't do anything to hurt them. They'll all turn up safe at home. You'll see."

But they didn't. Janice's car was gone. Inside the house, almost all traces of the children's existence had disappeared. Their clothes and snacks were gone—no teddy bears or blankets, no diapers, sippy cups, or push-and-pull toys. The house was neat, clean—and empty.

Mrs.Blackburn, the lady who lived next door, shouted across the hedge. "That must be quite a rummage sale your synagogue is holding, Sarah. Tell Janice I have some things in the attic I could donate if she wants to come by later this afternoon."

"What? Wait! You've seen Janice? When?"

"Oh, a couple of hours ago, I guess. She was loading the whole back end of her car with boxes—looked like baby things, mostly. She told me the synagogue has a lending closet for new parents and grandparents. I've been wondering why I've kept those old things of Jason's. I might as well send them somewhere to let others get some use ..."

David interrupted her chatty. "Wait, Mrs.Blackburn. This is important. Janice and her car are missing. Did you notice when she left here?"

"Oh, my goodness! I had no idea! It must have been around 11:00, I guess.

"Were the twins with her?"

"Come to think of it, they were already strapped into their car seats. I noticed because I could see them squirming around to watch what she was doing."

Now it was David's turn to panic.

CHAPTER 37

Amber Alert

October 10-11, 2012

Missing Twins
Jillian and Jeremy Cohen

Missing since: October 10, 2012
Missing from: Birch Falls, TN
Age now: 21 months
Race: Caucasian
Hair color: Light brown
Eye color: Brown
Height: 32"
Weight: 25 lbs.

A Tennessee AMBER Alert has been issued for Jeremy and Jillian Cohen (twins), last seen in the area of the College Nursery on the campus of Smoky Mountain University in Birch Falls, TN. They were wearing matching white tee shirts, dark blue coveralls, and white shoes.

The children may be in the company of Janice Highsmith. She is 24 years old, height 5'2", 120 pounds, with blond hair, and blue eyes. She is believed to be driving a 2004 Toyota Corolla Sportiva hatchback, license plate number CD9 7JR. Based on additional information provided by the Birch Falls Police Department and the District Attorney's Office, the Missing Child Alert that was issued at 11:00 AM on October 10, 2012, has been UPGRADED to an AMBER Alert.

David had taken only a quick look around the empty house before heading straight for his home computer to create the "all points" bulletin. The muscles in his jaw clenched as he revised the usual wording of an AMBER Alert to fit the description of his children. Somehow, seeing the words in print only intensified the fear he was feeling.

"Sarah, do we have a good headshot of the twins? We're going to need to circulate their pictures."

"The nursery took pictures of each of them when we enrolled them. I'm sure they have them on file. Should I call and ask them to send copies to ... to the police?"

"No, have them forward them to my email at the DA's office. I want to set up a separate command post there."

"Should you be trying to handle this yourself? Isn't that rather like a doctor not being allowed to operate on a member of his own family?"

"It's different, Sarah. In a situation like this—where the perpetrator is on the move across jurisdictions—there's no one with the authority to take charge. And I don't want to see the case get buried under the local police's pile-up of daily business—traffic tickets, shoplifting, jaywalking. We're going to need the full cooperation of local police, the Sheriff's Department, the State Highway Patrol, and law enforcement people from adjoining states. Luckily enough, we still have my old offices with an empty suite of well-equipped desks to use as a command post."

"And what do I do, while you're micro-managing all of this? Just sit here and chew my fingernails?"

"Of course not. I want you with me, making contact with friends and family—anyone who might be able to help. I can give you a list. The rumors will already be flying around the college as the word comes in that the nursery is a crime scene. Julia and Will can help with campus gossip. I want my dad at our house in case Janice decides to come home. And we need to bring Sheila Leibowicz into the picture since she and her ladies' interfaith group have worked with Janice and her classmates."

"Shouldn't we be out looking for the car?"

"And just where would you suggest we start? We have no idea where she's headed. If we drive around, we could be moving away from her rather than toward her. No, love, we need to allow the authorities to do the searching until we have a confirmed sighting."

It was a long afternoon. Most of the phone calls came from friends and family wanting to know if they had heard anything, which only increased the tension everyone was feeling. When the first helpful call came in, David put it on speakerphone so that Sarah and the police in the room could hear.

"Mr. Cohen? This is Joey Breckenridge, general manager at Sunset Motors in Knoxville. I think the woman you are looking for was here earlier this afternoon. She came in asking if she could trade her Toyota hatchback for a smaller car of equal value. She said the Toyota was just too big for her to handle, and I could see why. She was a little mite of a thing. She was particularly worried that she couldn't see to back up and she couldn't get turned around enough to see the two babies she had in car carriers in the back seat."

"Sounds like her, all right."

"Well, at the time, I didn't know anybody was looking for her. Then another guy came in asking who owned that Toyota Sportiva outside because he was looking for a car just like that to take on a hunting trip next month. Things got complicated because we were trying to buy her car so we could sell it to him. But first, we had to find a smaller car for her and make that trade. So, we were juggling paperwork, checking credit scores, and confirming VINs. The two kids were crying and fighting and wiggling, and the young woman was trying to make them be quiet.

"That's when our teenage receptionist handed me a folded note, telling me I'd better respond to that number. I thought it was a phone call from my wife asking me to pick up a loaf of bread or something, so I just pushed it aside. I didn't get around to looking at it until nearly closing time. That's when I saw the license number and the AMBER Alert and realized that I had been dealing with a kidnapper."

"Mr. Breckenridge, listen to me. Where is she now?"

"No telling. She left here around 5:30. A couple of our boys helped her transfer everything from her Toyota to an older, dark blue Nissan Sentra with temporary plates. The other guy—the hunter—went off with the car you were looking for. He is probably driving around Knoxville some-where. And the young woman? She told Johnny, our lot boy, that she was headed for Asheville and then Florida after getting some supper. So, she could be in a drive-in some-where or maybe headed east along I-40. Johnny told her it wasn't safe for her to be driving that stretch of mountain road in the dark, but she didn't seem to care. Sorry I can't be of more help."

"You've been very helpful. We now know what direction she's headed in and what she's driving. We'll change the AMBER Alert and start narrowing our search."

Sarah was bouncing up and down. "She's getting away. We've got to go after her."

"No. That's a job for the Knoxville police. They can check cars with dealer plates in hamburger joints and spot her before we could even get close"

"But if she's on her way to Asheville …"

"I've driven that road myself, Mrs. Cohen, and it's scary in the dark." The police chief patted her shoulder. "She won't try it. She'll be looking for a place to stop for the night, and that will give our guys time to catch up."

In truth, however, the police had a difficult job. In the dark, a lot of cars were dark sedans with blurry plates. The police investigated several suspects, but they never spotted the right vehicle.

False alarms continue to come in all night. Around midnight, Sarah curled up on a couch, unable to keep her eyes open any longer. But David remained alert to any possible clue. The next breakthrough did not come until nearly 9:00 AM when a state highway patrolman called in to report a sighting by a motel owner.

Jonah Smithers owned the Bide-a-Wee Motel just off the tourist route to Pigeon Forge and Gatlinburg. His disreputable establishment sported six small rooms whose furnishings dated back some thirty years. But what they lacked in amenities they made up for with low visibility from the highway and a bargain nightly rate.

On the night of October 10, only two of those six rooms were occupied—one by a down-on-his-luck book salesman and the other by a harassed mother with two squalling babies. Wisely, Jonah assigned the two rooms as far apart as possible, not wanting the children to disturb a regular customer. The motel owner then drank three beers and went to sleep in a room behind the counter where he would not be disturbed until morning.

Around 7:00 AM, he stepped outside and saw the young mother just getting into her car. She smiled, waved, and shouted across the parking lot.

"Any place around here to get a good breakfast?" she asked.

He pointed her toward a mom-and-pop diner just down the road. "Jenkins Diner is probably open by now."

"Thanks. See ya!"

The motel owner picked up his newspaper from the porch and walked back into the office, not noticing that the young mother in the dark blue Nissan Sentra drove right on past Jenkins Diner and took the ramp onto I-40. She did not return to pay her bill. It was that failure that led him to place an indignant call to the State Highway Patrol, but he waited too long to file the report. She was far away by the time the local cops went looking for her.

Two hours later, a gas station attendant outside of Asheville reported that someone named "Highsmith" had used a credit card to pay for a fill-up. He had not noticed the old car or its dealer plates until just before it pulled away. The tip was helpful, however, for it suggested a route change; the car had turned off of I-40 onto Route 26, headed for South Carolina. "That's a pretty deserted stretch of highway," the caller explained. "Nothing much out here except the Great Smoky Mountain National Park. She'll make good time because there's nowhere to get lunch until she gets to Spartanburg."

Sarah's eyes brimmed with tears. "South Carolina? She's

getting further and further away, while we sit here doing nothing."

"Patience, my love. It's going to be even easier to find her in South Carolina. So far, she's been moving through heavily populated communities, and it's easy to get lost in a crowd. But in the area she's passing through now, traffic is light. Little towns are few and far between, and strangers are just that—very, very strange. Somebody will spot her. Just wait and see."

As usual, David was right. When the phone rang around 1:30, a distinctly southern drawl brought exciting news. "Think we've got your kidnapper for you," the speaker said. "This is Patrick Kerrigan, chief of police in the fine metropolis of Inman, SC. Never heard of us, have you? I'm not surprised. We're just a little town of some 3000 citizens located at the edge of one of the craziest interchanges in the whole Interstate system. We're at the junction of I-26 and I-85 with several other smaller roads crisscrossing them. We have some thirteen intersections within a square mile.

"We're a typical southern town—a courthouse in the middle of the town square, with the important elements of civilization clustered around that central square—a church, a library, a school, a grocery store, a department store, a shoe shop, a newspaper corner, an all-day restaurant, and a gift shop.

"The young lady in question was trying to find the road to Columbia but found herself in the heart of Inman. She pulled into a parking spot in front of the courthouse, grateful to be out of traffic but surprised to see parking meters all around the square. We know what happened next because our meter maid, Mabel Bowers, was watching her from across the street. The woman got out of the car to investigate, only to discover that she would need nickels to feed the meter. She opened the car's back door and realized the two small children in the back seat were sound asleep. She quietly shut the door, locked it, and headed for the newspaper stand on the corner to get change. That's when Mabel descended.

"The meter maid notified the police desk that there were children in a locked car and asked them to send reinforcements. One uniformed patrolman tackled the job of unlocking the car by poking a plastic ruler down the side of the car window. The other cop stopped the driver as she came out of the store. He read the young woman her rights, handcuffed her, and then manacled her to the nearest stop sign. By the time the chief arrived to take charge, she was demanding a lawyer and the two children were awake and screaming in fright. The chief had quickly checked the woman's ID, the VIN of the car, and the dealer's license tags before announcing that they had just made the most important arrest of the month."

Back in Birch Falls, Sarah and David sagged in relief. The ordeal was over, and the children were frightened but safe. The chief explained what would happen next. Procedural rules required them to send the children to the local hospital to make sure they had not suffered any ill effects from being locked in the car. Janice was under arrest for child endangerment, and the FBI had been notified to take over the case because it involved transporting kidnap victims across state lines.

"We will handle the details, Mr. Cohen. You just come and get your kids."

CHAPTER 38

Trial and Reconciliation

October 2012

Within hours, the good news about the discovery of the kidnapped Cohen children had spread throughout Tennessee. David's political stance as an independent district attorney caught the attention of newspaper columnists across the state, and the story rekindled public interest. Even the governor became a part of the news when he offered to provide his private plane to fly David and Sarah to South Carolina to reclaim their children.

When they looked back on the trip later, Sarah and David remembered only a blur of being rushed from one point to the next—a frantic ride by police cruiser from Birch Falls to Nashville, where they met the governor's pilot; the up-and-down 35-minute flight from there to Spartanburg, SC; and another police escort to the local hospital in Inman. The reunion with the children in an emergency room cubicle began with shaky little voices crying 'Ma-ma' and 'Da-Da' and ended with everyone in tears when Jillian patted her mother's cheek and asked, 'Mama cry?'

"Your children are fine," the local doctor assured them. "They are grubby and flushed from crying, and they both could use a change of clothing. They are frightened and probably hungry, but they've suffered no long-term ill effects. The best thing you can do for them right now is to rush them home and into familiar surroundings. We're waiving most of the regulations here to make that possible."

"What's being done with their things—the car and everything in it—car seats, all the clothes, toys, and food that the kidnapper took with her?"

"Aah, yes. I've been told that all the baby things have been boxed, sealed, and taken to your waiting plane. We can take care of the paperwork later."

"Can we see Janice?" David asked.

"No," the chief responded. "She's currently undergoing questioning by our investigators. I suspect we'll be transporting her under guard to the nearest mental health facility soon. She seems very confused about her identity. As I mentioned to you on the phone, this case will be transferred to the FBI as early as tomorrow because it is now classified as human trafficking. And you will need to keep in mind that you are the victims, not the enforcers of the law."

"Of course, although that's easier said than done."

A nurse entered the cubicle, bringing graham crackers and cartons of milk to tide the children over the trip home. Now recovered from their crying spells, they ate with enthusiasm and then closed their eyes, dropping off into a deep sleep in their parents' arms. They barely stirred during the trip back to the waiting plane.

Sarah was unwilling to move as Jillian cuddled deeper into her arms. She noted that David was following Jeremy's example and nodding off after being awake for over 24 hours. Sarah, however, was having the opposite reaction to the release of tension; she was wide awake. She stared at the passing scenery, wondering about this part of South Carolina. She caught her breath as a huge billboard demanded her attention. "Cowpens?" she asked, not intending to speak out loud, but their driver reacted.

"Yes, ma'am," he said. "Folks around here make a big 'thing' about our Cowpens Battlefield. Brings in lots of tourists, especially in January, when all those northerners are wandering around the South to avoid going home to winter snows."

"What's so special about a cow pen?" David asked sleepily.

"It's a famous battle, dear. The Battle of Cowpens in January 1781 marked the turning point of the American Revolution. I always meant to look into the details, but I had no idea it was located here."

"Yes, ma'am," the trooper repeated. "Just outside of Spartanburg. If you come back in January, you can walk the whole battlefield, watch reenactments, and end up with lots of souvenirs."

"Once a historian, always a historian, even amid a family crisis," David mumbled.

"Or maybe it's once a novelist, always a novelist," Sarah responded. "I've always thought there must be great stories around that battle." She smiled to herself but let the discussion drop.

At home, the exhausted twins clutched their blankies and teddy bears and snuggled into their cribs without a protest. Sarah dropped into a rocking chair and let memories wash over her. The terror of kidnapping had passed, replaced by the sweetness of toddler kisses. She was still sitting with eyes closed and a smile on her lips when David returned from stashing the last box of Pampers.

"Are you ready to turn in?" he asked.

"Not tonight. I'm staying here. I've been remembering. The first time I saw these little creatures, we had just rescued them from a car wreck. And here we are again. They don't have to sleep in a drawer tonight, but they still deserve to have a mother keeping watch over them."

"On that night, you didn't know what would happen to them. This time, you can be sure they are safe."

"Can I? Can we ever be sure of their future safety? If I've learned one thing from this whole nightmare, it is the importance of the present moment. And at this moment, I simply want to savor the sounds of their breathing and the closeness of their warm little bodies."

David paused between the two cribs, letting a hand drop gently onto each little head. "There is one other important difference between tonight and the night of the accident. This time they have two parents to keep watch over them."

Monday, October 29, 2012

The Cohen kidnapping had so much publicity that it had to come to trial, even if all the parties involved would have preferred to settle it out of court. "You must not let your professional position sway the outcome of the case in any way," the police chief had warned David. "I don't want anyone to question the fairness of Miss Highsmith's settlement. No one must be able to say she got off easy because she worked for you. Worse, we don't want anyone to say she was treated too harshly because of your political prominence. She gets her day in court, same as anyone else."

The first arraignment hearing occurred just two weeks later on October 29, 2012. With the elections coming up on November 6, David was acutely aware that his term as district attorney was almost over. In any event, as a victim of the alleged crime, he would have had to recuse himself from the trial. But here, sitting in the back of the courtroom, he sensed that his separation had already begun. He listened to the proceedings like the lawyer he would soon become rather than the county official he had been.

"All rise. The Pullman County Court is now in session, The Honorable Judge Pearl McCutchen presiding."

A familiar figure, still dwarfed by her flowing black gown, entered a door concealed in the panels behind the podium. Judge McCutchen pounded her gavel once on the desk. "You may all be seated. We are here assembled to hear depositions concerning case number 58394: 'The County of Pullman and the State of Tennessee versus Janice Marie Highsmith.'"

She hesitated, looking out at the crowded courtroom. "I was not expecting there to be an audience at this stage of our proceedings. Today we will simply meet the people on prosecution and defense. Then comes the plea. After that, we will set our hearing schedule. Who represents the prosecution?"

A distinguished-looking gentleman stood. "Your Honor. I am Nathaniel Baywater, most recently of the Nashville District Attorney's Office. I have been asked to handle Miss Highsmith's case because of the obvious conflict of interest between her and the local DA. I have not yet had a chance to meet with the defendant I will not ask her to commit to anything on her own without the advice of counsel. I must hear from her as to the details of this case. I will be calling for a continuance to be sure the defendant gets an impartial hearing."

"The City of Birch Falls welcomes your participation, Mr. Baywater. I am Robert Q. Jones, founding partner of the Jones and Smithers Law Firm. We will be representing Miss Highsmith *pro bono* at the request of the court. We, too, prefer a continuance to review the case."

The judge frowned. "Am I understanding you both? Neither one of you has talked to the defendant. Then in fairness to this young woman, I want to hear what she has to say for herself. But let me be clear. I am not asking her to make any permanent commitments. I only want all of us to meet her and understand a little bit about who she is. Miss Highsmith, would you stand just where you are and introduce yourself to the court?"

For a few moments, Janice appeared to be confused. Then, as if she had suddenly made up her mind, she grasped the arms of her chair, stood up, lifted her head, and turned to face the curious audience.

"Good morning. My name is Janice Marie Highsmith. I was born and raised in Huntsville, Alabama. I arrived here in Birch Falls a year or so ago as something of a vagrant. At that time, I was still struggling with my decision to start a new life for myself. My story may be a familiar one. It's a tale of abuse—a dysfunctional family, children raised without purpose or self-esteem, a household devoid of ethics or morality.

"I won't go into great detail about the family I left behind except to tell you these basic truths. My mother is an alcoholic. My father is a cocaine addict and a drug dealer. I am the youngest child. My three older brothers have all spent varying lengths of time in local and state jails for criminal activities. Growing up, we knew only that life itself was a constant fight for survival. In my household, if there was food on the table, one rule prevailed. 'Grab it as quickly as you can or there will be nothing left. We took what we needed without consideration for whether it was right or wrong to do so. It was simply a matter of survival.

"Here in Birch Falls, however, I observed families leading quite different lives—loving parents, hard-working men, neat yards and clean houses, and well-behaved children. The people here seemed to follow unwritten rules of conduct—rules I didn't know existed. I stayed here because I wanted to be a part of their world. I found training and employment as a mother's helper and became entirely self-supporting.

"Still, I didn't know I could be someone important—not until I met the Cohens, who gave me my first taste of self-worth. And then I betrayed them. I wanted what they had, and for the first time, I realized I could get it. But I went about it in the wrong way. I let myself be guided by the lessons life had taught me growing up. So I took what I wanted instead of earning it. And by the time I realized what I had done, it was too late."

Judge McCutchen shook her head as if to reject the story she was hearing. "But why would you do such a thing? Why would you kidnap two small children?"

"I needed them. I have an aunt—my mother's older sister—who lives in Jacksonville, Florida. I am her only niece, her only heir, and now she is dying of cancer. Last year, shortly after she got her diagnosis, she wrote me a letter telling me she hoped I had grown up to be a credit to her family. Because her time was running out, I made up a story about being married to a sailor. I told her he was off on a six-month duty assignment in the Mediterranean. I also told her I had given birth to twins. She responded by saying she wanted to meet them before she died. So, I borrowed them."

"A child is not a cup of sugar. You can't just borrow one."

"I thought I could. And believe me or not as you will, I fully intended to bring them back after a couple of days. I'm not a kidnapper. I'm a caregiver, and I was taking good care of them. I hoped my aunt would die happily believing in my good fortune. I thought if I inherited her house, I could move there and start a new life to someday fulfill the promise she seemed to find in me.

"I was wrong. I see that. So now I pay the penalties. I intend to plead guilty, Your Honor. I did what they said I did. I will accept my punishment gladly, in the hope that I can use my time in prison to find a healthier plan for the rest of my life."

David quickly passed a note to the defense attorney, who stood to attract the judge's attention. "In light of this extraordinary testimony, we respectfully ask the court to remit the defendant to a mental health facility during the continuance requested earlier."

"So ordered. Court adjourned."

As they left the courtroom, David watched Sarah's expression change from non-committal to anger and then frustration.

"What's wrong, sweetheart? Are you disagreeing with the judge's order or with my interference?'

"I'm not questioning what happened just now in the courtroom, although I was a bit surprised to see you interject yourself into the proceedings. When I saw you pass that note, I saw a district attorney taking charge. And it made me realize that Janice has more clarity about her life than either of us has about our own."

"How so?"

"Well, no matter how hard you try to be impartial, you are still wearing three different hats this morning. You are the father whose children were kidnapped. That makes you a victim. You may not be running for re-election, but you'll continue to be the district attorney until mid-January. You still feel your responsibility for seeing to it that the court functions as you think it should. And you are thinking like the defense lawyer you hope to become."

"You're right. I have to admit I was itching to step in and take charge. But why are you feeling conflicted this morning? You have a single role in this drama—that of the victim."

"I'm looking at our lives as a whole, not just as a scene playing out in a courtroom. And out in the rest of the world, I'm wearing more hats than I can count.

"I'm back in the classroom, even though I'm not sure I want to teach anymore. My children are back in the campus nursery, although I still don't completely trust their staff. I have an idea for a new book, but I can't make myself finish the one I'm currently writing. I'm scheduled to go up for tenure in the fall, but I don't know if that's a label I want to wear. I have everything I ever wanted—marriage, children, good health, friends, a comfortable home, a professional career, and a creative outlet. But now I don't know which ones I want. And that makes me angry."

"Can I help? Or am I just in the way—a part of your problem?"

"I don't think anyone can help, except maybe … maybe the mother superior has a formula for finding closure. I think I want to read what she has to say about the closing of the nunnery."

CHAPTER 39

Compline—The Seventh Hour

From the journal of Maggie Anne Wiggers, later known as Sister Margaret, and now, by the grace of God, as Mother Margaret, Mother Superior of this Convent of Our Lady St. Walburga:

September 21, 1948

Summer has run its course, and its heat has dissipated. Rain has fallen softly all day, not a downpour but a gentle washing of our dusty world. Our summer flowers have shed their petals, but a bundle of autumn chrysanthemum buds made their appearance today. The last hummingbird has abandoned the basil blossoms to begin its annual journey to the warmer climates of Central America. In the nearby woods, the poplar trees are wearing crowns of gold rather than green. I look across our cloister garden and marvel at God's plan. Summer's glory fades, and the next season steps confidently into its place to bring us new joy.

But how do I get through this day of change? How do I say farewell to my sisters and to this house that has sheltered us for so long? It is appropriate that on this day my thoughts are devoted to change and completion, for it closes a century of service and prayer for the nunnery of St. Walburga. Our predecessors, six intrepid ladies, arrived here in 1843 to find a grubby village clinging to the foothills of a misty mountain range. Its inhabitants were day laborers struggling to tame a wilderness and turn it into a commercial center. They did not welcome a gaggle of nuns, but within five years those nuns help turn Birch Falls into a thriving little town. For the next hundred years, the women of St. Walburga served the needs of their community both on a physical level and on a spiritual one. Now we move on.

Like the crops of summer, our projects have yielded their bounty. Thanks to our efforts, the citizens of our town have used our social services to provide help when they needed it. Our maternity house offered a safe environment for unwed mothers, and our orphanage placed hundreds of parentless children into welcoming adoptive homes. The older children who came to us received good educations. From the Civil War onward, our hospital wing offered assistance to those wounded in the service of their country. And most recently, we have provided a safe and caring environment for the elderly whose families can no longer handle their frailties. The examples we have set have served as guides when governments assumed more responsibility for the welfare of their citizens.

The expansion of state-run institutions, however, has brought other changes to our world. No longer must a young woman settle for marrying or remaining in the family home as an old maid aunt. A nunnery is no longer her only other escape. She is now free to choose among many occupations and careers. But, as one of our diocesan priests recently pointed out to me, St. Walburga has failed to recruit a single new novice in the past twenty years. And as a result of that failure, the nunnery now has an aging staff to care for a population that continues to grow beyond our ability to serve it.

The priests of the diocese agreed back in 1938 that the nunnery of St. Walburga had outlived its usefulness. But thanks to the intervening war effort, we have had ten years' warning. We've spent those years getting used to the idea—arranging new accommodations for those who rely upon us, finding new religious houses to accept our sisters who will be displaced, and deciding what is to be done with all of our buildings and equipment. My final task comes tonight in the refectory when I lead my sisters through the final prayers of Compline. But what shall I say?

As I pondered that question, a knock on my office door interrupted my thoughts. My visitor was our youngest nun, Sister Cicely, a local woman who began as a hired helper for our kitchen and later begged to join our shrinking band. This afternoon, she came seeking my advice one last time.

"Mother Margaret, I am worried about Sister Elizabeth. I went up to the dormitory to sit with her for a while this afternoon and found her crying softly in her bed. The other sisters tell me she's been crying all day. Oh, she's not wailing or sobbing or carrying on. There's only a quiet waterfall of tears running down her cheeks. She's not in pain. She's not hungry. There's nothing she wants or needs. She just can't stop the tears."

"It's a sad day for all of our sisters. St. Walburga's

Nunnery will close forever when we blow out the last candle tonight. It's a momentous event, one worthy of a few tears, I think."

"Of course, it is, Mother Margaret, but her grief seems excessive. Sister Elizabeth is responsible for my being here, and in many ways, I owe her my life as well as my calling. I cannot bear to let her lie there and cry."

I shook my head. I understood what the young sister was telling me, but I also understood the deep sadness our former mother superior had to be feeling this day.

"What is your relationship with the sister, if I may ask? Are you family?"

"No, nothing like that. It's just ... my mother died in 1919 of influenza, after successfully nursing all of her children through the illness. I was a young teenager, shaken beyond reason by her death. My father was so devastated that he was of no help to any of us children as we tried to make sense of the fact that we were now motherless waifs.

"One night my father came into my bedroom. He talked about how much he missed my mother and how much I resembled her. Then he asked if he could just lie next to me on my bed for a few minutes to find some sort of family companionship. I agreed and eventually we both fell asleep. And then, in the middle of the night, he ..."

The young woman cringed, looked away, swallowed hard, and did not finish her sentence. She didn't need to. I understood what had happened, and I told her it was not as uncommon as she might think.

"Oh, but it frightened me beyond reason. I couldn't talk to my brothers, so I sought counsel elsewhere. I was employed as a kitchen maid here at the nunnery after I finished school, and eventually, I talked to Sister Elizabeth, who was by then the new mother superior. I told her what had happened and how frightened I was of my father. She offered me a solution. She said if I became a novice, he would never again be able to touch me. I agreed.

"She became the mother I had lost, my spiritual guide, and my best friend. That's why I'm so concerned about her today. I've done everything I can think of to make her smile again." She gave me a shaky smile as she continued.

"I even offered to sneak out to the barn and get her favorite cat. I hoped I could bring Whiskers in so that they could have a cuddle. Sister Elizabeth laughed at that through her tears—although the tears didn't stop—and then she said no. She could not allow me to break the rules of the nunnery for her sake. She said she would be fine, and it was comfort enough to have me there holding her hand for a while. But I still don't understand why she is crying."

"My child, Sister Elizabeth was the prioress of our house for ten years and mother superior of the nunnery for twenty years, and for all of those thirty years, she had to swallow her feelings to put the concerns of the nuns under her care ahead of her desires. Now that I've taken her place, I'm learning just how often we have to do that. We bury our feelings to do what is best for our sisters. Now, I imagine, Sister Elizabeth recognizes that she is coming to the end of her own life. And she also realizes that the nunnery itself will cease to exist after today. All of that buried sorrow and grief has washed back over her. She now has time and permission to let her feelings flow, and that's what's happening.

"You must not deprive her of her great need to grieve. You may be sure, however, that having you there to care about her is helping her, even though you cannot see a difference in her behavior. So, stay with her as long as you can this afternoon, love her, and be there for her. Know that you are doing what you can to help her reach her final destination."

"Thank you, mother."

"Oh, and Sister Cecily, one other thing. "Go find Whiskers. Get her that cat."

Again, I wonder. How do I say farewell to my sisters and to this house, which has sheltered us for so long? I have no greater wisdom than the words of the Compline service. St. Benedict, the founder of our monastic order, suggested a simple outline for the celebration of Compline. There should be, he said, three psalms chosen by the individual priest or church official according to their circumstances.

For example, I often choose Psalm 121: "I will lift up mine eyes unto the hills, from whence cometh my help." It is meaningful here in the foothills of the Smoky Mountains, although it might not be for someone, say, on the coast of the Carolinas. Another favorite choice is Psalm 30: *In manus tuas, Domine* ("Into Thy hands, O Lord"), for it teaches that at the end of the day, we must surrender our wills to that of the Lord.

A hymn and a lesson follow the Psalms and a three-part closing.

The usual responsive reading is *Kyrie Eleison*. The Greek words translate roughly to "Lord, have mercy upon us." And because they are spoken by the whole congregation, they emphasize the unity of a group like the nuns of our house.

Next comes the Benediction, which involves displaying the holy sacrament on the altar and using it to bless the congregants. A chant or reading such as this one accompanies the blessing:

Down in adoration falling,

Lo! the Sacred Host we hail,
Lo! o'er ancient forms departing
Newer rites of grace prevail;
Faith for all defects supplying,
Where the feeble senses fail.
To the Everlasting Father,
And the Son Who reigns on high
With the Holy Ghost proceeding
Forth from Each eternally,
Be salvation, honor, blessing,
Might, and endless majesty.

And finally comes the Dismissal or *Nunc dimittis*:

Lord, now lettest thou thy servant depart in peace according
to thy word.
For mine eyes have seen thy salvation,
Which thou hast prepared before the face of all people;
To be a light to lighten the Gentiles and to be the glory of thy
people Israel.

With those words, the celebrants will file out of the choir and go to their beds in reverent silence. As the mother superior, however, I feel a need to offer one last prayer to the nuns who are witnessing the closing of their nunnery on this night.

"My sisters, as you close your eyes tonight, take comfort in the words of the first prayer of your childhood. Let them banish your doubts and fears, and surrender to what will be, knowing that the wisdom of God supersedes all."

Now I lay me down to sleep.
I pray the Lord my soul to keep.

If I should die before I wake,
I pray the Lord my soul to take.

"Sleep well, my dear sisters, and God bless you on your journeys."

CHAPTER 40

New Insights, New Doors

Nov. 28, 2012

One morning shortly after Thanksgiving, Sarah found a telephone message slip in her office mailbox summoning her to the dean's office following her morning class. With a sudden surge of relief, she realized this was her moment of closure. The doubts and second guesses that had plagued her thoughts for so long disappeared in a breath, and she knew which door she wanted to open. She didn't have to think about her answers to whatever the dean wanted this time. Her decision was set.

Instead of worrying about his reactions, she enjoyed the beauties of the cloister garden, noticing the changing colors of the leaves, the last flowers on the mum plants, and the emerging red berries on the holly bushes. Ready for whatever was about to happen, she took a deep breath outside the administration offices and entered with a determined smile. She gave the dean's secretary, Martha Wright, a quick hug.

She scratched the office cat's ears and squared her shoulders as she entered the dean's inner sanctum.

"Good morning, sir. You wanted to see me?"

"Yes, Professor Chomsky. Thanks for being so prompt. Do have a seat and relax. It's not bad news. How are your children, by the way? Have they recovered from their trauma?"

"Apparently so. They seem to remember the kidnapping as a great adventure. Now they're happily downstairs in the nursery again, playing with blocks and coloring pages as if nothing had ever threatened their little world. I envy them."

"Yes. Well, you have some good news of your own."

"I do?"

"I received a letter from the Catholic diocese this morning, commending the tremendous work you have done for them. They have expressed their entire satisfaction with the manuscript—except for a couple of cosmetic capital letter changes. The letter also contained a check with a hefty bonus for you. They called it a payment 'in place of royalties.'"

"I wasn't expecting that."

"Nor was the college, but I'm sure you'll accept it as a way of easing back into your regular salary."

"About that, sir ..."

"What? Getting ready to hit us up for a raise?"

"On the contrary, I'm not sure when or if I'll be coming back to work."

The dean looked shocked. "Are you serious?"

"Yes, sir. If it doesn't upset the teaching schedules too much, I'd prefer this to be my last semester. In any event, I won't be teaching next year, nor will I be coming up for tenure."

"Have you received a better job offer?"

"No. Let me explain. Someone once told me that I couldn't have it all. She said the time would come when I would have to choose between family and career. I didn't entirely believe it then, but it's true. My moment arrived last month when I came very close to losing my family. Now I want to be at home for as long as my children need me. I also want to try my hand at writing historical fiction. I can't do a good job at either one of those if at the same time I'm trying to do my best as a full-time professor. I have to choose. And right now, I see family and personal development as more important than my academic career. I'm sorry if that disappoints you."

The dean leaned back in his chair, his hands steepled in front of his face to partially hide his expression. "I'll be sorry to lose you. It's a choice I can't fully understand because society does not make that demand upon males in the profession. However, I will respect your decision unless you change your mind."

"Thank you."

"But let me make a practical suggestion. Don't announce that you are quitting and walk out of here, letting the door slam on your heels. When you have a long journey ahead of you, it's not a good idea to lock the doors behind you. You can never be sure what you may need in the future. Take an extended leave of absence and postpone any request to be considered for tenure but keep your options open. Some day you may want to come back to the classroom, either full-time or as an adjunct."

"That time may come. I'll always be a historian, and I plan to keep up with the latest developments in my field. My writing career will not lead me further astray than fact-based historical fiction. I also intend to stay in touch with my friends here at the university. I still believe it possible to open all the doors that call to me—just not all of them at the same time."

"Well, I will tell you this. As an outstanding teacher, you would have received tenure next year without any difficulty. Choosing not to apply is a personal decision, not something that will leave a black mark on your record. Don't worry about upsetting the spring teaching schedule, either. I had already warned Dr. Chalmers not to assign you to spring classes until we heard from the archbishop. If at some point, you decide to come back to the classroom, you will find a welcome in the history department here. Until then, I wish you well. Oh, here. This check is still yours. Use it to fund your new writing career."

Sarah blinked back tears as she left the inner office. Somehow guessing what had just been decided, Martha Wright gave her a comforting hug. "Call me if you need me," she murmured. "I'm still here as your friend."

That evening, Sarah greeted David with the news that a delivery dinner was on the way from their favorite Asian restaurant. "It's my treat tonight. A small windfall has earned me a night off from cooking. But I'm not ready to leave the children with a new sitter, so I've ordered take-out."

"So, are you going to tell me the details, or do I get to guess, starting with what we're about to eat?"

"How does this menu sound? We start with your favorite fresh spring rolls and then share a platter of 'Happy Family' over fried noodles. And for dessert, there will be fortune cookies, including some for the children, along with a couple of slices of mango pie for us."

"It sounds wonderful, but tell me again what goes into a

plate of Happy Family? This is the second time you've suggested it, although we didn't get to eat it the last time."

"Sarah laughed. "It's nothing more than a traditional Chinese stir-fry, except it has a little bit of everything in it—steak, pork loin, chicken, shrimp, maybe even some tofu—to keep everyone happy."

"Does wishing for happiness make it so? And, yes, I get the double message. I take it you've had some good news."

"The dean handed me an unexpected victory this morning—a ten-thousand-dollar bonus check from the Catholic diocese. They liked the book."

"Sounds like they loved every word of it, which doesn't surprise me. But from the grin on your face, I'm guessing there's more to the story."

"Well, I wasn't hoping for more money, and it didn't affect any of the decisions I made today. But I'll admit that it gives me confidence that what I've decided is the right choice. It provides a small cushion of financial support for some of the changes I'm going to make around here. I'm more than ready to allow my imagination to run free for a while. And that may mean I'll be dragging the family off on some research trips. I also want to provide wifely support for your new venture into the law firm. And to make sure that everyone is happy, the children get a bit more than a cookie. Their fortunes will offer them a stay-at-home mom for as long as they need her."

"Does that mean ...?"

"Yes, I gave the dean my notice this morning. I will be finished on December 17th when I've turned in my semester grades. I'm taking an extended leave of absence with the full approval of the college and an open invitation to come back to full-time teaching whenever I feel I'm ready. But for now,

I'm taking the first steps toward having it all by choosing a couple of the closed doors I want to open at this moment."

"Is this still a secret, or are you planning to tell everyone your decision?"

"I don't intend to make a big deal out of it. I prefer to think of the move as a natural choice for this period of my life. I'll mention it if the question arises, but it will not be accompanied by a humongous drumroll. Of course, I'll tell our families and closest friends, but I don't see it as 'big news' except for those in our inner circle."

David smiled in agreement. "My folks will be thrilled for you. You know that as grandparents, they are united in believing that family must come before career or reputation. And Rabbi Leibowicz and Sheila will thank HaShem for allowing us the freedom to choose what's best for each of us."

"I wish I felt as confident about my parents. My mother will understand. She and I had long discussions about this during their visit last Hanukkah. My father, the other rabbi in my life, will be surprised that I am turning my back on tenure because his vision for me has been that of a dedicated scholar. But he's always allowed me to make my own decisions, and this one will be no different."

Again, David agreed. "I suspect he will also know that the issue is common. Three of your colleagues in the history department have faced the same questions in the past couple of years. They came up with different answers, but each of them would understand your position. Among our friends, you'll have full support from Julia and Will, who know from experience that you can love an adopted child as intensely as a natural one. Who knows? Maybe Julia will decide to follow your example into full-time motherhood."

"She may, indeed. Little Maddie Rae is her life right now.

But it would be different for her since she already has tenure. She's now in those ten years when nobody expects her to accomplish much except show up on time for classes. In any event, my choices will not affect our friendship. Our bonds go beyond the university and beyond being new mothers together, as well.

"My only public announcement will come when I hand in my resignation as an advisor at the next meeting of the Smoky Mountain Historical Society. A few of my students may have a hard time accepting the news because they haven't yet been tested in the same way. I think this is a decision that comes with becoming a grownup, and the undergrads are not finished doing that. But the older graduate students, like Jean and Matt, are already learning to set their own goals, and not blindly accept the ones the school sets for them. I'm hoping they'll see my choice as approval of their options."

David suddenly looked serious. "I need to make one pronouncement regarding my role in all of this. You have not asked me for my reactions. I assume that's because you trust me to support you. And of course, I do. But my feelings go deeper than that. We have each made a life-altering decision in the last few weeks, and we have done so independently, not asking each other for permission to seek the things we need. I see that as an affirmation of our lives as a couple. We are equal partners, strong and independent precisely because we think alike and share our mutual goals and values. You may have found the perfect formula for a happy family."

Recipes for a Changing Lifestyle

SESAME SALAD DRESSING

Ingredients:

- 1/2 cup rice vinegar
- 1/2 cup sesame oil
- 1/4 cup soy sauce
- Finely chopped garlic and Vidalia onion (to taste)
- 2 tbsp. toasted sesame seeds
- Crushed red pepper flakes (to taste)

Preparation:

- Beat well or mix in a blender.
- Serve over butter head or Boston bibb lettuce.

~

GREEN ONION LATKES

Ingredients:

- 4 ½ cups shredded peeled baking potato (about 1 1/2 pounds)
- ½ cup finely chopped green onions
- 2 teaspoons all-purpose flour
- ¾ teaspoon salt
- 2 large egg whites
- 2 tablespoons olive oil, divided

Preparation:

- Combine potato and onions; squeeze moisture from potato mixture over a sieve.
- Combine potato mixture, flour, salt, and egg whites in a large bowl.
- Divide mixture into 12 equal portions, and squeeze out any remaining liquid
- Discard liquid. Shape each portion into a 1/4-inch-thick patty.
- Heat 1 tablespoon oil in a large nonstick skillet over medium heat.
- Add 6 patties to pan; cook 5 minutes on each side or until golden.
- Repeat procedure with remaining 1 tablespoon oil and 6 patties.

～

BAD DAY HAMBURGER GRAVY

Ingredients:

- 1 lb. lean ground beef
- 1 Vidalia onion, chopped
- 2 packets beef gravy mix
- 8 oz. sliced mushrooms (canned or fresh)
- 2 cups water
- 1 tbsp. minced garlic
- Salt and pepper to taste

Preparation:

- Brown beef and onion together until onion is soft and beef is no longer pink.
- Add mushrooms and garlic and heat (longer if mushrooms are fresh)
- Add seasonings to taste.
- Sprinkle mixture with gravy mix
- Stir in water and heat to boiling for one minute.
- Serve over mashed potatoes, rice, or cooked noodles

BEAN AND TOMATO STEW

Ingredients:

- ½ cup basil leaves, chiffonade
- 2 teaspoons lemon zest (from 1 large lemon)

- 2 (10-ounce) containers of cherry or grape tomatoes
- ¼ cup olive oil, plus 2 tablespoons and more for drizzling (optional)
- 1tablespoon fresh thyme leaves
- Kosher salt and black pepper to taste
- 1 medium Vidalia onion, thinly sliced
- 3 large garlic cloves, thinly sliced
- ½ teaspoon red-pepper flakes
- 2 (15-ounce) cans of white beans (such as navy or cannellini), rinsed
- 1 ½ cups vegetable or chicken broth, or water
- 1 or 2 cups baby spinach leaves, depending on personal taste

Preparation:

- Heat the oven to 425 degrees. In a small bowl, gently toss together the basil and lemon zest with your hands until well combined; set aside.
- On a sheet pan, toss the tomatoes with 1/4 cup oil and thyme; season well with salt and pepper. Roast tomatoes until they have collapsed and begin to turn golden around the edges, 20 to 25 minutes.
- When the tomatoes are almost done roasting, heat 2 tablespoons oil in a large (12-inch), deep electric skillet or Dutch oven over medium heat. Add the onion, garlic, and red pepper flakes and cook until the onion is softened and the garlic is fragrant, 4 to 5 minutes.
- Stir in the rinsed beans and broth and bring to a simmer. With the back of a spoon or spatula,

gently smash about ½ cup of the beans so they slightly thicken the broth.

- If you want a thicker stew, crush some more of the beans. Season with salt and pepper.
- When the tomatoes are finished roasting, add them directly to the stew along with any juices that have been released. Simmer for 5 to 10 minutes more so the flavors become friendly; season to taste with salt.
- Stir in spinach leaves until they wilt.
- Ladle into shallow bowls. Top each serving with some of the lemon-basil mixture and drizzle with more olive oil.

VIETNAMESE FRESH SPRING ROLLS

Ingredients:

- 2 ounces rice vermicelli
- 8 rice wrappers (8.5 inch diameter)
- 24 small, cooked shrimp – peeled and deveined
- 1⅓ tablespoons chopped fresh basil (Thai is best)
- 3 tablespoons chopped fresh mint leaves
- 3 tablespoons chopped fresh cilantro
- 2 leaves romaine or leaf lettuce, chopped)
- 4 teaspoons fish sauce
- ¼ cup water
- 2 tablespoons fresh lime juice
- clove garlic, minced
- 2 tablespoons white sugar
- ½ teaspoon garlic chili sauce

- 3 tablespoons hoisin sauce
- 1 teaspoon finely chopped peanuts

Preparation:

- Boil rice vermicelli 3 to 5 minutes, or until al dente, and drain.
- Fill a large bowl with warm water. Dip one wrapper into the water for 1 second to soften. Lay wrapper flat.
- In a row across the center, place 3 shrimp, a handful of vermicelli, basil, mint, cilantro and lettuce, leaving about 2 inches uncovered on each side.
- Fold uncovered sides inward, then tightly roll the wrapper, beginning at the end with the lettuce. Repeat with remaining ingredients.
- In a small bowl, mix the fish sauce, water, lime juice, garlic, sugar and chili sauce.
- In another small bowl, mix the hoisin sauce and peanuts.
- Serve rolled spring rolls with the fish sauce and hoisin sauce mixtures.

ELEGANT TZIMMES

Ingredients:

- lb. carrots
- tbsp. oil, divided
- ½ cup honey

- ½ onion, diced
- ¼ cup raisins
- ¼ cup golden raisins
- 6 dates
- Sea salt

Preparation:

- Peel and slice the carrots into sticks. Toss the carrots with the honey, 2 tbsp. oil and sprinkle with sea salt.
- Spread the carrot sticks out over a baking pan, cover with foil and bake at 375°F for 40 minutes.
- Increase oven temperature to 425°F, uncover the carrots and bake for another 30 minutes. Transfer carrots to a serving dish.
- Heat frying pan, add 1 tbsp. oil, onions, a sprinkle of sea salt, and sauté until the onions are golden in color.
- Add the raisins and dates and cook until the fruit is soft—about 5 minutes.
- Spoon mixture over carrots and serve warm.

CUCUMBER AND CORN SALAD

Ingredients:

- 1 tbsp. unsalted butter
- 1 cup freshly cooked corn kernels
- 3 tbsp. lemon juice
- 1 tbsp. olive oil

- $\frac{1}{2}$ tsp. sugar
- 1 tsp. toasted sesame oil
- Kosher salt and freshly ground black pepper
- 3 small cucumbers (about 1 lb.), thinly sliced crosswise
- $\frac{1}{4}$ cup pomegranate seeds
- 1 tbsp. poppy seeds

Preparation:

- In a large skillet, heat the butter over medium-high heat. Add the corn and cook, stirring, until tender, about 3 minutes. Scrape the corn into a large bowl and set aside to cool to room temperature.
- In a small bowl, whisk the lemon juice with the olive oil, sugar, and sesAMe oil, and season with salt and pepper.
- Add the cucumbers to the corn along with the pomegranate and poppy seeds, and then add the dressing and toss to combine. Transfer to a platter and serve at room temperature.

SHEILA'S BABY BREAKFAST COOKIES

Ingredients:

- 3 mashed bananas
- 1/3 cup unsweetened applesauce
- 1 tsp vanilla
- 2 cups old-fashioned or quick oatmeal

- 2 tbsp. milk (adjust according to dryness of oatmeal)
- tsp cinnamon

Preparation:

- Preheat oven to 350 degrees.
- Peel and mash bananas into a mixing bowl.
- Add applesauce, milk, and vanilla. Stir well.
- Add oats and cinnamon. Stir well.
- Add one of these optional add-ins, if desired, depending on child's age, allergies, and personal preferences: 1 tbsp. honey, ½ cup golden raisins, chocolate chips, chopped walnuts, flaked coconut, or dried cranberries.
- Drop onto an ungreased cookie sheet. Makes 15-20 cookies.
- Bake for 15-20 minutes.
- Cool on wire racks.
- Store in refrigerator or freezer.

~

FOUR-CHEESE SOUFFLÉ

Ingredients:

- 1 diced onion (plus your choice of pre-cooked green pepper, spinach, crispy bacon bits, chopped chives, and/or grated garlic)
- 4 tablespoons butter

- 4 tablespoons all-purpose flour
- 1 cup whole milk
- 1/2 cup shredded Cheddar cheese
- 1/2 cup shredded Swiss cheese
- 1/4 cup shredded Monterey Jack cheese
- 1/4 cup shredded Muenster cheese (Or substitute Asiago, Brie, Gruyere, Emmental, or Manchego for any of the four cheese varieties, keeping amounts the same.)
- Salt and pepper to taste
- 5 separated eggs

Preparation:

- Preheat oven to 350 °F.
- Sauté onion in butter until translucent. Pre-cook any additional flavoring additions.
- Whisk in flour to form a roux. Gradually whisk in milk until thickened.
- Add cheeses. Allow to melt and then season. Remove from heat and beat in yolks.
- Allow to cool.
- While egg yolks are cooling, beat whites to stiff peak. Gently fold in whites to cheese mixture.
- Add to buttered 1 1/2-quart casserole dish and bake for 35 to 40 minutes.
- Serve immediately.

Add crusty bread or rolls and a fruit salad.

DECONSTRUCTED FRUIT SALAD

Ingredients:

- 6 oz. flavored yogurt (like strawberry, peach, or raspberry, but not "fruit on the bottom!)
- 3 tbsp. apple cider vinegar
- tbsp. honey

Add Per Person:

- 5 oz. spring greens or chopped romaine
- 1 banana, sliced
- 1 cup assorted berries (strawberries, raspberries, blueberries, blackberries)
- 1 slice of pineapple, cut into narrow wedges
- ½ apple or pear, cut into thin slices
- ½ cup canned mandarin orange wedges
- ¼ cup chopped pecans or walnuts
- ¼ cup crunchy granola crushed into small chunks

Preparation:

- Mix dressing and refrigerate for no more than 2 hours.
- Arrange fruits in separate piles on top of greens.
- Top with nuts and/or granola
- Serve dressing on side.

〰

INSIDE-OUT CARAMEL APPLE CAKE

Ingredients:

For Apples:

- 4 tbsp. butter (if using unsalted, add ¼ tsp. salt)
- 2 large Granny Smith or Honeycrisp apples
- ½ cup dark brown sugar

For Cake Batter:

- ½ cup softened butter
- and $1/3$ cups dark brown sugar
- large eggs
- 1 and $2/3$ all-purpose flour
- ¾ tsp. baking powder
- ½ tsp. salt
- ½ tsp. Cinnamon
- ¼ tsp. nutmeg

For Frosting:

- 1/3 cup butter
- 2/3 cup dark brown sugar, firmly packed
- 1/3 cup milk
- 3 cups powdered sugar
- teaspoon vanilla
- pecan halves or flaky salt

Preparation:

350-degree oven; buttered 10-inch cast iron skillet. Prepare up to 2 days ahead; keep leftovers for up to 5 days.

For apples:

- Melt butter in saucepan.
- Peel, core, and dice apples.
- Add sugar and cook until apples soften slightly, 4 to 5 min.
- Cool to room temperature.

For cake:

- Cream butter and brown sugar until fluffy (4-5 minutes).
- Add eggs, one at a time, and beat to incorporate.
- Stir in vanilla.
- Whisk dry ingredients together, add to wet ingredients, and mix to blend.
- Spread evenly into buttered skillet.
- Bake for 30-35 minutes until browned and set. Do not overbake.
- Cool.

For frosting:

- Melt butter in saucepan over medium low heat.
- Stir in brown sugar, cook and stir for 2 minutes.
- Add milk and continue cooking until mixture boils, stirring constantly.
- Remove from heat and gradually stir in powdered sugar.
- Add vanilla and blend well.
- Spread over cooled cake. If icing gets too thick, add a little milk and blend well.

- Garnish with pecan halves or flaky salt if desired.

HOT WATER CORNBREAD

Ingredients:

- 2 cups yellow cornmeal
- 2 tsp granulated sugar
- 1 tsp salt, or more if you want more for taste
- 1 3/4 cups boiling water; adjust, depending on the texture of cornmeal
- vegetable oil for frying

Preparation:

- Add cornmeal, sugar, salt, and boiling water to a medium-sized bowl and whisk until combined.
- Add oil to coat the bottom of a 10-inch cast iron skillet.
- Heat over medium-high heat until the temperature reaches 375 degrees.
- Drop 2 tablespoons of batter into oil and fry on both sides until golden brown.
- Drain on paper towels and serve while hot.

OMELET

There are as many omelets as there are omelet-makers. If you add ham, it's a Denver Omelet. If you add potatoes, you can call it a Spanish omelet. Or choose your favorite combination and name it after your favorite city.

Ingredients:

- 2 or 3 large eggs at room temperature
- 1 tbsp. butter
- ½ cup chopped vegetables (green peppers, onions, mushrooms, cherry tomatoes, potato slices, zucchini, spinach), ham, fresh herbs
- salt and freshly ground black pepper to taste
- ⅓ cup shredded cheese, preferably a white variety such as cheddar, provolone, parmesan, or brie.
- 1 pinch cayenne pepper

Preparation:

- Beat eggs with a little water in a small bowl until just combined; do not overbeat.
- Prepare chosen fillings. In a small, buttered skillet, sauté chopped vegetables until softened and meaty bits have started to caramelize. Season with salt and pepper; set aside.
- Melt butter in a 10-inch non-stick or oiled cast-iron skillet over medium-high heat. Reduce heat to medium-low and pour in eggs.
- Mix briefly with a spatula while shaking the pan to ensure eggs are evenly distributed. Quickly run the spatula along edges of omelet. Sprinkle cheese, chopped herbs, and cayenne pepper over omelet.

- Cook, shaking the pan occasionally, until top is still wet but not runny, about 5 minutes.
- Spoon filling onto one side of omelet; use a spatula to fold omelet in half and transfer it to a plate.

HAPPY FAMILY STIR-FRY

Ingredients:

- 1/2 lb. beef, sliced thinly
- boneless, skinless chicken breast, sliced thinly
- 6 large prawns, shelled with tail on
- 1/2 cup scallop
- 2 cups broccoli florets
- 1/4 cup carrots, sliced
- 1/2 cup straw mushrooms
- 1/2 cup water chestnuts
- 1 cup baby corn
- 1/2 cup snow peas
- 1/2 cup green, yellow, red bell peppers, chopped
- 3 green onions, sliced

For sauce

- 1/2 tablespoon garlic, minced
- 1/2 tablespoon ginger, minced
- 1 teaspoon sesame

Sauce

- 1/2 cup beef broth
- 1 1/2 tablespoons oyster sauce
- 1 1/2 tablespoons thin soy sauce
- 1 1/2 tablespoons sweet/thick soy sauce
- 3 tablespoons sugar
- Pepper to taste
- 1 tablespoon cornstarch mixed with 2 tablespoons cold water

Preparation:

- Combine the sauce ingredients except for the cornstarch slurry.
- Over medium-high heat in a wok or big pan, saute the garlic and ginger until fragrant.
- Toss in the beef, chicken, prawns and scallops and stir-fry until the beef is browned, chicken is no longer pink and prawns turn pink.
- Toss in the vegetables, leaving out the broccoli and green onions, and toss to combine, stir-frying for 2 minutes.
- Pour in the sauce mixture and stir to mix thoroughly.
- Pour in cornstarch slurry and simmer until the sauce thickens.
- Toss in the broccoli and green onions and stir-fry for another minute.
- Remove from heat, drizzle with sesame oil and add a dash of pepper, mixing well.
- Dish and serve hot.

www.ingramcontent.com/pod-product-compliance
Lightning Source LLC
Chambersburg PA
CBHW071427130726
47998CB00016B/1518